If a man were looking ~~~~ ready-made family...

he couldn't hope to do better. Andy was a super kid, and Jennifer was a pretty, sexy woman.

But Cliff *wasn't* looking for a ready-made family!

Still, he couldn't get mother or son off his mind. Wherever he went, he saw ten-year-old boys and thought about Andy. He had dreams about Jennifer—and woke up aroused.

Cliff cursed. He was in deeper than he wanted to be. And more than conscience was involved. Something compelling was tapping needs in him. Needs that scared him. He wanted to know his son. He wanted to make it up to Jennifer for not having been there for her.

But what the wary bachelor *didn't* want was to make a commitment he couldn't possibly live up to....

Dear Reader,

Welcome to Silhouette **Special Edition**...welcome to romance.

Fall is in full swing and so are some of your favorite authors, who have some delightful and romantic stories in store.

Our THAT SPECIAL WOMAN! title for the month is *Babies on Board,* by Gina Ferris. On a dangerous assignment, an independent heroine becomes an instant mom to three orphans in need of her help.

Also in store for you in October is the beginning of LOVE LETTERS, an exciting new series from Lisa Jackson. These emotional stories have a hint of mystery, as well...and it all begins in *A Is for Always.*

Rounding out the month are *Bachelor Dad* by Carole Halston, *An Interrupted Marriage* by Laurey Bright and *Hesitant Hero* by Christina Dair. Sandra Moore makes her Silhouette debut with her book, *High Country Cowboy,* as **Special Edition**'s PREMIERE author.

I hope you enjoy this book, and all of the stories to come!

Sincerely,

Tara Gavin
Senior Editor
Silhouette Books

Please address questions and book requests to:
Silhouette Reader Service
U.S.: 3010 Walden Ave., P.O. Box 1325, Buffalo, NY 14269
Canadian: P.O. Box 609, Fort Erie, Ont. L2A 5X3

CAROLE HALSTON
BACHELOR DAD

Silhouette ®

SPECIAL ▼ EDITION ®

Published by Silhouette Books
America's Publisher of Contemporary Romance

SILHOUETTE BOOKS

ISBN 0-373-09915-0

BACHELOR DAD

Printed in U.S.A.

Books by Carole Halston

Silhouette Special Edition

Keys to Daniel's House #8
Collision Course #41
The Marriage Bonus #86
Summer Course in Love #115
A Hard Bargain #139
Something Lost,
  Something Gained #163
A Common Heritage #211
The Black Knight #223
Almost Heaven #253
Surprise Offense #291
Matched Pair #328
Honeymoon for One #356
The Baby Trap #388
High Bid #423
Intensive Care #461
Compromising Positions #500
Ben's Touch #543
Unfinished Business #567
Courage to Love #642
Yours, Mine and...Ours #682
The Pride of St. Charles Avenue #800
More Than He Bargained For #829
Bachelor Dad #915

Silhouette Romance

Stand-In Bride #62
Love Legacy #83
Undercover Girl #152
Sunset in Paradise #208

Silhouette Books

To Mother with Love 1992
"Neighborly Affair"

CAROLE HALSTON

is a Louisiana native residing in a rural area north of
New Orleans. She enjoys traveling with her husband to
research less familiar locations for settings but is
always happy to return home to her own unique
region, a rich source in itself for romantic stories about
warm, wonderful people.

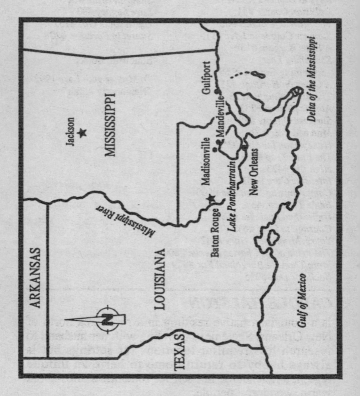

Chapter One

"Let's park the car down by the yacht club, Mom," Andy urged, just as Jennifer had known he would.

"It's always crowded at that end of the lakefront, especially on a Sunday," she objected.

"We can drive by and see if there's a parking place. Please, Mom. It's my birthday weekend."

Yesterday he'd turned ten years old. Like every one of his birthdays, it had been a deeply meaningful occasion for her. Each year when her blond-haired, blue-eyed son went through his birthday-cake ritual, making his wish and blowing out the candles, Jennifer silently rejoiced in the decision she'd made all those years ago not to give up her unborn child for adoption.

Thank heaven that she'd found the courage somewhere in her meek soul to rebel. Four months' pregnant and with no one to lend support, she'd left the home for unwed mothers in Alabama where her guardians had taken her, traveled to a new town and changed herself into a different person, someone proud and independent. She'd put the past behind her, including mistakes, wiped the slate clean of shame and regret, and started over. It hadn't been easy, but it had been worthwhile beyond words.

In a way, Andy's birthday was Jennifer's birthday, too. He'd changed her life.

Today's outing was entirely his idea. He and his best friend, Kevin, and Jennifer were headed for the Mandeville lakefront with a Frisbee. But the real attraction, she knew, was the harbor and sailboats. Jennifer seriously wondered if a love for sailing could be passed along in the genes.

It was uncanny that as a small tyke, Andy had selected picture books with illustrations of boats—and not tugboats or rowboats or ships, but sailboats. Certainly she hadn't encouraged the fascination. In fact, she'd discouraged it, without making an issue. Today she'd suggested alternative excursions, to no avail.

"Hey, neat! Look at all the big sailboats!" Andy marveled when the small, picturesque harbor came into sight. "Slow down, Mom!" he begged as they passed the boat launch over on their left and approached the municipal dock, which was lined with boats tied up two or three abreast.

Tall aluminum masts glinted in the bright late-morning sunshine. Stainless-steel rigging formed a dense triangular web. Jennifer turned her head to look across the street at the Pontchartrain Yacht Club. A huge banner read, Welcome, Southern Yacht Club. There evidently had been a regatta from New Orleans to Mandeville the previous day, and the local yacht club was playing host to their yachting neighbors on the south shore of Lake Pontchartrain. Even someone like her with no interest in boating knew that Southern Yacht Club was an old New Orleans organization.

"Look, Ms. Anderson, that truck's about to pull out," Kevin offered helpfully.

"*Great!* We can park right here close! I guess it's my lucky day," Andy exulted.

"I guess it must be," Jennifer said resignedly. She would much rather have driven farther along the lake-front, away from the harbor. The scene wasn't reminiscent of a marina in Fort Lauderdale, but it still had threatening associations.

After all this time, even a glimpse of a sailboat from the car when she was driving on the Lake Pontchartrain causeway served as a reminder of her one fateful sailing adventure. Jennifer had carefully buried the memories, which touched off such disturbing emotions. She always felt a little shiver of purest pleasure, a flush of shame, and a dull pain in her heart.

How dearly she'd paid for a single day of stolen bliss with a handsome, fun-loving sailor bent on seeing the world. Yet she had Andy as a result.

As expected, he insisted on touring the dock and inspecting all the boats, making wistful comments.

"One of these days I'm gonna learn how to sail. Mom, couldn't I take sailing lessons this summer? They're not that expensive."

"You'll be taking a tennis clinic and playing in several junior tournaments. And you're signed up to compete on the swim team at the club," Jennifer reminded him. "That should be enough to keep both you and me busy this summer."

"I sure wish we belonged to Northshore," Kevin remarked enviously. Most people referred to the Northshore Health and Recreation Club as simply Northshore. "You sure are lucky, Andy, that your mom works there."

One of the benefits of Jennifer's job was use of the club facilities for herself and her son.

"Yeah, I am lucky," Andy agreed. "I've got it pretty good, all right."

He flashed his mother a sheepish, endearing smile and said no more about sailing lessons. Possessed of a sunny, outgoing personality, he wasn't the type to whine and nag as some children did. Aside from loving him with her heart and soul, Jennifer truly enjoyed his company.

"I feel pretty lucky myself," she said, ruffling his blond hair.

They'd paused beside a red-hulled yacht. A bald man lounged in the awning-shaded cockpit, conversing with another man in the cockpit of the yacht tied up alongside.

"Where did Cliff go?" the latter asked.

"He went jogging on the lakefront. You know Cliff. Never makes a big deal about keeping in shape, but he eats healthy and goes light on the booze and gets his exercise."

"I noticed he nursed a couple of beers last night and left the party around midnight. The guy's some sailor, huh?"

"He ought to be. He's sailed all over the world. He raced in the SORC."

Jennifer realized that she was listening intently to the conversation, her heart racing. What was this Cliff's last name? Surely it couldn't be—

"Come on, Mom." Andy tugged at her arm. "Let's see the rest of the boats and then go play with the Frisbee."

Her knees were weak. In all these years she'd never entertained the possibility of encountering Andy's biological father here in Louisiana. Or anywhere else. He'd sailed away into oblivion for her, as surely as if the earth were flat, and he'd fallen off.

Jennifer was shocked to realize that her panic was mixed with a thrill of hopefulness. Only a silly romantic fool would cling to hope for almost eleven years when there was absolutely none.

"Why don't we leave now and go and have lunch?" she suggested, speaking in as normal a voice as she could manage.

"But we just ate breakfast a little while ago." She'd taken the two boys to a popular family restaurant for the breakfast buffet, where they'd stuffed themselves. "I'm not hungry yet. Are you?"

Jennifer leveled with her son. "No, I'm not hungry, but I'm also not finding this very much fun. I would rather do something else with you and Kevin."

"You just don't like sailboats, do you, Mom?"

"Not at all," she admitted honestly. "I feel about as much enthusiasm for looking at sailboats as you feel for cleaning your room."

"Okay. We won't look anymore. We'll go play with the Frisbee on the grass. Come on, Kevin." He dashed away with his friend.

Jennifer raised her hand in protest, then lowered it. She was overreacting, going into a state of alarm over the mention of an expert sailor named Cliff. The odds were overwhelming that he was a stranger, not the carefree sailor she'd known ever so briefly. This Cliff who was jogging on the lakefront probably bore no physical resemblance to Cliff King, who in his early twenties had been tall, with a rangy, muscular build. He'd been deeply tanned with sun-streaked blond hair and blue eyes with laughter crinkles at the corners.

In ten or twelve more years, Jennifer would look at Andy and see a twin of the attractive image imprinted in her memory. But she hoped that her son wouldn't use his charm and good looks to take advantage of naive girls who fell for him and forgot their morals. She hoped that he grew up with a more responsible code of sexual conduct and didn't regard sex as casual pleasure, his for the taking. God knew how many Andys had been conceived during his biological father's travels from port to port around the world.

Jennifer gave her head a hard shake, clearing her mind of the whole troubling train of thought, and crossed the street in pursuit of the two ten-year-old boys. They were taking a shortcut through a small playground teeming with preschool children.

She didn't plan to stay longer than an hour before she loaded Andy and Kevin back into the car. After today, she wouldn't be talked into coming back to the lakefront, and especially not on a weekend when she might be subjected to a similar scene as this one. It simply wasn't an excursion she could enjoy.

Andy would understand. He was a sweet-natured boy, considerate for his age, though not docile and desperate for approval, the way she'd been as a child. It pleased Jennifer deeply that he was well-adjusted and happy. There wasn't any sign of the low self-esteem she'd had to overcome.

"Hold up, you guys," she called.

Andy turned and grinned back at her, gesturing with a pinwheel motion of his arm for her to hurry up.

Jennifer's mood lightened. It was a perfect spring day, and the lakefront truly was a parklike setting, dotted with occasional shade trees and providing a peaceful vista of open water. There was room along its grassy expanse, extending a mile and a half from end to end, for a whole variety of leisurely activities. Today there were joggers and walkers and people romping with dogs, no one getting in anyone else's way. Farther down someone was flying a huge kite that soared high into the blue sky.

"Catch, Mom!" Andy skimmed the Frisbee in her direction with unerring accuracy.

Laughing, she caught it with both hands. The two boys went into hysterics when she threw the Frisbee back and it arced toward the lake instead of returning to them.

"Oh, *no!*" Jennifer shrieked. "It's going to go into the water!"

A male jogger coming from the opposite end of the lakefront had evidently finished his run and was walking briskly to cool down. Reacting quickly, he extended a long arm, leapt high and snagged the Frisbee before it sailed past him out into the lake.

Jennifer turned to stone. "Dear God, it just can't be him," she whispered, staring with disbelief at a more mature Cliff King. With a flick of his wrist, he sent the Frisbee through the air to her son.

"Thanks, Mister!" Andy shouted. His engaging grin was a carbon copy of the one on the face of this man who was a total stranger to him. But he was no stranger to Jennifer.

Rooted to the spot, she gazed helplessly, part of her reveling in the sight of him, part of her trembling with eager uncertainty. He was really here, in Mandeville. The reality was almost more than she could take in. She'd been so sure that she would never see him again.

What should she do? For the moment Jennifer wasn't capable of acting. Paralyzed by her emotions, she watched as Andy motioned with the Frisbee, silently asking the stranger, *Want to join in the game?*

Sure, kid, was the good-natured answer, signaled with a raised hand.

The scene didn't seem real, Andy and his friend Kevin tossing a Frisbee with Andy's father, his real father, not the man in the wallet-sized photo on Andy's bedside table. When he was four years old, Andy had asked to see a picture of his dad, whom he believed to be dead. Jennifer had produced Frank Jennings's photo, stuck away in a drawer with her other few photographs. She hadn't had a picture of Cliff except the one etched in her memory.

After much agonizing during Andy's infancy, Jennifer had decided that she simply couldn't tell him that he was illegitimate. Her own sordid background had caused her too much shame. It was better to lie and create a respectable background. And that's what she'd done, never dreaming that the truth could come out, as it could today.

"No," Jennifer whispered, shaking her head in horrified protest. She couldn't bear Andy's knowing that he'd been an unfortunate accident, born out of wedlock. He believed that his parents had loved each other and had been married. When he was older, he could find out the true facts, but not at his impressionable age.

Eventually Cliff would surely glance her way. Jennifer waited, her heart pounding with the horrible suspense. Would he recognize her instantly as she'd recognized him? Would he look at Andy, see the resemblance and put two and two together?

"Please, God..." Jennifer prayed despairingly as her golden-haired son tucked the Frisbee under his arm and ran pell-mell to strike up a conversation with his biological father, who had no idea that Andy existed.

If by some miracle Cliff didn't notice her and walked on, none the wiser, it would be the best thing for her and Andy. Jennifer was all but certain of that.

And yet, heaven help her, the thought brought the familiar dull pain to her foolish heart.

"Hey, Mister, did you sail over from New Orleans?" the youngster asked Cliff eagerly.

"Why, yes, I did," Cliff replied. "How'd you know?"

"Your T-shirt says Southern Yacht Club."

Cliff glanced down at his chest. "So it does."

"Did your boat win the race?"

"The boat I sailed on won the race. Unfortunately, I don't own it. Is your dad a sailor?" It was an educated guess. The kid obviously was familiar with SYC and knew there'd been a race from New Orleans to Mandeville. Cliff wouldn't be surprised to learn that he'd met the boy's father—and his mother, if the latter was the pretty brunette keeping a close eye on the two boys. She definitely looked familiar, and virtually all his social contacts in the New Orleans area—a part of his sales territory—were boating acquaintances.

"My dad's dead."

"I'm sorry," Cliff said, laying his hand on the boy's head. The matter-of-fact answer touched him more than he would have expected. Perhaps the reason, he realized, was that the kid reminded him so much of himself at the same age. In fact, it was damned strange. Except for the clothes, the youngster might have stepped out of one of Cliff's mother's old photo albums.

The smaller brown-haired boy, who'd hung back a little, volunteered, "My dad's alive. He takes Andy and me on camping trips."

"I'm Andy and he's Kevin, my best friend. That's my mom over there." Andy waved at the brunette woman, who'd stood motionless during the past few minutes. She didn't crack a smile in response, but gestured for her son and his friend to break up their visit and come to her.

"Did your mom attend the yacht-club supper and party last night?" Cliff inquired, more certain than ever that he'd met her. Did she recognize him and wish to give him the cold shoulder for some reason?

"No, sir. Yesterday was my birthday," his youthful lookalike explained hurriedly. "I was ten years old. My mom had a party for me at a pizza restaurant with five of my friends. Then last night she took me and Kevin to a movie."

"I spent the night," Kevin added.

"We'd better go, Kevin," Andy said reluctantly. "Mom's probably ready to leave." He added for Cliff's benefit, "She doesn't like coming here to the lakefront. She hates looking at sailboats." Remembering the Frisbee, he waggled it and grinned. "Thanks for catching my Frisbee."

"Wait. I'll walk along with you," Cliff surprised himself by saying. He couldn't analyze his own motivation.

"Sure," Andy agreed, falling in step with him. "You can meet my mom. Her name is Jennifer."

Jennifer, Cliff repeated silently. The name had a ring of familiarity. He'd probably known several Jennifers, but...

"You live over in New Orleans?" Andy asked.

"No, I come to New Orleans periodically on business. I'm a sales rep for a large company that sells marine hardware."

"Where're you from?"

"Originally Savannah, Georgia. Now I'm based in Atlanta, but I don't spend much time there. I travel a lot in my job."

As he carried on conversation with the personable kid, Cliff did some mental backtracking. Where *was* he ten years and nine months ago? That would have been the summer after he got his engineering degree at Georgia Tech. He'd spent a couple of months in Fort Lauderdale, giving sailing lessons, then gone down to Saint Thomas.

Had he known a Jennifer in Fort Lauderdale? *Yes, he had. Jennifer Anderson.*

Cliff stopped in his tracks about ten yards away from Andy's mom, who'd stood her ground as he approached, flanked by the two boys. *Man, don't even think such a crazy thing!* he told himself. *You're not this kid's father!*

"Hello, how are you today?" She greeted him in a strained voice, backing away several steps. "Boys, I'm in a big hurry. Let's go."

"May I introduce myself?" Cliff asked quickly as she half turned to lead them to her automobile. He came closer. "I'm Cliff King. Correct me if I'm wrong, but I think we might be old acquaintances. Did you ever live in Fort Lauderdale, Florida, by chance?"

"I'm quite certain we haven't met before," she replied, not answering his question. "If you'll excuse us—"

"Mom, didn't you and Dad get married in Florida?" Andy spoke up.

"It wasn't Fort Lauderdale," she informed her son crisply.

"What town was it?" he persisted.

"We'll discuss it in the car. You boys come along." She'd been avoiding eye contact with Cliff. Now she gave him a quick parting look before she departed hastily with the two youngsters in tow.

Andy glanced back and waved at Cliff, "Bye, Mr. King."

"Bye, Andy," he called back, hearing the gravity in his voice.

Had she been lying when she denied recognizing him? God, he hoped not. He hoped it was a case of misidentification on his part. It had been ten years, after all. He hoped his instincts were all wrong, that she really had an urgent appointment and wasn't fleeing the lakefront, getting Andy away from him.

"You're off your rocker, man," he muttered, shaking his head. "That kid's not yours. He said his dad was dead."

Cliff was too shaken to go back to his host's sailboat. Finding an empty bench, he sat down and gazed blindly out at the lake, seeing the bluer water of the Atlantic. Traveling back in memory was surprisingly easy. The long-forgotten details of his brief acquaintanceship with Jennifer Anderson seemed incredibly vivid and fresh.

He'd met her in a secondhand bookstore. They'd reached for the same book in a bin. Their hands had touched. She'd blushed and gotten flustered. He'd found her shyness appealing, found *her* appealing with her big brown eyes and long, dark brown hair plaited in a French braid.

He could even remember what she'd been wearing that day. A sleeveless yellow dress and white sandals.

He'd struck up a conversation with her, then invited her to go to a nearby fast-food place for a soda. With some persuasion, he'd talked her into coming along the next day, a Saturday, on a sailing lesson he already had scheduled. The lesson was cancelled, as it turned out, and he'd gotten permission from his boss to take Jennifer out sailing.

From his point of view, it had been the perfect date: a day out on the water with a pretty girl, a steady breeze filling the sails, a six-pack of cold beer, sandwiches and chips to munch on. Jennifer had looked sexy and yet sweet in her relatively modest pink bikini. Cliff had kissed her. She'd responded and they'd ended up making love. Passionate and yet tender love that had scared him.

The last thing Cliff had been interested in then was a serious relationship. He didn't intend to settle down until he'd seen some of the world and gotten his fill of adventure. It was only fair to explain his position to Jennifer, and he had.

When they'd returned to the marina and she was leaving, he'd asked if he could see her again. She'd answered that she didn't think it was a good idea. Cliff had known she was right.

He'd let her drive off without giving him her address or phone number. Unable to get her out of his mind, he'd cut short his stay in Fort Lauderdale and headed down to the Caribbean a week later. Leaving the area had been the only surefire way of keeping himself from playing detective and tracking her down.

It had taken him a year or two to forget her. After all this time, his memories still roused a poignant regret.

Had he used a condom that day when they made love? He didn't think he had. In those days, he hadn't been as careful as he was now. He'd taken precautions only when his female partner called it to his attention that he needed to. Quite possibly he'd assumed that the Jennifer he'd met in the bookstore was on the Pill, if she hadn't told him otherwise.

Was this woman he'd encountered today, ten years and nine months later, the same Jennifer? Had he gotten her pregnant on that one date?

Cliff had to find out.

"Mom, are you mad?" Andy caught her hand as he trotted along beside her.

Jennifer gave it a reassuring squeeze. She swallowed hard at the tears clogging her throat. "No, I'm not mad. I'm just in a hurry. I have a lot to do at home this afternoon."

Her answer was a truthful reply to his question. She wasn't angry, just overwhelmed with humiliation and hurt. If he'd asked whether she was upset, she would have had to say yes. Jennifer had never lied to her son, except for creating a respectable background story to give him the warm security she'd never had, the security of knowing he'd been wanted.

Whatever doubts she'd had about not telling him the truth were gone, erased by the meeting with Cliff. Andy's biological father had only a vague recollection of her. He'd taken her at her word when she denied having any recollection of him. He'd let her walk away again, out of his life.

I think we might be old acquaintances, he'd said, uncertainty in his voice. The words had cut into Jennifer like a razor.

Their date had been just another date with good sex for him. She'd always known that and accepted it. Or so she'd told herself. Why, then, did she feel as though her heart were breaking?

What Jennifer should be feeling was relief. It had been a close call, encountering Cliff, but Andy was none the wiser. He wouldn't have to know—or, at least, not until he was older, and it didn't matter—that his real father barely remembered his mother. No, not his "real" father, his biological father.

The sad truth was that Andy didn't have a father, only a mother who put his well-being above all else.

Thank heaven, he would go on believing that he was wanted by both parents, who'd been man and wife. That was what was important, not Jennifer's foolish aching heart.

Chapter Two

At the Pontchartrain Yacht Club, Cliff consulted a Northshore phone book and found a listing that read *Jennifer and Andy Anderson.* He copied down the number and the address, 231 Pinewood Street, Mandeville.

With the slip of paper in hand, he returned to *Sinbad,* where he informed Ken Perez, the owner, of his sudden change in plans: he wouldn't be sailing back across Lake Pontchartrain that afternoon. After showering and changing clothes, he collected his duffle bag, said his goodbyes and rode back to New Orleans with a crew member from one of the other yachts, whose wife had driven over to pick him up.

Cliff's rental car was parked at Southern Yacht Club. He tossed his duffle bag into the trunk, got behind the wheel and headed for the twenty-four-mile-long causeway he'd just ridden across.

Reaching Mandeville, he kept an eye out for a real-estate office, spotted one almost immediately, and stopped to make inquiries. A helpful agent provided him with the information he sought, the name of the subdivision where Pinewood Street was located and directions that would take him there.

Back in his car, he felt his stomach rumbling. He hadn't eaten breakfast or lunch. He decided to have a quick meal at a restaurant before he proceeded. It might be a long haul. If Jennifer Anderson wasn't home, Cliff intended to park in her driveway and wait for her.

He'd been coming to New Orleans for six years and knew that there were some expensive country-club subdivisions on the Northshore. But Jennifer and Andy's house wasn't in one of them. The lots were small and the houses modest, though fairly new. The yards were all neatly tended, if not manicured. Children played in the street, as advertised by signs: Children at Play. Cliff slowed his car down to a cautious crawl and had to stop twice.

He waited patiently for an adorable little girl to pedal her plastic bike to safety. Although she was sweet, she produced no tremendous yearnings in him. These young-family neighborhoods were foreign territory to him; he found it hard to imagine ever feeling at home in a place like this.

His mother asked from time to time when was he going to settle down, get married and give her grandchildren to spoil? His stock answer was, "Whenever I find the right woman." So far, at age thirty-three, Cliff had never come close to wanting to propose marriage.

Did his mother have a ten-year-old grandchild named Andy whom she didn't know about? Cliff prayed that she didn't.

Turning onto Pinewood Street, he regretted his decision to put food in his stomach. His hamburger had given him a rare case of heartburn. If no one was home, he would find a convenience store and buy a roll of antacid tablets to get some relief. The best relief would be learning that he was on a wild-goose chase.

The odd-numbered houses were on his right. Cliff spotted a mailbox up ahead with the digits 231 painted on the side. He braked in front of the house. It was a one-story beige brick ranch style with decorative shutters painted forest green. A paneled front door and the posts and railing of a narrow recessed porch were painted to match the shutters. The house had a one-car garage, the door of which was closed. Like most garages in middle-class subdivisions, it was probably utilized for storage, he reflected.

Parked in the driveway was a small economy car that was several years old. Cliff identified the make of the car, a typical mode of transportation for the neighborhood. Sold by an American automaker, it was reliable and got good gas mileage. Jennifer Anderson had made a smart choice among lower-priced automobiles, if the car belonged to her, as he assumed it did.

The house she owned or rented had a cozy air. There were curtains in the windows. White petunias cascaded from a terra-cotta pot on the sidewalk by the porch. The lawn was mowed. From all the outward indications, Andy's mom was doing a commendable job of providing a home for her son. The best testament was the boy himself.

Should Cliff just drive on and leave her in peace to carry on her life?

Maybe he should, but he couldn't. He had to *know*, damn it.

Cliff pulled into the driveway and parked behind the sensible economy car, which brand-new couldn't have cost half of what his little sporty high-performance car back in Atlanta had.

On the porch he pressed the doorbell and heard faint chimes within. The paneled door had a peephole. He stepped to one side, out of its range. The door swung open in less than a minute and Jennifer Anderson stood framed in the opening, wearing the same outfit she'd worn on the lakefront, red slacks and white blouse. She clutched the edge of the door and stared at him, her face mirroring disbelief and horror.

"It's *you*," she whispered. "You've *found* me."

Cliff put out one hand and braced himself against the door frame. Her reaction removed all doubt: she was the Jennifer he'd known in Fort Lauderdale almost eleven years ago.

On this second meeting, the image of the younger Jennifer was fresh in his mind, following his bout of remembrance. The woman standing before him had a new, shorter hairstyle. The simple, bouncy, unpermed look was extremely becoming. Her dark brown hair hadn't lost its healthy sheen. And her complexion and features were as fresh and pretty as he recalled. Her figure was still slim, though the figure of a grown woman, not a nineteen-year-old girl.

Even in his present state, this Jennifer Anderson appealed to him. Under different circumstances, very different circumstances, Cliff would have been attracted to her all over again.

"Can I come in and talk to you?" he asked hoarsely.

"There's nothing to talk about. *Please* go away."

He shook his head. "Sorry, I'm not going to go away. Is Andy inside?"

"No. He's at a friend's house in a different part of town." Her voice gained strength. "You can't see him again. It wouldn't be good for him."

"I just asked in case you wanted to go somewhere else where we could talk privately," Cliff hastened to explain. "I didn't come to see Andy."

She let his words sink in. "What is there to talk about? Surely you can piece the story together for yourself. I got pregnant, making love to you that one time. Don't worry—I don't hold you in any way responsible." She still grasped the door, but was standing straighter, as though strength had come back into her legs. Cliff's own legs felt wobbly. This was all so unreal.

"But I was responsible. Or we both were. That is what you're telling me, isn't it?" He needed more courage before he could spell out in plain words that Andy was his kid.

"You're Andy's biological father, if that's what you're asking."

Cliff could feel himself turning pale at the confirmation. He glanced toward the street, where two young mothers were walking past, pushing strollers. "Look, why don't we carry on our discussion inside your house?"

"There's nothing to discuss. *Please,* just go away and forget all about today."

"Forget about today," he repeated incredulously. "You can't be serious."

Her body sagged again in the face of his insistence. Slowly she opened the door wider and moved aside so that he could enter.

Cliff stepped inside a small tiled entryway that was separated from a carpeted living room by a waist-high partition and spindles. While she was closing the door, he glanced into the living room and noted a chintz-covered sofa and love seat in an L-shaped grouping. There was a television set in the corner and a fireplace on one wall. The mantel of the fireplace was lined with framed photographs. From that distance he could see that the pictures were of Andy at various ages.

For ten years he'd had a kid and hadn't known it. Things like this didn't really *happen*.

"Any minute now I'm going to wake up and find out this is all some crazy dream," he said, his sheer disbelief in his voice.

She'd turned around and stood with her back to the door, leaning on it for support. "It must be a shock."

"I'm not sure shock is a strong enough word. You weren't on the Pill, I take it."

"No, it was my first time."

"Your first time?" Cliff stared at her, unnerved by the revelation that she'd been a virgin. "Why the hell didn't you say something?"

"I should have," she replied. "But I was swept away by the moment and took the chance so many girls take that I wouldn't get pregnant, having sex once. I don't blame you. I never blamed you. So don't blame yourself. Just go and let Andy and me carry on with our lives."

"You must have a pretty low opinion of me, if you think I could do that." He jammed his hands into his pockets. Obviously she thought Andy was better off with no father than with him for a father. "You told him that his dad is dead?"

She nodded. "I made up a story. He thinks his father and I were married. He has a picture I gave him of a man he believes is his dad."

"A picture? Of whom?"

"Frank Jennings. He was the man I was dating... when I met you."

"You were involved with another guy and went sailing with me? Made love with me?"

"If you remember, there were supposed to be other people along." She continued before he could tell her there was no need to refresh his memory; he remembered everything about that day. "Originally you'd had a lesson scheduled. I certainly never meant to make love with you. But, you're right, I wasn't free to date you. It was wrong, and I suffered the consequences."

"So Frank Jennings was the reason you didn't think it was a good idea to see me again. I thought—" Cliff pulled his hands out of his pockets and jammed them back in again, completing the sentence for himself. He'd thought they were on the same wavelength that day, both of them in danger of falling in love.

Jennifer shook her head, rejecting the whole line of conversation. "None of that matters now. What matters is the present."

"Did you even try to contact me when you found out you were pregnant?"

"Yes, I went to the marina. But you had gone, leaving no forwarding address."

"What did you do?"

She sighed. "It's a long story. I was raised by an aunt and uncle. They were terribly disapproving of the fix I'd gotten myself into. They took me to Alabama, to a home for unwed mothers. At their insistence, I signed papers to put my baby up for adoption after it was born.

"In my fourth month, though, I left the home, took a bus here to Louisiana and got a job. Andy was born, and we've lived here ever since. The schools are good. Andy's a happy, well-adjusted child. I have no regrets whatsoever for bringing him into the world. There's no reason for you to feel any guilt," she assured him at the conclusion of her bare-bones summary of her experiences. Reading between the lines, Cliff could guess what she'd been through.

"But I do feel guilty. I haven't paid a nickel of child support all these years," he pointed out. Not to mention the other kinds of support, like facing the music with her and sharing the blame for carelessness.

"You didn't know Andy existed."

"But I do know now. And I certainly mean to start giving you some financial support. If you'll give me a deposit slip from your checkbook, I can set up a direct deposit."

She stiffened, as though he'd insulted her. "That's generous of you, but Andy and I don't really need any financial assistance. Not now. I earn a good salary at my job. We have a comfortable life-style."

"Put the money in a college fund. Spend it however you want—on extras. I'm sure you can find some use for it," Cliff stated reasonably. His words obviously had no effect.

"Andy already has a college fund. The balance in it is no secret to him. Our state of finances isn't a secret. He helps me balance my checkbook when the statement comes." Maternal pride warmed her voice and a mother's love softened her features as she divulged, "Math is his favorite subject in school. He makes *A*'s and *B*'s in all his classes. And he's gifted athletically. When the time comes for college, he shouldn't have any trouble getting a scholarship to a good university."

"My favorite subject was math," Cliff reflected. He'd made all *A*'s and *B*'s in school, too, and played varsity sports in high school. He'd scored high on the college entrance tests and had the option of attending half a dozen top universities with the aid of scholarships. It sounded as though Andy had inherited more than Cliff's looks.

The kid probably would get along fine in the world without any help from him. Cliff couldn't really argue the point with Jennifer. But, damn it, he had a moral responsibility to contribute somehow to Andy's upbringing, now that he knew about him.

"Look, Jennifer, I'm in a fairly high income bracket for a single man." It occurred to him that she hadn't inquired whether he was married and had legitimate children. From the moment he'd shown up, her one concern had been to get rid of him. "I can easily afford to pay child support. I couldn't live with my conscience if I didn't pay it."

"To salve your conscience, Cliff, you would destroy my peace of mind? Is that fair or right? I don't want checks from you coming in the mail or deposits showing up on my bank statement. I want to blot out this chance meeting today. Do what's best for all three of us, Andy and me and yourself," she pleaded with fervor and conviction. "Go about your life and let us go about ours."

He sighed, combing his fingers roughly through his hair. "Let me think this whole thing through. In a day or two, we'll talk on the phone—" She was shaking her head adamantly. Frustration welled up in him. "What are you afraid of, Jennifer? That down the line, I'll take you to court and file for partial custody? I'll never do that."

She'd paled at his words. "What I'm afraid of is that the truth will come out and Andy will be hurt. Please. Do as I ask. If you owe me anything, you owe me that." Tears glistened in her lovely brown eyes, making them luminous.

Cliff struggled with an unfamiliar sense of helplessness as he gazed at her. "That's really what you want?"

"Yes," she whispered and opened the door wide.

What the hell choice did he have, but to leave? With a last lingering glance at the pictures on the fireplace mantel in the living room, Cliff strode past her out the door, hearing it close quietly behind him.

In the yard across the street, a man younger than Cliff by a few years was pitching a red plastic softball to a little preschool boy, who swung at the ball with an orange plastic bat. Cliff observed the scene as he headed to his car.

"That was a good swing, son," the man encouraged. "Now watch the ball and hit it this time."

"I'm gonna hit a home run, Daddy!"

The little boy connected and his triumphant cries blended with his father's hearty praise.

Andy hadn't had a father to play ball with him when he was the little boy's age. He didn't have a father now to toss a football with him, to do all those typical father-son activities with him. Trying to escape the thought, Cliff drove as fast as he dared through the family neighborhood, retracing his route.

On the causeway he could see the sails of the yachts returning across the lake to New Orleans. Andy had said with regret in his boyish voice that his mom "hated looking at sailboats" and avoided the lakefront. Cliff had given her that aversion. The knowledge made him feel rotten. In fact, he couldn't recall ever feeling quite as rotten as he felt right now.

Jennifer walked numbly into the living room and watched Cliff leave, his haste evident. After his car had disappeared from sight, she sank down on the sofa and wept anguished tears, seeing his sick expression when she'd opened the door and he'd realized that there wasn't any mistaken identification. She was the Jennifer Anderson he'd been "acquainted" with in Fort Lauderdale.

Plainly he'd held out some hope that she was a stranger, that Andy wasn't his offspring.

On Andy's behalf, she felt an overwhelming sense of rejection. How could he meet his son, see for himself what a wonderful little boy Andy was, and not want to claim him? Before today, she hadn't resented Cliff, hadn't held him in any contempt, but her estimation of his character had sunk very low.

Often during those months in the home for unwed mothers in Alabama, she'd asked herself how he would have reacted if she'd been able to contact him and tell him that she was pregnant with his baby. Would he have insisted on marrying her? she'd wondered hopefully. She'd even tortured herself with daydreams about his coming to the home and heroically rescuing her.

The sad realist in her had known even then that Cliff wouldn't have wanted to be saddled with a wife. Today's encounter left little doubt about what his reaction would have been. Eleven years ago Cliff would have offered her what he'd offered today—only financial support.

God knows she could have used some supplemental income during those early years as a single mother, but she didn't need Cliff's money now. She and Andy lacked for none of the essentials.

What Andy needed from a father wasn't checks sent in the mail. Among other things he needed a role model, and that role model wasn't Cliff, still the footloose bachelor.

Jennifer wiped her wet cheeks, reflecting dully that it hadn't come as any surprise that Cliff wasn't married at thirty-three. In her mind, he'd remained single, the perfect date, the perfect lover, adventurous and carefree. At first sight of him on the lakefront, she'd sensed that he was still unattached.

Sending him away had been the right thing to do. This moment he was probably thanking her, realizing as she realized that he wasn't cut out to be a father.

Would she ever hear from him again?

No, she didn't expect to. But if she were wrong, she would deal with him more decisively than she had today. Cliff had forfeited any rights as a father with his reaction. Jennifer was Andy's only parent, and she would protect him at all costs.

A muffled sound in another part of the house brought Jennifer to her feet. The clothes dryer had finished its cycle. Enough sitting and moping. She had household chores to get done before she picked up Andy. Her budget didn't stretch far enough for maid service.

With working a full-time administrative job at Northshore Health and Recreation Club, teaching several aerobics classes for extra income and being homemaker and mom, Jennifer stayed constantly busy. Living in an apartment or a condo would have eliminated yardwork, but she thought it was important that Andy have a bona fide nice home, not just a dwelling.

And Andy helped her with the yardwork. This spring he'd taken over mowing the grass. He liked operating the lawnmower and had delegated her to his former task, collecting branches and pine cones that had fallen from the trees and sweeping the grass clippings off the driveway and paved walkway. He was keen on trying his hand at trimming with the weed-eater, but Jennifer insisted he wait another year or two.

He had other chores to perform on a regular basis, such as wheeling the garbage can out beside the street on garbage pickup days. He was responsible for keeping his room reasonably neat and was required to pick up after himself, not kick off his shoes anywhere and leave his discarded clothes strewn hither and yon.

They had a harmonious life-style, she and Andy. Today, out of the blue, it had been threatened. Months would pass before she could feel safe again.

Jennifer shrugged aside her anxiousness and lingering sense of depression as she drove to the subdivision where Kevin lived. Andy could read her moods. If she acted tense and distracted, he would sense that something was wrong and ask her what was the matter.

A part of her personality change had been to make herself into an upbeat, positive person. She hadn't wanted Andy to grow up with gloom and negativism, as she had.

He came bounding to the car when she pulled into the driveway. Her heart swelled with her adoration.

"I had a great time," he volunteered as he fastened his seat belt. "Kevin's dad hung out with us all afternoon. We played touch football until Mr. Pritchard got out of breath. Then he worked with us on throwing passes and making running catches. It was *fun*, Mom."

Jennifer shifted into reverse and looked over her left shoulder, checking to see if the coast was clear to back out and also hiding her expression from him. As hard as she tried to be both mother and father to him, she couldn't fill all his needs.

"I'm so glad you enjoyed yourself," she said.

"This was my best birthday weekend ever," he mused happily when they were driving along.

"You said the same thing last year," Jennifer recalled, giving him a smiling glance. "Where were Kevin's sisters?" Andy's friend had twin five-year-old sisters, whom both boys considered major nuisances.

"Mrs. Pritchard took them somewhere with her in the car. They sneaked into Kevin's room last night while he was at my house. Guess what they did."

"There's no telling. What did they do?"

He related the latest mischief of the twins. Jennifer paid close attention, his boyish voice music to her mother's ears.

What a joy he was to her.

At his suggestion they picked up fried chicken dinners at his favorite chicken franchise on their way home. After supper, he had a homework assignment. The next day being a school day, he was in bed by nine o'clock without her having to remind him.

Jennifer went into his room to say good-night. He lay on his back, holding the small framed picture of the man he believed to be his father. His wistful expression hurt her unbearably.

"Thinking about your father tonight?" she asked, sitting on the side of his bed.

He nodded. "It's too bad he had to die, huh, Mom?"

Jennifer smoothed his blond hair back from his forehead. "It's too bad that your dad had to miss out on a wonderful son like you."

"If he was alive, him and me could do things together like Kevin and his dad, go camping, play touch football."

"*He* and *I*," she corrected, her throat tight with emotion.

He put the photograph on his nightstand and burrowed his head lower in his pillow. "Don't look sad, Mom. It's not your fault."

"Maybe you and I could go camping this summer. I'm willing to give it a shot. And I'm in pretty good shape, you know. I could play touch football with you and Kevin and probably not get out of breath like Mr. Pritchard. Don't grin at the idea!'' she admonished, pretending to be insulted.

''You're in good shape, all right, Mom, but you're not too great at throwing or catching.'' His grin widened. ''You should've seen yourself catching the Frisbee today on the lakefront. Then when you threw it, you almost fell down and it went wild. Lucky for us, Mr. King came along and saved it from going into the lake.''

''That wouldn't have been tragic. I would have bought you another Frisbee.'' Jennifer would rather have bought him a hundred Frisbees than have that one rescued by Cliff.

''That was fun, throwing the Frisbee back and forth with him. I bet he can throw a football real good, too.''

''Really well, you mean.'' Jennifer tucked the sheet around him.

''Mom, what town in Florida *did* you and Dad get married in?''

''Boca Raton,'' she lied.

''Wasn't it weird that Mr. King thought he knew you a long time ago? You think maybe you forgot him?''

''No, I doubt I would have forgotten Mr. King. Now it's time for us to say good-night and let you go to sleep.'' Jennifer bent to kiss him on the cheek. ''I love you a whole bunch.''

He hugged her around the neck. ''I love you, Mom.''

His words eased her guilt over the necessity for telling him lies. She would willingly suffer the pangs of conscience to protect him from truths that could do him no good to know.

The conversation didn't undermine her conviction that she'd acted wisely today in sending Cliff away. It took more than skill in throwing a Frisbee to be a real father.

It took more than being able to pass a football, which, as Andy had conjectured, Jennifer was sure Cliff King could do better than the average dad.

If Cliff had true fatherly instincts, he wouldn't have left on her terms today.

Chapter Three

Jennifer smiled a friendly greeting at an attractive, well-built man entering the club, carrying a typical athletic bag.

"Hi. How are things going?" he asked, dropping the bag to take out his wallet and remove his membership card. "Parking lot is almost full out there."

"Ladies' tennis-league day," she explained, glancing at his card and then typing the membership number into the computer.

An employee scheduled to work at the entrance desk had called in sick that morning, and she was helping out. Normally she worked in the business office, but she willingly filled in wherever she was needed. In a pinch she would report to the nursery or step behind the counter in the snack bar and take food orders. A change of pace was always welcome, and she took a personal pride in making the club a top-notch facility.

The owners, Bailey and Brenda Philips, were a couple in their mid-thirties, both actively involved in management, both sincerely committed to being healthy and fit themselves. They treated their employees very well. Jennifer was appreciative.

"Have a good workout, Richard," she said pleasantly to the man. His name, Richard Mackey, was printed on the membership card.

"Thanks." He leaned on the counter after he'd stuck his wallet back into his pocket. "You're one of the aerobics instructors, aren't you?"

"Yes, I am," Jennifer confirmed.

"I've noticed you around the club." He grinned and confessed, "I checked out the sign-in sheet of one of your classes. You're Jennifer, right?"

"Right."

"The sheet was full, and the exercise studio was jam-packed. You must be one of the popular instructors."

"Most of our classes are full."

He chatted a few minutes more. Jennifer was friendly, but not encouraging. Several more club members arrived, and she turned her attention to them.

"Nice talking to you," Richard said and moved along.

When the reception area was clear again, she looked around behind her, feeling herself under scrutiny, and met the gaze of Marlene Turner, a petite redhead, who was unpacking a shipment of T-shirts and hanging them on a rack in the retail shop. There was no partition separating the shop and the U-shaped counter that formed Jennifer's work station.

"Why didn't you flirt with that nice man?" Marlene chided. "He was dying to ask you out. Isn't he your type?"

"No man is my type right now," Jennifer replied, suddenly seeing an image of Cliff King. "There isn't room in my life for a relationship that doesn't include Andy."

"You're not even thirty!" Jennifer's age, twenty-nine, was common knowledge since her co-workers had thrown her a surprise party at the club this year with Brenda and Bailey's assistance. "Don't you feel the need for some male companionship?"

"It's not that simple, Marlene. No man is going to be satisfied with just an occasional date when Andy's spending the night with a friend. I'm not going to stick him with sitters. For now, I'm content to have male friends here at work." To mollify her fellow employee, who meant well, she added, "When Andy goes away to college, there'll still be plenty of time for me."

Marlene shook her head slowly in bafflement. "Don't you ever meet a guy and feel a strong physical chemistry?"

"Never any overwhelming attraction."

A group of women in exercise togs was exiting, several of them holding small children by the hand. Jennifer welcomed the interruption. She busied herself and didn't resume the conversation.

But Marlene's question nagged at her. *Don't you ever meet a guy and feel a strong physical chemistry?*

Jennifer had met one man in her twenty-nine years who'd bowled her over with his masculine appeal. Cliff King. When she was eighteen, she'd liked everything about him, his looks, his voice, his smile, his personality. Almost eleven years later, she found him just as attractive.

Every time she visualized him as he'd looked on the lakefront, as he'd looked standing outside her door and in her entryway, she felt a quiver of pleasure in her midsection. And during the past five days, she'd visualized him all too often.

It disturbed her deeply to realize that she could make a fool of herself over Cliff all over again.

At noon Jennifer went home for lunch, as she did frequently. Fixing herself something to eat was more economical than eating at the club, even with her employees' discount, and she lived only ten minutes away.

The mail had come. She took the sheaf of envelopes and a couple of catalogs and junk mail inside without glancing through the assortment. It was bill time, which accounted for the bulk. Jennifer rarely received personal correspondence. Her uncle and aunt had disowned her and didn't even have her current address. Other than them, she had no relatives that she knew about, and she hadn't kept in touch with school acquaintances.

Lunch was a large green salad and a glass of skim milk. As she ate, Jennifer thumbed through the catalogs that had come in the mail. One of them was a favorite wish book of Andy's, with sporting equipment of all kinds and specialized clothes for a variety of sports. She flipped quickly through the pages aimed at sailing enthusiasts, closed the catalog and tossed it aside.

How long, she wondered, before she could put Sunday out of her mind? How much time had to pass before she could return to normal and not constantly be reminded of Cliff King?

The top envelope in her stack of mail was the telephone bill. Ripping it open, she remembered Cliff's suggestion that he call her in a few days. He hadn't called, thank heaven. She stuffed the bill back in the envelope after noting the amount she owed.

The next envelope was company stationery that she didn't recognize. It had been addressed by hand. Jennifer's heart skipped a beat as she read the name of the company, International Marine Hardware. The branch-office location was Atlanta, Georgia.

Andy had reported the information that Cliff King lived in Atlanta and worked for a marine-hardware company. *Was this envelope from him?* Picking it up, she studied the handwriting as though it would give her a clue. The penmanship was bold, with hurried strokes. The postage wasn't metered. The sender had moistened a stamp and stuck it in the corner a little askew.

Jennifer slid her placemat to one side, her appetite completely gone. The food she'd eaten formed a lumpy mass in her stomach. Carefully she opened the flap and took out a folded page of paper. A check fell to the table, face up so that she could read the amount, five hundred dollars.

The paper was company stationery, like the envelope. It crackled when she unfolded it. He'd handwritten a note. *I'm sorry, Jennifer, but your solution just won't work for me. Call me collect at my office or home number, and we'll discuss it.* In parentheses were both numbers. *Leave a message if I'm out, and I'll call you back. In case of emergency, please know that I'm concerned.* The word *please* was underlined. *Sincerely, Cliff.* A postscript read, *I would prefer a direct deposit for the sake of convenience.*

Jennifer read and reread the note and then gazed at the check, obviously written on his personal checking account. On the line at the bottom he'd scrawled, *Month of May.*

Did he plan to pay this large a sum of money monthly?

Such a generous supplement to her and Andy's income would definitely come in handy. She quickly banished the thought, upset with herself. Of course, she couldn't cash the check.

It didn't seem moral to take his money and not openly acknowledge him as Andy's father, something she *wouldn't, couldn't* do.

Jennifer didn't want a tie with him, which regular payments would establish. She wanted to forget about him and have him forget about the two of them. How could she sleep well at night, worrying that he might show up at any time?

She would return the check with a note. Jennifer got up immediately and went to Andy's room to use the computer that he'd gotten for his birthday present. Her fingers hovered over the keyboard. *Dear Cliff* seemed far too personal. *Am returning your check,* she wrote. *For reasons I explained, I simply cannot accept money from you.* She underlined *cannot* and then typed her initials.

On her way back to the club, she mailed the note, folded around the check and sealed in a hand-printed envelope. The address was his home address, which she'd copied from the check. Jennifer hesitated before dropping the envelope into the drive-by mail receptacle at the post office. He'd requested that she contact him in an emergency, obviously meaning some life-threatening situation involving Andy.

Should she copy down the address? She'd torn up his note with the phone numbers.

No. She didn't want to have Cliff's address, hidden away in a secret place. If, God forbid, there ever was a serious emergency involving Andy, she knew how to track down his biological father. That knowledge in itself was disturbing enough.

The world had shrunk and become very small since Sunday.

Jennifer dropped the envelope into the slot and drove on.

Cliff paid for his purchases in the men's department of a major department store in an Atlanta shopping mall. He'd bought half a dozen shirts, a couple of ties, a supply of socks and underwear. It hadn't taken him long to make his selections. Shopping wasn't his thing.

Carrying his one large bag, he made his way toward a door opening into the mall. While he was here, he would check out the music store and the sporting-goods store, then be on his way.

His route took him past the boys' clothing department. A boy-size mannequin in khaki shorts and a blue striped knit shirt grinned at him. Seized by some impulse he didn't understand, Cliff stopped midstride and then strolled among the racks of clothes, thinking about Andy. The youngster had been almost constantly on his mind.

"Can I help you find the size you're looking for, sir?" inquired a middle-aged male clerk.

"I don't really know the size," Cliff replied.

"How old is the boy?"

"He's ten, but I think he's probably big for his age."

"If you buy something that doesn't fit, it can always be exchanged or returned."

"He lives in Louisiana. I'm actually just browsing." Why hadn't he said those last words to begin with? Cliff asked himself and knew the answer. *He wanted to talk to some other human being about Andy.*

"Let me know if I can help you." The clerk moved away.

Cliff left the department, angry at himself and disturbed over his feelings of regret. So he wouldn't ever buy his kid any clothes. So he wouldn't ever take him to a department store like this one to shop. So what?

The child-support money he paid would clothe Andy as well as any other kid. It wasn't any deep-seated desire of Cliff's to go on father-and-son shopping excursions, for heaven's sake.

Out in the mall, he saw families everywhere he looked. His eyes seemed to spot boys about Andy's size. In the music store, he found himself glancing over the shoulders of preteen kids at cassette tapes of groups and singers popular with the young generation. In a few years, Andy would be a teenager. He would ask for a stereo for his birthday or Christmas present.

Cliff knew something about stereos. He could pick out a good one for the kid, when the time came. But he wouldn't be picking out a stereo for Andy or giving Andy's mother any input, not unless her attitude toward Cliff changed in the interim and they established amicable communications about Andy.

Is that what he wanted? Cliff asked himself. Did he want to be in communication with Jennifer Anderson and share parenting decisions with her? Hell, no, he didn't want that! So why was he moping around in this damned music store?

Out of sheer stubbornness, Cliff refused to let himself flee the mall. He'd meant to go by the sporting-goods store, and, by jove, he would. So what if he walked up and down aisles and saw item after item that would make a ten-year-old boy's face light up?

Cliff wasn't going to eliminate sporting-goods stores from his life, or department stores with boys' departments, or music stores, just because he'd discovered he had a kid living in Louisiana, a great kid who was getting along just fine not having him as a father. These regrets he was experiencing would go away. He was quite sure they didn't arise from any deep-seated desire to be a parent.

For the next twelve or thirteen years, until Andy was out of college, Cliff was firmly committed to rendering financial assistance. Otherwise, he would adhere to Jennifer's wishes and stay out of the picture.

Now, on with his single man's life.

Leaving the shopping mall, Cliff deliberately thought about his date that night with Whitney Blair, a successful corporate career woman who was beautiful enough to have made it big in modeling. He'd met her his last time home from being on the road. It seemed a long time ago now.

They had dinner reservations at a good restaurant. Afterward he would take her to a night spot with live music, where they could dance. Dancing usually put him in the mood for romance. If Whitney was similarly affected, maybe they would end up spending the night together. Cliff dwelled on the prospect, trying to stir up male anticipation. Had the mental stress of the past few days weakened his sex drive?

That had to be the explanation, because he'd been strongly attracted to Whitney. Seeing her in person again would undoubtedly do the trick, he told himself.

It should have been sound reassurance. Whitney Blair looked gorgeous and sexy that night when she opened the door of her upscale townhouse. She wore a red silk dinner suit that clung to her tall, willowy figure. The neckline of a filmy white blouse dipped invitingly low, showing cleavage. But Cliff's gut reaction wasn't admiration. A vivid picture of Jennifer in red slacks and a more prim white blouse flashed before his eyes, and he cursed silently. Damn, why had Whitney picked out that same color combination, red and white?

It was necessary for him to fall back on a seasoned bachelor's acting skill as he whistled appreciatively. Whitney was giving him a frankly approving once-over.

She smiled and informed him in an apologetic tone, "I'm on the phone. I'll be finished with my conversation in just three minutes. I promise."

"No rush," Cliff said.

He stood a moment in her elegant foyer. The floor was tiled in black-and-white marble. A black lacquered table held a simple silk flower arrangement. *Nice,* he thought and walked over to the doorway leading into the living room to glance inside. The furnishings were expensive, the decor a sophisticated eclectic blend of contemporary and period. The marble fireplace didn't have a mantel. Over it hung a large abstract painting.

Cliff admired the painting, admired the whole ambience of the place. Whitney's townhouse was very much to his liking, comfortable enough without any suggestion of hominess. It was a setting for adults, not for family life. Cliff's kind of setting, as opposed to the house in which Jennifer and Andy lived.

Whitney returned, and once again he fell back on his considerable experience in the dating game. The spark of attraction just wasn't there tonight.

The fault lay with him. There was no reason he shouldn't be absorbed in getting to know her better. She was as intelligent and interesting as she was beautiful.

Also, she was obviously perceptive. Over coffee, following an excellent dinner, she asked, "Do you have something on your mind, Cliff?"

He opened his mouth to deny that he did, then nodded instead. "Sorry to be such poor company," he apologized sincerely.

"Would you like to talk about whatever the problem is?"

Again Cliff started to answer in the negative. Instead, he found himself pouring out the whole story to her.

"No wonder you're distracted," she remarked when he'd finished. "What a shock to discover that you have a ready-made family off in another state!"

"I have a son, not a ready-made family," he corrected her.

Her eyebrows shot up at his sharp tone. "I didn't mean to hit a raw nerve."

Cliff grimaced. "I didn't mean to bite your head off. Thanks for listening."

"If you'd like to call it an evening, I'll understand," Whitney assured him.

He insisted that he didn't want to call it an evening. They left the restaurant and went to a popular night spot and danced, as he'd originally planned.

"You're a marvelous dancer," Cliff complimented during a slow number.

"So are you," she replied. "You're just the right height for me."

"And you for me."

They danced together well. He should have felt an urge to tighten his arm and hold her body closer to his. Instead it was something he did because he hoped to kick start his male libido. To no avail. Any man in the room would probably have loved to be in his shoes, but Cliff inhaled her perfume and didn't respond.

He'd read once that the mind was the main sex organ. Tonight he couldn't keep his mind on Whitney. That was his problem. His thoughts kept wandering to Louisiana, where Andy would be asleep by now, and Jennifer—was she home with him or out on a date? This minute was she dancing in some man's arms, snuggling close?

Cliff missed a step and jerked his thoughts back to the present. Damn it, he should be enjoying himself thoroughly. It annoyed the hell out of him that he wasn't. He didn't care one way or another whether Andy's mom— and that was all Jennifer was to him, Andy's mom—was out with a man, as long as she'd hired a trustworthy sitter. And Cliff had every confidence that she wouldn't venture from the house at night, leaving Andy, unless she had.

Whitney suggested leaving about fifteen minutes later, and Cliff didn't argue. When they arrived at her townhouse, she didn't invite him in, much to his relief.

"Will you go out with me again in a few weeks and give me another shot?" he asked her.

"Absolutely," she replied and pressed her mouth lightly against his in a good-night kiss. "I think it speaks well of you as a man that you're not taking being a father in stride. If your pregnant girlfriend had been able to track you down years ago, I bet you would have done the old-fashioned, honorable thing and married her."

"I don't know what I would have done," Cliff admitted honestly.

Driving home, he got angry all over again, because the evening had been such a bust, needlessly. What had happened all those years ago had happened. There wasn't any changing anything.

Jennifer didn't want Cliff to upset the applecart now. Nor did Cliff want to upset the applecart. He would pay his child support, not a minimal amount, and know that he was assuming responsibility for Andy in the only way that was open to him, in the way that was best for all concerned.

Cliff left for Pensacola, Florida the next day, a Saturday. On Sunday he spent the day on the water, sailing on the company yacht of a man who was both client and friend. Monday he took care of his business in Pensacola and Tuesday he drove to Tampa where, as always, he combined work with pleasure.

His work was pleasure for him, for the most part. He enjoyed visiting boatyards and marinas and retail stores that sold boating equipment and supplies. The owners were usually yachting enthusiasts, Cliff's kind of people.

In every city in his territory, he got invitations to lunch, to dinner, to parties at local yacht clubs. He reciprocated and played host himself at restaurants. He had more opportunities to go sailing than he could possibly take advantage of. And the whole time he was representing his company very well.

It was a great job, tailor-made for his talents and interests and personality.

The week went by fast. On Thursday he returned to Atlanta for a sales meeting, pleased that he hadn't brooded about the new development in his life. The shock was fading and his sense of guilt was lessening. He was getting used to the idea that he had a son off in Louisiana. He was starting to accept his status as an anonymous parent.

Then he went through his accumulation of personal mail and found his returned check, along with Jennifer's brief note. Cliff completely blew his cool.

When he'd calmed down, he picked up the phone and punched out her number, which he didn't need to look up. He remembered it.

After three rings, an answering machine clicked on. Andy's boyish voice delivered the recorded message. Cliff felt an odd, disturbing pang of emotion and clenched his jaw, waiting for the beep.

If his call aroused Andy's curiosity, so be it. Cliff intended to set things straight with Jennifer, not try to reason with her. He meant to pay child support.

"Hand me your keys, Mom. I'll unlock the door."

Jennifer complied with her son's instructions and stood back, while he let them into the house. More and more of late, he was taking the initiative, not satisfied with being her little boy. It made her sad in a way to realize how fast he was growing up.

Inside he relocked the deadbolt and headed immediately for the kitchen, asking over his shoulder, "Want me to pour you a glass of milk, too?"

"No, thanks," she refused. "I'm going to jump into the shower."

In her bedroom Jennifer shed her wraparound skirt and peeled off leotard and tights. Her schedule as an aerobics instructor varied from month to month, but currently she taught classes on Tuesday and Thursday nights from seven to eight.

She eyed the bathtub longingly as she turned on the tap in preparation for taking a shower. It would have been nice to treat herself to a soak in the tub, but she preferred to spend the extra half hour with Andy before he went to bed.

Wearing a cotton caftan, she joined him in the living room, where he sat on the floor by the coffee table, sipping milk, munching a handful of cookies and watching TV. He'd done his homework at the club in her office.

"Any phone messages for me?" she asked as she sank down on the sofa. The answering machine was in the kitchen. If there'd been messages, he would have listened to them, since they usually were for him.

"Just one. Guess who called you? That Mr. King we met on the lakefront." He crammed the rest of a cookie in his mouth and picked up the TV remote to change channels.

Jennifer waited a few seconds for the shock waves to subside. "Did he say what he wanted?"

"No. He just said to call him back tonight. I saved the message so you could hear it for yourself."

"Later on I'll listen to it," she said, trying to convey a lack of interest.

"Are you gonna call him?"

"I doubt very much that I will. Especially not if the number's long-distance."

"It wasn't our area code. It was probably Atlanta, Georgia. Remember, that's where he lives."

Jennifer didn't reply, again hoping to seem indifferent rather than alarmed and panicky. Cliff had had time to receive his check back in the mail. Without any regard to raising Andy's curiosity, he'd called and left his name.

Andy finished his last cookie and drained his glass of milk, then got up to go and prepare for bed. Jennifer carried the empty glass to the kitchen and played the message. In a grim tone, Cliff commanded more than requested that she phone him long-distance at his home number.

With a troubled sigh, she wrote down the number, tucked it into her caftan pocket and erased the message. Later tonight she would return his call, after Andy had gone to bed. In the meantime, she would leave the phone off the hook. Cliff would get a busy signal if he called again.

Regardless of how her conversation with him went, tomorrow she would arrange for an unlisted number. Her nerves couldn't take it knowing that it wasn't safe for Andy to answer the telephone.

That it wasn't safe for her to pick up the receiver without wondering whether she'd hear Cliff's voice.

family.

Chapter Four

Jennifer sat on the edge of her bed, gazing at Cliff's phone number. She was tired and didn't feel up to talking to him tonight. Her emotions were too close to the surface.

It had been an effort for her to try to act as though nothing was wrong when she'd said good-night to Andy earlier and tucked him in. His trust in her, his confidence in her, his respect for her were all in jeopardy because of Cliff.

Maybe Jennifer had been wrong to make up a fictional family history for her little boy. She would admit to being fallible. But she'd done it for the right reasons, not wanting him to experience the shame that she still felt when she thought about her parents, her real family history. Her own relatives, who'd grudgingly raised her, had thrown it in her face that her biological father was a felon.

And that was all he'd been, her biological father. Estranged from her mother, his common-law wife, and serving a prison term when Jennifer came into the world, he'd ignored her existence. She'd been an unfortunate accident, just like Andy, the difference being that Andy had been loved in the womb, wanted in the womb, by *her*, his mother.

Jennifer doubted seriously that her mother had wanted her during pregnancy or afterward, though she had taken care of Jennifer after a fashion and shown her affection before she'd died. Sad to say, Jennifer was probably fortunate that her mother hadn't lived to raise her, considering the environment she would have grown up in.

Could anyone blame her for not sharing that kind of background with her innocent, impressionable child?

She hadn't made up wonderful memories such as visits to a now deceased grandma and grandpa. She'd simply omitted the sordid and ugly and glossed over the miserable.

Someday when Andy was grown-up and secure in his own identity, Jennifer would tell him the truth about her background, including how she'd got pregnant with him. By then he could understand her motives for lying.

But not now. Not any time soon. The truth would only harm him.

Andy was better off believing that his parents had been married and his father was dead. Jennifer sincerely believed that. If Cliff King truly wanted to do what was best for Andy and her, he would leave them alone. He would go about his life as usual and let them do the same.

Why couldn't he see that?

Sighing wearily, she put the slip of paper with his phone number in the drawer of her bedside table. She wouldn't call him tonight. It wouldn't do to talk to him when she was feeling so vulnerable.

Jennifer's worried state of mind didn't keep her awake. She'd had more than her share of worry during those first few years of being a single mother and had learned that getting her rest was essential for coping. Problems would always be there the next day.

When the phone beside her bed rang, she was soundly asleep. Groping for it, she wondered what time of the night it was. Her only concern was stopping the noise, to keep Andy from being disturbed.

"Hello," she mumbled into the mouthpiece, expecting some stranger's voice to apologize for calling the wrong number.

"Hello, Jennifer. Cliff King here. I guess I woke you."

Her fingers had gone lax, and she almost dropped the phone with the shock of his voice in her ear. Gripping it tighter, she mumbled indignantly, "It's the middle of the night." Her surprise was swirling the fog in her brain, but not clearing it away.

"It's only a quarter of eleven. That's hardly the middle of the night."

Jennifer peered at the illuminated face of her digital clock. It took her a few seconds to verify the time. When she didn't answer immediately, he continued talking. Even with the grim tone, his deep, resonant voice was pleasant to hear. She'd liked his voice so much eleven years ago.

"I've been sitting by the phone waiting for you to call me," he was saying. "Didn't you get my message?"

"Yes, I got it. But not before Andy heard it. That was very thoughtless of you, Cliff, calling and leaving your name like that." Keeping her voice low, Jennifer admonished him fiercely, her speech still not distinct. "He might hear me now and come in here and ask who I'm talking to at this hour."

"If you're afraid of waking him, go to another phone. Our conversation shouldn't take long. Then we can both get some sleep," he added, completely without remorse or sympathy.

"Hold on, then."

Her coordination wasn't fully at her command, either, as she put the phone down, sat up, turned on the lamp and climbed out of bed. Squinting at the brightness of the light, she trudged over to the doorway, leading into the hall, paused and carried on a groggy debate with herself. Should she go out to the kitchen? Or just close the bedroom door?

She closed the door and trudged back to the bed, aware of her bare feet sinking into the carpet. It was ridiculous, but she felt immodest wearing only her nightgown, with Cliff waiting on the line. Her caftan lay draped over a chair. She took some extra time to slip it over her head and then sat primly on the side of the bed and picked up the phone again.

"You can go ahead and say what's on your mind now." The last word was muffled in a yawn. Her sleepiness wouldn't dissipate.

"I was beginning to wonder if you hadn't dropped off to sleep," he said, sounding annoyed and impatient.

"I'm not functioning very well," she admitted.

"Your house isn't that big that it would take you more than a minute to go to any room in it."

"Our house is plenty big enough for Andy and me."

Her cheeks were warm with a silly embarrassment. Though there was absolutely nothing intimate about the call, she didn't want him to know that she'd stayed in her bedroom.

"I'm sure it is. My comment wasn't meant to be critical. Your house is quite nice."

His compliment was stiff.

"We like it. And I can afford the rent, if you're wondering." She had to get her wits about her. Too much was at stake not to be focused on the grave harm he could do to her and Andy.

"What do you do for a living, anyway?"

"I'm employed at a health-and-recreation club."

"How much do you earn?"

Jennifer bit off the words *None of your business* and named the amount of her last year's gross income on her tax return, rounding off the figure.

"What exactly is your job there?"

"I work in the business office. I'm also a part-time aerobics instructor. That's where we were tonight. I was teaching a class, and Andy was doing his homework. We were home by eight-fifteen."

"At which time you played my message and ignored it."

"I didn't ignore it," she objected. Would that she were capable of ignoring any message from him. "It wasn't convenient to call. And I've explained my feelings to you."

"I explained mine in the note that accompanied my check. I plan to put the check in the mail again tomorrow. You admitted just now that you work two jobs. On your income, you can damn well use the money."

How dare he talk to her like that. Jennifer held back a hot retort. As much as she wished she could tell him what he could do with his money, too much was at stake for her to flare up and let go of her self-control. Somehow she had to reason with him, *not* be argumentative or hostile.

"Whatever pay I earn for teaching aerobics classes is more in the nature of a bonus. Or what we call *lagniappe* here in Louisiana. I would work out regularly anyway, to get exercise and stay healthy. It would have to be at night, since, like most of the working mothers in my classes, I hold down a regular job." She continued with calm emphasis, "As for being able to use extra money, anyone can, no matter what their income is. The point is, I'm able to support my child and myself adequately."

"God, you're stubborn!" he muttered.

Jennifer didn't answer, not trusting herself. She'd left the opening for Cliff to say *He's my child, too,* but he hadn't spoken those words. He didn't claim Andy in his heart, and thus he had no rights, no obligations. On her little boy's behalf, she felt anew a sense of hurt and rejection.

It didn't matter. She loved Andy enough to make up for his father's not loving him on sight.

"Look, Jennifer," Cliff said wearily. "I can see where you're coming from. I wasn't there for you when you may have really needed financial support. The fact remains that this whole thing has really messed up my head. I *can't* walk away from it, like you seem to expect. I have a responsibility. So cash the damned checks I send you and put them to some good use for him."

He hadn't called Andy by name. The realization brought a pang of sadness and removed all uncertainty.

"I won't cash any checks you send, Cliff. It's wrong of you to insist. How can you expect me to take money from you against my conscience simply to ease your guilt feelings? Put yourself in my place, for heaven's sake."

"Put yourself in *my* place."

"That's impossible, I'm afraid." Jennifer tried her best not to sound accusing. "Tell me honestly. What was your reaction when you learned he was your son? Were you glad? Are you glad now?"

"I sure as hell didn't feel like rushing out and buying a box of cigars. He's a great kid, but it hit me like a ton of bricks to learn that he was *my* kid. I think the majority of guys would react the same way," he defended himself strongly.

"Probably they would," she concurred in fairness. He hadn't responded to her final question about his present state of mind. He didn't need to. After the worst of the shock had worn off, he still wasn't glad. He hadn't yet and probably never would think of Andy with a thrill of pride mingled with joy.

Suddenly the strain of the conversation was too much. Any moment she would break down and start crying. That would never do. She had to hold on to her composure long enough to restate her position calmly and rationally.

"It was very unfortunate that we had to run into you, Cliff. Otherwise you'd never have known. Let it be enough that you were more than willing to pay child support. Your check was very generous. Now I'm going to hang up. It's late, and I have to get up early. Please don't call again or try to communicate with me. Do what's best for all three of us, even if it's not easy."

Jennifer cradled the phone gently and let her body sag. She felt utterly drained.

Had she convinced him? She thought maybe she had. She prayed she had.

Perhaps he would make another attempt or two to pay child support. Eventually, though, he would give up, because he had no real interest in being a father to Andy. That was the message she'd gotten from tonight's phone conversation.

She hadn't expected any sudden change of attitude in Cliff. Why, then, did she feel such deep disappointment?

It was late, and she was too tired for soul-searching. Jennifer rose and drew the caftan over her head. Wearily she plodded over to her bedroom door to open it again. On impulse she continued down the hall to Andy's room. Looking in on him would cure this heartsick feeling.

He was sleeping restfully, the sheet still tucked around his waist. She tiptoed over and gazed down at him. The maternal love and tenderness that welled up in her heart left no room for any other emotions.

Bending down and pressing a kiss to his forehead, she felt a renewal of her single-minded purpose in life, nurturing and protecting her child.

By Wednesday of the following week, no envelope from Cliff had arrived. Jennifer made a point of coming home at noon to check the mail.

Then on Thursday there it was in the mailbox, the same company stationery. This time he hadn't hand-addressed the envelope but had stuck on a computer-printed label. Or someone had stuck it on. A secretary perhaps.

Her name and address had been entered in a mailing-data file that could generate identical labels on command. That Cliff was implementing such businesslike efficiency awoke alarm in Jennifer. It bespoke resoluteness.

Had she read him wrong in their phone conversation? she asked herself, hurrying into the house. Dear God, she hoped this hadn't turned into a battle of wills for him.

He hadn't written a note this time. The page of paper enclosing his check was blank.

Jennifer stared a long time at the check. His bold masculine scrawl looked familiar. If only he'd jotted some message to clue her in on his state of mind.

Should she just go ahead and cash the check? Was that the wisest course of action in the long run? Put aside her strong sense of conviction, and humor him?

His good intentions probably would weaken after he'd had his way, if this was a battle of wills. Before long, the checks wouldn't arrive regularly. Eventually they undoubtedly wouldn't arrive at all. But there would be that possibility that an envelope would turn up in the mail, that Andy might see it, might discover its contents.

Jennifer couldn't take the risk.

And it wasn't fair, wasn't right that she should go against her conscience, her convictions. For ten years Andy had been her sole responsibility, and he still was. Cliff was offering only money. If he were offering more, then it would be an entirely different matter.

She *wouldn't* cash the check.

So what to do? Send it back or simply tear it up? Better the latter, she decided. Returning the check could affect him like waving a red flag in his face, and that wasn't her intent at all. By the time his bank statement arrived, he might be preoccupied with other matters in his bachelor's life.

For all Jennifer knew, Cliff might be living with a current girlfriend at this address. Banishing the pointless speculation, she ripped up the check into tiny fragments, replaced them in the envelope, crumpled it and buried it deep in her kitchen garbage pail. Still not satisfied, she removed the plastic liner, knotted the top and took the half-filled bag to the garage, where she deposited it in the large garbage container.

There, she told herself. *That's taken care of, for now.*

Her stomach was in knots and she had no appetite, nevertheless Jennifer fixed herself a light lunch and ate it because she believed in good nutrition just as she believed in exercise. A healthy regimen made for a healthier person, and as a single parent she couldn't afford to let herself get run-down or stressed out. It wouldn't be fair to Andy.

She had to be strong and well and capable and wise for him.

The next garbage pickup was on Saturday. Jennifer was relieved to return home from grocery shopping and find their garbage container empty at the edge of the driveway. The secret item of garbage had gone to some landfill.

Now she could relax.

The rest of May passed. At the end of the month, she received her bank statement and knew that Cliff's bank had probably mailed out statements, too. She had a couple of outstanding checks that should have cleared. Perhaps he would have several and maybe the one written to her wouldn't be so noticeable in its absence among his canceled checks.

Now he couldn't pick up the phone and call her. Jennifer had gotten an unlisted number. He would have to write her a letter if he wanted to communicate with her.

She began checking the mail daily with a nervous feeling in the pit of her stomach. Sure enough, an envelope from him arrived. Inside was a handwritten letter and a check. Intent on reading the former, Jennifer put aside the check without looking at it.

Dear Jennifer, he'd written in his bold penmanship, *Enclosed is a check for $1000. It's money for Andy. Put it to some good use for him. There are no strings attached, if that's what you're worried about. Hope you and Andy are both well. Cliff.* He'd included home and office numbers again.

A sad bitterness welled up in Jennifer as she re-read the letter. No, there weren't any strings attached. There wasn't any attachment involved, just conscience. His check was conscience money.

He'd said that he was in a high income bracket. Apparently he was, judging from his persistence in paying such a generous amount of child support. Jennifer picked up the check and gazed at it. As he'd indicated, it was for the sum of one thousand dollars. At the bottom, he'd penned the notation, May, June.

Next month would he send a check for May, June, and July in the amount of $1500? Alarm flared up as she considered another alternative—Cliff could deliver a check in person. He'd told Andy that he came to New Orleans on business. It was only a thirty-minute drive across the causeway.

He could show up here at her house unannounced.

For a few panicky moments, Jennifer entertained desperate thoughts. She could move to a different address, a different town, a different state, even. No, of course, she wouldn't move. She and Andy were happy here in this house, this neighborhood, this town.

To ensure their happiness, she really had no option other than to cash Cliff's check before the month was out. And cash any others that he sent. He was in the driver's seat because he didn't seem to care about Andy's real wellbeing. It was a bitter realization.

Jennifer hid the check away in her handbag and then managed to get down some lunch before she returned to her job.

Cliff decided that he wasn't going to wait and stew in suspense until his bank statement came before he took action. He was due to make a trip to New Orleans and had a business-related matter to take care of in Mandeville. While he was on the Northshore, he would look Jennifer up at her place of employment and settle things with her, once and for all. Then maybe he could settle down and get back to normal.

If he wasn't thinking about Andy these days, he was thinking about Jennifer. He would bet he'd gone over his two conversations with her—the first on that Sunday at her house and the second on the phone—at least a thousand times. He'd relived over and over the scene on the lakefront with Andy.

This whole situation was turning Cliff into a basket case. He was so damned sick of feeling guilty.

Arriving in Mandeville, he found a pay phone with a Northshore phone directory and turned to the yellow pages. Jennifer had said she worked at a health club. He found the listings and began calling them in order and asking to speak to her. On the third call, the person answering responded, "Hold on, and I'll ring her extension." Cliff hung up, knowing he'd hit pay dirt.

He studied the ad of the Northshore Health and Recreation Club. It would seem to be the club to join in the area. It had tennis courts, racquetball courts, basketball courts, Olympic-sized swimming pool for adults and full-sized fun pool for children, up-to-date fitness equipment, aerobics classes, nursery, snack bar, even a retail shop selling athletic clothing and shoes. At the bottom of the ad was the location, with a simple map that made asking for directions unnecessary.

Cliff found the club without any difficulty. He parked his rental car and got out. It was a quarter to twelve. If she was gone on her lunch hour, then he would wait for her to return. His appointment at the yacht club wasn't until two-thirty.

He wouldn't need more than ten minutes of Jennifer's time. Cliff hadn't come to negotiate.

The club building was a two-story structure with cedar siding. A bright blue canvas canopy shaded the entrance. Healthy-looking shrubs and annuals in full bloom grew in raised beds that were typical here in Louisiana, with all its rainfall. A nice facility, judging from the outside, Cliff thought, getting out of his car and glancing around the large parking lot, which was almost full.

Through a tall wire-mesh fence, he could see tennis games in progress and hear the thunks of rackets connecting with balls. From the far side of the building, where presumably the swimming pools were located, came the shouts and laughter of children and an occasional loud splash.

It occurred to Cliff for the first time that Andy probably wasn't in school today. Summer vacation would have begun the first week in June.

Where was he today? Could he be *here?*

Cliff stood in the parking lot, hands in his pockets, suddenly ambivalent about going inside. Encountering Jennifer face-to-face again was one thing. Encountering mother *and* son was something else entirely.

His kid. By now he should be used to the idea, but he wasn't.

His judgment told him that it was unlikely that Jennifer often brought Andy to work with her. No employer was that tolerant, and this wasn't a mom-and-pop operation.

Cliff headed for the canopied entrance, passing a stream of club members making their exit. The majority of the adults were female, with children in tow.

The glances at him were curious, understandably. He'd gotten dressed that morning to call on clients, in a red-striped button-down shirt open at the neck, khaki trousers, navy blazer and bone-colored deck shoes with navy socks. In the course of doing business, he routinely went aboard yachts, so hard-soled loafers, his regular street shoes, weren't suitable. While his attire was casual for most sales reps, he stood out in this setting, not wearing exercise clothes or carrying an athletic bag.

Or maybe it was his expression that was attracting attention, Cliff realized, reaching the glass doors and seeing his reflection. He hardly recognized himself with the set jaw and frown. Generally he was a laid-back kind of guy.

His blond hair was windblown. He'd driven across the causeway with the car window rolled down. Since he didn't have a comb on him, his fingers would have to do. Cliff shoved his hair back and smoothed it down and tried to look less fierce as he entered the club.

A cute college-age girl wearing a blue T-shirt was stationed behind a counter. The name of the club was emblazoned on the front of her shirt. She flashed him a bright smile and greeted him with a friendly "Hi."

He smiled back at her and felt more like himself. "Hi. I'm Cliff King. Could you direct me to the business office?" he requested pleasantly. "I'm here to see Jennifer Anderson."

She jotted down his name on a clipboard. "Take a right and go up the stairs. The business office is on your left."

On his way to the stairs, Cliff passed through a wide glass-walled corridor with racquetball courts on either side. So far he was as impressed with the inside of the club as with its exterior.

Reaching the second floor, he immediately spotted an open door with the word "office" painted in black block letters. He walked into the room, a typical modern business office with desk and computer and file cabinets. No one was there, but Cliff could hear female voices coming through a door leading into what he assumed was an adjoining office. Neither of the voices was Jennifer's.

Was this her desk? he wondered and walked over nearer. A small framed photograph provided him with his answer. Cliff picked it up and gazed at a picture of Andy. Self-conscious grin. A good-looking kid.

It was probably his school picture. If she was like Cliff's mother, Jennifer bought the packet every year and had extras in some drawer. Maybe she would give the picture to him.

Abruptly Cliff set the frame back on the desk, as though it had burned his fingers. He strode over to the doorway toward the voices. "Excuse me."

The conversation stopped, then one of the women inquired, "Can we help you?"

Remembering his reflection in the plate-glass doors at the entrance, Cliff tried for a calm, pleasant expression.

"Hello." He greeted the two women from just inside the door. They were both in their mid-thirties. One sat behind a desk, and the other sat perched on it, wearing nylon warm-up pants and a club T-shirt. "I came by to see Jennifer. I gather she's on her lunch break."

Both pairs of female eyes were appraising him with open curiosity. Cliff resisted the impulse to smooth back his hair.

The woman in the warm-up pants spoke. "Jennifer went down to the snack bar a couple of minutes ago to have lunch with her son. He's enrolled in our junior tennis clinic. You know Andy?"

"Yes, I've met him." He'd *met* his own son. He didn't *know* him and probably never would.

She stood and approached Cliff, holding out her hand. "I'm Brenda Philips. My husband and I own Northshore."

He shook her hand. "Cliff King."

She introduced the other woman, presumably a coworker of Jennifer's. "This is Gretchen Sawyer."

Cliff nodded to her. "Nice to meet you." He glanced at his watch to indicate time pressures. "I'll drop by the snack bar." Before either of them could offer to take him there, he turned and left.

What now? he asked himself outside in the corridor.

The wall at the head of the stairs was partially glass, affording a view of the tennis courts as well as letting in natural light. When he'd passed this way before, Cliff had barely glanced down to take in the activity. He'd been too intent on his mission.

Now he walked over and gazed out. Two courts to the far left were occupied by youngsters and a couple of adults, obviously instructors. Without any trouble, he picked out Andy.

My kid, he thought.

Cliff was a fair tennis player and a fair golfer. If he'd played either sport with more regularity, he could have been better than average. He'd been endowed with good hand-eye coordination and natural athletic ability. Unknowingly, he'd passed those genes along to Andy. That was evident from watching a few minutes of the tennis clinic.

Good forehand, kid, he applauded silently with an emotion oddly like pride.

So what was he going to do? Leave the club without seeing Jennifer or go to the snack bar and find her?

He was going to the snack bar.

It was down on the ground level. Cliff had noted a sign with an arrow and found his way without asking anyone for directions.

He saw her immediately, standing with her back to him at the station for ordering and picking up food. In a different state of mind, he could have appreciated the view of her figure in her summery outfit, especially from the waist down. A sleeveless yellow blouse was tucked into a narrow white denim skirt, the hemline just above the knees. Her legs were bare and she wore sandals.

Cliff came to within a few yards and stopped, waiting for his chance to alert her to his presence.

"What would you like to drink, Jennifer?" the college-age fellow waiting on her inquired. He looked like a bodybuilder.

"Two low-fat milks, Brad," she replied. "Or make it one low-fat milk and one regular soda."

He grinned at her. "Soda's for Andy?"

She nodded, her glossy dark brown hair bouncing with the motion. It was hair that invited touching, unlike so many women's hair these days. "He'll probably be thirsty."

"Kid's a good little tennis player, isn't he? I was watching the clinic earlier from the weight room."

"He plans to be the next Jim Courier or Pete Sampras. He can't decide which," she said laughing, maternal pride and affection in her voice. The comment had obviously pleased her no end.

It had pleased Cliff, too.

"One low-fat milk and one regular soda. And your food's ready." Brad inventoried her order as he loaded her tray. "Hamburger and fries, veggie melt on whole wheat bun. Enjoy, as they say."

"Thanks, Brad."

Brad glanced past her at Cliff. "Can I help you, sir?"

"No, thank you," Cliff refused.

Jennifer had picked up the tray and was turning around, a smile on her lips. At the sound of his voice, she jerked to a stop, the smile fading and her brown eyes widening with shocked disbelief.

"*Cliff . . .*" she murmured faintly, all the healthy color leaving her pretty face.

"Hi, Jennifer." Cliff quickly stepped forward and took the tray from her hands before she dropped it. "There's an empty table over there." He nodded in the direction of the table and led the way. She followed at a distance.

Cliff set the tray down and pulled out her chair for her. She sank into it as though her knees were weak.

"You can't stay, Cliff," she objected in a low, panicky voice when he pulled out a chair for himself. "Andy's here at the club. He'll be joining me for lunch any minute."

"I know he's here," Cliff replied, dropping down across from her. "I saw him out on the tennis courts."

"You went out there? He saw you?"

He shook his head. "No, I glanced out the window upstairs when I went to your office looking for you."

"You have to go," she pleaded. "He'll remember you. You made a big impression on him. Don't you *care*—" She broke off and answered her own unfinished question with bitter recrimination. "Obviously you don't."

"It didn't occur to me that Andy would be at work with you," Cliff said in his defense. "I'll say what I came to say and leave."

"If you're here to discuss paying child support, you've won. I intend to cash your check."

"You do?"

"Yes. I just haven't done it yet."

"Well, then, I guess there's nothing to discuss. I can be on my way." But Cliff made no move to rise.

The snack bar was separated from a busy passageway by a wrought-iron railing. From his vantage point, Cliff could see the whole length of the passageway. At the far end, double glass doors led outside to the tennis courts. He saw the crowd of youngsters with tennis rackets coming inside. He spotted Andy among them, carrying his racket on his shoulder.

Cliff had time to get up and slip away. But he didn't. He sat there.

"Andy is headed this way," he warned Jennifer, who grew even more pale. "Try to act natural and let me do the talking."

Andy eyed him curiously as he approached the table, coming up behind his mother. He wore baggy white shorts and a T-shirt several sizes too big, in tune with the current fashion.

"Hi, Andy," Cliff greeted the boy. Another impulse took hold, and he held out his hand. "You probably don't remember me."

Andy pumped Cliff's hand. Cliff could feel the sweaty warmth of his son's small hand, the calluses on his palm. He'd wanted to make physical contact with the kid, he realized.

"Yeah, I do," Andy replied. "You're Mr. King. You threw the Frisbee with Kevin and me on the lakefront. And you called my mom and left a message on the machine." He dragged out a chair for himself. It scraped on the ceramic floor.

Jennifer spoke up, "Before you eat your lunch, Andy, you should shower in the locker room and change clothes."

"But, Mom, my hamburger and fries will be cold!" Andy protested.

"He's right," Cliff remarked, knowing that he really had no right to put in his two cents' worth. Jennifer glanced at him reproachfully.

"I'm starving, Mom."

"I guess you are." She gave in, and Andy sat down and immediately started unwrapping his hamburger.

"Aren't you having any lunch, Mr. King?" he asked.

Jennifer answered for him. "Mr. King doesn't have time to eat." She began to unwrap her sandwich.

"I have an appointment with the commodore of the Pontchartrain Yacht Club," Cliff explained, watching the boy bite hungrily into his burger. "Ketchup?" He pushed the bottle closer.

Busy chewing, Andy nodded and dumped ketchup on his fries. "Have some," he offered generously when he'd washed down his food with a swallow of soda. Before Cliff could refuse, he moved the paper plate between him and Cliff.

"Thanks." Cliff picked up a french fry and ate it.

"What's your appointment with the commodore about?" Andy inquired.

"It's not polite of you to ask," Jennifer mildly scolded her son. She'd managed to choke down a small bite of her sandwich with obvious difficulty.

"The nature of my business isn't confidential," Cliff said. "The company I work for supports youth sailing programs. I have a check for the commodore to be spent on enlarging the yacht club's fleet of small sailboats, which is used for teaching sailing and is used also by members and their children free of charge."

"How much is the check for?"

"One thousand dollars."

"Wow! That's a lot of money."

Jennifer was grasping the edges of the tray, making no pretense of eating. Cliff guessed that she was thinking of his check to her written in the same amount. Up until now, paying child support had been something his conscience insisted upon. That had changed somehow. Sitting here with Andy, he suddenly *wanted* to pay child support for reasons other than conscience.

"I'll bet sailing is lots of fun, huh?" Andy speculated wistfully.

"I love it," Cliff said simply.

"How old were you when you learned?"

"Twelve years old. My best friend's father bought a sailboat, and I went out sailing with them every weekend."

"You own your own sailboat now?"

"No, but I plan to in a few years, when I can afford it. The kind of sailboat I plan to buy is very expensive."

"Like those fancy boats that race over from New Orleans?"

Cliff nodded. "Like those fancy boats." Right now he could afford a smaller, less "fancy" sailboat.

"I'm only ten," Andy mused. "Maybe in a couple of years, I can take sailing lessons." He glanced guiltily at his mother, as though conscious of some disloyalty to her, and added stoutly, "I'm too busy this summer, what with tennis and swimming, huh, Mom?"

She leaned toward him and smoothed his mussed blond hair from his forehead. "By the time you're twelve, if you still want to take sailing lessons, then you can. Okay?"

"*Okay!*"

He munched happily on his burger and fries. Cliff met Jennifer's solemnly questioning gaze. Her *Okay?* had been meant for him, too. She'd conceded on the issue of his financial obligation to Andy. Now, would he go away and stay away?

Cliff nodded slightly. He'd succeeded in his purpose for coming here today, but he felt anything but good about it.

"When you called our house, Mr. King, what did you want to talk to Mom about?" Andy asked curiously.

"Andy." Jennifer spoke his name as a gentle reproof. "Son, you're getting old enough to learn that you can't ask adults just any question that pops into your head."

"Sorry. I just wondered what was so important. Mr. King called long-distance."

Cliff reached over and squeezed his shoulder. "Your mom is right. Some questions are impertinent. I got that same lecture many a time."

"You had trouble telling the difference, too?" Andy picked up a french fry, and Cliff helped himself to another one.

"Finally I figured out that the questions that had me the most curious were the ones I shouldn't ask. As for my calling long-distance, most of the phone calls I make are long-distance. So I think nothing of it. Since I'd met you and your mother on the lakefront, I hadn't been able to get her off my mind." From Jennifer's expression, she assumed he'd made up a glib lie, but it wasn't a lie. Just not the whole truth—that he hadn't been able to get either of them off his mind.

"Because you thought you knew her before."

"Right. But it must be a fairly common occurrence for a man to phone your house. Your mom is a pretty woman, and she's single."

Andy angled a grin at Jennifer. "She is real pretty."

"It's *not* a common occurrence for men to call our house," she stated. Her cheeks had gotten some attractive color in them.

"Mom doesn't go out on dates. She'd rather do things with me."

"Well, I certainly have to commend her. She's doing a fine job raising you alone." Cliff pushed back his chair and rose. "I enjoyed talking to you, Andy. Keep up the good work with your tennis, and one day I may be watching you on television. Now I'd better shove off."

"Will you be coming back to Mandeville some time?"

Cliff met Jennifer's gaze and read nothing but anxiousness in the soft brown depths. He shook his head. "Not in the foreseeable future." After a last, lingering glance at the bright, likable ten-year-old who was his kid, he turned and left.

"Bye, Mr. King," Andy called after him.

Chapter Five

"How did Mr. King happen to come here, to the club, Mom?"

Jennifer was watching Cliff walk away with long, hurried strides. This was the last they'd see of him. The thought brought not comfort, but an emotion like despair. It had taken her so by surprise for him to appear out of nowhere. All her woman's defenses had been down, leaving her vulnerable to his rugged handsomeness, his likeableness.

Andy was sitting there waiting for an answer. She had to pull herself together and satisfy his curiosity with as much of the truth as she dared tell him.

"Mr. King came here looking for me," she said to her son, trying to sound normal and calm. "That same night he left his message on our machine, he called again after you'd gone to bed. He asked about my job. That's how he was able to find me at work."

"Our phone number isn't listed now. He couldn't call you again because he doesn't know it." Andy put two and two together for himself.

"That's right. Mr. King was part of the reason I got an unlisted number. Now not just anyone can call and bother us."

He nodded and sighed. "You don't like Mr. King at all, even though he thinks you're pretty and likes you. Do you, Mom?"

"I certainly don't *dis*like Mr. King. He seems like a nice man."

"I like him," Andy reflected. "I wouldn't mind if you went out on some dates with him. Then I would get to see him, too."

Jennifer's heart squeezed painfully at the note of regret in his young voice. She was feeling her own complicated regrets.

"Would you like some dessert? Some ice cream?"

"I'm full now, but can I have some later?"

"Yes, you may. Just sign the ticket. Tell me about the clinic while I finish eating. Brad was watching you from the weight room and said what a good tennis player you are."

He glowed at the praise, which meant more coming from Brad, Jennifer knew, than from Marlene or Gretchen or even from one of the women fitness instructors. Lacking a father's attention, Andy valued praise and attention from adult males.

Had she let him down by not dating more, by giving up on finding a man she could care deeply for, who would also be a wonderful stepfather?

That afternoon Jennifer had no opportunity to brood. Cliff's visit to the club had created a small sensation. Who was he? When and where had she met him? Repeatedly she was grilled by her curious and thrilled co-workers, and by Brenda. Jennifer stuck to a simplified version of the truth, that she and Andy had run into him on the lakefront some time ago. He was in Mandeville on business and had looked her up.

"He's *gorgeous!*" Brenda Bailey rhapsodized.

At least three of the well-intentioned inquisitors who'd popped into the office, including Brenda, picked up Andy's photograph from her desk and remarked without suspicion on the chance resemblance.

"Why, if you were to end up marrying him, Jennifer," Brenda mused, "hardly anyone would believe Andy wasn't his son."

"I'm not going to end up marrying him. I doubt I'll ever see him again."

Her only communication with him would be checks sent through the mail. With his conscience at ease, he could go about his life now and forget them. It was what Jennifer had urged him to do from the outset.

But not what she'd wanted deep in her heart.

Cliff hadn't eaten any lunch, and there was enough time to go to a restaurant before he met with the commodore. But he wasn't really hungry. The taste of the fries he'd eaten off Andy's plate lingered in his mouth.

It was the closest he would come to having a meal with Andy, he couldn't help thinking.

Pulling out of the club parking lot, he drove without any clear destination, generally in the direction of the yacht club and the Mandeville harbor. He felt so damned lousy, so dissatisfied.

What he needed to shake his mood was to walk the docks of a marina, Cliff decided. A marina with sailboats. There was one tucked away near the causeway.

He'd noticed the cluster of masts, always as beautiful a sight for him as a virgin forest was for a camping buff.

After a few wrong turns, he located the marina behind a two-story building with a restaurant. Surrounding it were new-looking condo buildings. A sprinkling of realtors' signs indicated that some of the units were for sale.

Not a bad setup, Cliff thought, owning a condo a few steps away from a nice marina by the lake. If things were different—

What the hell was he thinking?

After discarding his blazer and leaving it in the car, Cliff walked along the network of piers, soothed by the sights and sounds of the marina. He stopped and examined a pretty sloop in pristine condition with a For Sale sign on it, about a thirty-footer. The owner had written his asking price on the sign, along with his phone number.

A damned good price. Cliff could buy the sloop outright. He wouldn't need to finance it.

That's what he would do, too, if he were going to come to Louisiana regularly to see Andy. He would buy a boat, teach the kid how to sail himself. If he took to it, Cliff would join the yacht club and give Andy a taste of racing. He just bet the kid would love it.

But none of that would happen because Cliff wasn't going to come to Louisiana even occasionally to see Andy. Jennifer would never be in favor of it, and the idea scared Cliff every bit as much as it appealed to him.

For one thing, seeing Andy meant seeing Jennifer. Mother and son seemed to be a package deal. Whitney Blair's words came back to Cliff: *ready-made family.*

If a man were looking for a ready-made family, he couldn't hope to do better. Andy was a super kid, and Jennifer was a pretty, sexy woman. She would undoubtedly make as good a wife as she was a good mom and homemaker. Cliff had reason to know that sharing a bedroom with her would be a pleasure.

But he *wasn't* looking for a ready-made family. Nor was he at all confident that he had it in him to be the kind of husband and father those two deserved. He couldn't imagine himself living with them in their cozy house in their family neighborhood. The very thought put him in a hurry to see the commodore and get back to New Orleans.

Cliff couldn't travel fast or far enough to get mother or son off his mind for very long during the next week or the week that followed. Not even sailing seemed to put his life back on track. Wherever he went, he saw ten-year-old boys and thought about Andy. He had dreams about Jennifer and woke up physically aroused as well as disturbed.

When it occurred to him that he hadn't been with a woman in months, not since that fateful day on the lakefront, he went out on several dates that turned out to be flops. Angry at himself and also angry at Jennifer, he stewed and cursed.

Hell, he might as well be married to her, if he were going to *feel* tied down. And that was his problem. He was carrying around a guilty conscience the size of a boulder, feeling a commitment to a woman who clearly wanted no part of him.

Eleven years ago when Jennifer got pregnant, Cliff might have found himself a groom in a shotgun wedding if he hadn't already moved on. It was all in his mind, he knew, but he felt as though he was confronted with entrapment now.

Paying child support wasn't going to get him off the hook, as he'd hoped. Cliff was in deeper than he wanted to be, and more than conscience was involved here.

Something compelling, which tapped needs in himself that
scared him.

Despite his qualms, he wanted to know his son, be a
part of his life. He wanted to be on friendly terms with
Jennifer, earn her respect and trust, make up for not having been there for her the last eleven years.

What he *didn't* want was to make a commitment he
couldn't live up to.

"You've been a big help. We're almost finished." Jennifer smiled at her son, who was busily stuffing newslet-
ters into envelopes.

"I don't mind doing this," he said. "I can stick the labels on, if you want."

"We can do it together."

They worked companionably at the table in her office.
Usually Jennifer commandeered a couple of the high-
school or college workers to help, but today she'd had to
tackle the job alone. Andy had volunteered his services.

When they'd finished stuffing the envelopes, she let him
help her print out the labels with names and addresses of
club members. Before they sat down again at the table,
she excused herself to make a trip to the rest room.

"Be right back," she promised. "You can catch the
phone, if it rings, and take down any messages."

When she returned, he was seated behind her desk,
talking animatedly on the phone.

"Who is it?" she mouthed.

"Hold on, my mom's back." Without covering the
mouthpiece, he spoke to her, "It's Mr. King. He's calling
from New Orleans."

Jennifer's heart stopped. When it started beating again,
much too fast, a jittery sense of gladness was mixed with
her surprise and alarm.

Andy resumed his conversation. He'd broken off in the midst of telling about the recent junior tennis tournament at City Park in New Orleans that he'd won in his age group. She walked around behind the desk, composing herself and letting him finish his story before she butted in.

"Let me talk to Mr. King."

"Okay." With obvious reluctance, he laid the phone down and scooted out of her way. "If Mr. King asks you out on a date, Mom, say yes. I can spend the night with Kevin."

Jennifer grew hot with mortification, knowing that Cliff had surely heard. "Why don't you go down to the snack bar and get us a cold drink?"

He obediently obeyed her request.

"Hello, Cliff." She managed to inject a note of reproof into her voice.

"Hi, Jennifer. How are you?"

His slight hesitancy made embarrassment well up in another hot tide, along with the sheer pleasure of hearing his voice again. "I'm fine. Why are you calling?"

"As I heard Andy mentioning, I'm in New Orleans. I called to ask if you and I could get together this evening. We need to talk. If you're free, I would like to drive over to Mandeville. We could have dinner."

He might as well have added with the same cautious earnestness, *Please don't mistake my intentions.. This isn't a date.*

"I am free," she replied with as much dignity as she could scrape together. "But what is there that we need to discuss?"

"Actually, a great deal. Jennifer, my thinking has changed radically over the past weeks, since that Sunday I came to your house."

Jennifer gripped the phone tight, his grave words making her blood run cold. "Cliff, you're not planning on getting a lawyer and—"

"Nothing like that," he assured her quickly. "Don't go jumping to wrong conclusions. No lawyers. I want to work out a friendly agreement between us. So, can I pick you up at seven-thirty?"

"Yes, I suppose," she said.

"That's great." He sounded enormously relieved. "Thank you for seeing me, Jennifer."

"Couldn't you have called from Atlanta, Cliff, and given me a little more advance notice?" Indignation had started to set in. "I'm tired of being taken by surprise like this. You just show up or call when the urge strikes. I guess you had to come to New Orleans on business." And had just worked her in, at his convenience.

"No, this isn't a business trip. I came at my own expense."

At least he'd made a special trip solely to discuss Andy. That made Jennifer feel a little better. The radical change in his thinking had to do with pressing for visitation rights. What else could it be?

She would have to agree. What choice did she have, despite her worries and fears about doing what was best for Andy?

"I'd better hang up. Andy will be back," she said, all her mother's anxiety in her voice.

"I need to hang up, too," Cliff answered, his tone gently apologetic. "I'm meeting someone in forty-five minutes."

Who was the person he was meeting? A woman friend in New Orleans? He'd said he hadn't come on business. Added to all her other emotions, Jennifer felt a jealous pain squeezing her heart.

* * *

Cliff sighed as he cradled the phone. He didn't guess he could blame Jennifer for treating him like a case of plague. It was going to be a slow process, gaining her respect and confidence.

At least she hadn't balked at seeing him tonight. *So far, so good.* Now on to the next step in his weekend plans, buying a sailboat.

His appointment was with the owner of the sloop he'd admired in the Mandeville marina. They'd already come to a gentleman's agreement. Today they were meeting at a notary's office to sign the bill of sale, at which time Cliff would hand over his cashier's check.

Yesterday morning the sloop had been hauled out at a Mandeville boatyard and examined by a marine surveyor, at Cliff's expense. The survey had uncovered no structural or mechanical defects. In the afternoon Cliff and the owner had taken the sloop out for a trial sail, so that Cliff could see for himself how she handled.

After about thirty minutes on the water, Cliff had sat back in the cockpit with a grin, knowing that he was soon to be a boat owner. It was a damned good feeling, if different from what he'd always imagined.

The sloop wasn't the super racing yacht he'd dreamed of owning someday, but she was perfect for the kind of sailing he wanted to do now. With Andy. With Andy *and* his mom, if she could get past her bias against sailboats and sailors and chose to come along.

Cliff's only reservation about having Jennifer as a crew member was that the idea was much too appealing. When he thought of it, he had to block vivid flashbacks of the long-ago sailing trip with her. The sailing trip that had made him a father.

He'd done some serious thinking about his relationship with Jennifer. Whatever the temptation—and it was
going to be strong, he knew—rushing into any kind of
man-woman thing was unwise. Theirs was going to be a
relationship of long duration, one that couldn't be broken off when it went sour. And all Cliff's romances had
eventually gone sour.

Jennifer was always going to be Andy's mother, and he
was always going to be Andy's dad. They needed to establish a solid base of friendship first and proceed very
slowly, if they proceeded at all, to become intimately involved.

Because down the road would be marriage. No doubt
about it, the realization made him nervous and cautious,
and it wasn't just a typical bachelor's wariness. Cliff
couldn't stand the thought of making a commitment and
falling short and letting Jennifer and Andy down.

Fortunately, he could count on her cooperation to keep
him in line. Making friends with her wasn't even going to
be easy. Whatever she'd seen in him originally had definitely died. The message he'd gotten from her repeatedly
was, *Go away and stay away. We don't need you.*

Well, Cliff was going to change her low opinion of him.
He was going to be there for her and Andy from now on.

"Mom, you look real *pretty.*"

"I'm glad you think so." Jennifer patted her son's
cheek in grateful appreciation for his compliment.
"You're prejudiced."

"I'll bet Mr. King thinks you look pretty, too."

"Mr. King is a very handsome bachelor. He undoubtedly goes out on dates all the time with beautiful women."

It was a fact she would try not to lose sight of tonight.
While her first and foremost concern was the discussion

she and Cliff would have about Andy, Jennifer didn't want to make a fool of herself.

She'd refused to let herself wear her new sundress. She'd overcome the temptation to take extra care with her makeup, the temptation to fuss with her hair. Tonight *wasn't* a date, she'd kept reminding herself as she got dressed.

The yellow skirt and blouse she'd finally selected was a standby of her summer wardrobe. After she'd slipped it on, she'd almost taken it off again, remembering that she'd worn a yellow dress the day she'd met Cliff in the secondhand bookstore in Fort Lauderdale. But, of course, he wouldn't remember such a minor detail.

"A car just pulled into our driveway," Andy announced. "It's probably Mr. King's car."

"Why don't you open the door for him?"

Before she could get the words out, Andy was halfway to the front door. It had been all his idea that she not take him ahead of time to Kevin's house, but have her and Cliff drop him off. He'd wanted to see Mr. King. Jennifer had agreed without argument. Tonight was about Andy. He might as well be here when Cliff arrived.

Now she knew as she trailed behind her son that she'd also welcomed his presence as a buffer when his father came to pick her up.

"Hi, Mr. King." Andy had the door open before Cliff could ring the doorbell.

"Why, hello, Andy. I didn't know I'd get to see you tonight."

Jennifer could hear Cliff's note of faint surprise, faint relief and also genuine gladness. His reaction to seeing his son—*their* son—did strange things to her.

"You and Mom are taking me to Kevin's," Andy explained.

"Good enough."

"Here's Mom now." Andy stood aside as Jennifer approached.

"Hello, Cliff."

"Hello, Jennifer." He greeted her pleasantly, his gaze skimming over her. "Are we ready to go?"

"I'll get my duffle bag," Andy announced and dashed off to his bedroom, leaving the two adults standing there.

"He's quite a kid," Cliff said.

"I'm biased, but I think he is."

"You've done a great job as a parent."

"Thank you. I've done my best."

Andy's return interrupted the stilted conversation between his two parents.

The three of them trooped to the late-model sedan parked behind Jennifer's car in the driveway.

"The Johnsons who live down the street have a new car just like this," Andy remarked as he settled into the backseat and fastened his seat belt.

"This is a rental car. I flew into New Orleans," Cliff explained.

"What kind of car do you have?"

Jennifer was curious to hear the answer, too. It didn't come as any surprise that Cliff owned a sporty high-performance car, a two-seater. A bachelor's car.

"Oh, *neat!*" Andy exclaimed. "Maybe you'll drive it to Louisiana some time when you come."

Cliff glanced indulgently over his shoulder into the backseat. "Maybe I'll do that. And if it's okay with your mom, you and I will go for a spin."

"You won't care, will you, Mom?"

"Mr. King said *maybe* he would drive his car here," she pointed out. "It wasn't definite."

"How about some directions to Kevin's house?" Cliff asked, backing out onto the street.

Andy obliged. Typically, he didn't sulk or nag her for the permission she hadn't given him, as many children his age might have done. Jennifer hoped that Cliff took note of his son's good disposition.

At Kevin's house, Andy unclipped his seat belt, leaned between the bucket seats and gave her a goodbye kiss on the cheek.

"Bye, Mom. Bye, Mr. King."

"I'll call you in the morning," Jennifer said, letting her tone convey, *I love you.*

Cliff had twisted sideways in his seat. He stuck his hand back to grasp Andy's. "Good night, Andy."

They watched him run full speed to the front door, ring the doorbell, turn and wave, and then disappear inside the house when the door opened.

Cliff looked over at her. "Tomorrow night I'd like for all three of us to go out to eat."

"You don't have to include me," Jennifer replied. "I'll agree to letting you take him out to eat by yourself. It isn't necessary for us to go to a restaurant tonight, for that matter. We can go back to my house and talk and put our cards on the table."

"I *want* to include you tomorrow night. I want us to have dinner tonight. To have an enjoyable evening, if possible. I want us to be friends," he declared earnestly. "But all in good time. I don't expect it to happen overnight."

He backed out onto the street and drove slowly through the residential neighborhood, heeding the twenty-five-mile-an-hour speed limit.

"Am I right in concluding that you're no longer satisfied with just paying child support?" Jennifer asked.

"You're right in concluding that," he answered, glancing searchingly at her. "Am I being overly optimistic in picking up positive vibes from you?"

"I'd rather hear your feelings before I tell you mine."

"Fair enough. But let's wait until we're at the restaurant to talk about it, shall we? Is Andy's tennis clinic still going on?"

He engaged her in conversation about her favorite subject and the only thing they had in common, their son, on the drive to Madisonville, a small, picturesque neighboring town. Nestled on the bank of the Tchefuncta River, Madisonville boasted several popular seafood restaurants, and Cliff had made reservations at one of them located on the riverfront.

It was still daylight as he drove across the drawbridge and parked the car beneath the spreading branches of an aged live oak tree. Jennifer opened her own door and got out before he could come around. He took a minute to gaze appreciatively up and down the street at old-fashioned white-painted houses with picket fences.

Along the water's edge was a municipal dock where visitors by boat could tie up. There was usually an interesting variety of vessels, and tonight was no exception. A shrimp boat bobbed gently next to a big motor yacht that reared high out of the water. Farther along was a wooden sailboat with gleaming paint. Cliff's glance rested longest on it.

"What a quaint, pretty little town," he remarked. "It's like a picture postcard."

Jennifer bit her lip. It was so tempting to play guide, to tell him about the Mardi Gras boat parade and Santa arriving in December by boat. But this wasn't a social occasion, and she didn't dare relax and enjoy his company. "Madisonville is a quaint town," she said.

They stood with the car between them. Cliff came around the front to her side. Jennifer waited for him, since the restaurant was across the street and behind the car. She braced herself as he reached her, her pulse quickening.

He wore a knit shirt open at the throat and tucked into cotton duck slacks, with the navy blazer he'd worn when he came to the club. Jennifer responded to his clean-cut good looks and his masculinity with an involuntary female pleasure that she was afraid she couldn't hide.

Cliff glanced at his watch. "Our reservation is for eight o'clock, so we're early. What do you say we sit for a few minutes outside here on the riverfront and have our talk?"

Jennifer stepped carefully over exposed tree roots and accompanied him across the grass to a bench overlooking the river. She sat at one end and he dropped down at the opposite end, leaving a space between them.

Anyone seeing them wouldn't make the mistake of thinking they were romantically involved, Jennifer thought as she turned sideways to face him.

"Let me start at the beginning," Cliff said. "It's not overstating things to say that learning I had a kid completely disrupted my life. I couldn't think about much of anything else." He gave his head a little shake. "Not that I expect sympathy, but I lost interest in dating. Not even sailing was the same."

Jennifer kept silent, noting his use of the past tense, which suggested he'd probably regained his enjoyment of his bachelor's life-style.

He went on. "I hoped that paying child support would get me off the hook. And who knows? Maybe it would have, if you'd gone along with it. It might not have. But I've come to feel that I want to know Andy. I want to do things with him, be a part of his life. I'm the first to admit that I'm not the best father he could have drawn, but I am his father."

"Yes, you are his father. And Andy could have done a lot worse when it came to inheriting genes. He's handsome and bright and personable—just like you." Jennifer chose her next words carefully, not wanting to offend him any more than she could help. "I'm sure you have many good character traits, too, Cliff, but quite frankly, I don't want Andy to turn out to be a carbon copy of you."

He winced. "Damn it, Jennifer, I'm honestly not a bad guy. If you'll give me half a chance, you'll find that out for yourself."

"It's not myself I'm worried about. It's Andy. He's very impressionable and ripe for hero worship. And how long are you going to want to be a part of his life? What if in a year or two or in five years, things happen in your life so that you stop paying attention to him? You could get married in that time, have other children. I don't want Andy hurt, Cliff."

"I can appreciate your worry." He sighed, rubbing his hand across his face. "The problem is that nothing I say is going to erase it."

"I guess not." Jennifer looked away, realizing anew how terribly vulnerable she was, as well as Andy. The thought of Cliff happily married to another woman was truly unbearable.

"Will you give me the benefit of the doubt?" Cliff asked earnestly. "I'm not insisting that we have to square with Andy."

Jennifer gazed at him stupidly. "You mean not tell him you're his father?"

He shrugged. "It's not a big deal for me that he know who I am. In fact, I would probably be more comfortable getting to know him as Mr. King."

"Cliff, you can't try out the role of father to see if you like it! Either you want to be Andy's father or you don't."

"Jennifer, I *am* Andy's father, whether I ever wanted to be or not. There's nothing equivocal about my commitment. I just don't have a lot of confidence at this point," he admitted. "This is all new to me and scary as hell. Do you think that Andy should be told? I was assuming that you would be adamantly against it."

"And I was assuming that you would insist. Exactly what is the agreement you want to make with me?"

"Just that you allow me to see Andy at least every other weekend. I'd also like to be able to call him and visit with him on the phone. Maybe spend some holidays with the two of you. I want to buy him presents for his birthday and Christmas. That sort of thing."

Jennifer nodded, mutely giving him her consent. What he had in mind was being a surrogate uncle, not a father. Cliff might sincerely believe that he was committed to being a parent, but he wasn't. She was still Andy's only parent.

It was up to her to protect him as best she could, while she tried to protect herself.

Chapter Six

"You're quite a woman," Cliff said gently. He ached to move closer and touch her reassuringly. She looked so troubled. But she might not welcome his touching her, and he needed to keep his distance. "I knew somehow that I could count on you not to be petty. To put your own feelings about me aside and give me a fair hearing."

She stiffened. "My feelings about you?"

"You think I'm a pretty lightweight individual, but I intend to win your respect. I want us to be friends." He stood and held out his hand to her. "Let's go have dinner now."

Trust me, he wanted to say to her. *I won't let Andy or you down.* But well-intentioned words from him wouldn't reassure her. Cliff had to prove over time that he wasn't a lightweight individual.

Tonight he hoped to get her to relax and have a nice evening. It was a chance for them to get better acquainted. He knew virtually nothing about her and vice versa.

Inside the restaurant, they were shown to a table and presented with menus. Cliff ordered a beer and Jennifer ordered tonic water with a squeeze of lime.

"I'm driving tonight," he told Jennifer before the waitress left. "Would you like to make that a gin-and-tonic or vodka-and-tonic?"

She refused politely.

"Are you a non-drinker?" he asked when they were left to peruse their menus.

"I might have a glass or two of champagne at a New Year's Eve party or special celebration, but other than that, I'm a non- drinker. I've never developed a taste for alcohol. The reason probably is that I grew up in a non-drinking environment."

"Were your aunt and uncle opposed to alcohol for religious reasons?" At her look of surprise, he reminded her, "You mentioned them that Sunday when I showed up at your house and you filled me in."

"I'd forgotten," Jennifer said. "To answer your question, they weren't regular churchgoers, but they didn't allow alcohol or smoking in their house. They didn't approve of dancing. They were very strict, puritanic people."

The picture she was painting seemed rather grim to Cliff. "How old were you when your parents died?"

"I was seven when my uncle and aunt took me in."

"You must have rebelled at some point before I met you," he suggested.

She looked embarrassed. "My behavior not being very puritanical, you mean."

"No criticism intended," Cliff objected. "I just recall that we had a few beers that Saturday we went out sailing and—"

"And had sex in broad daylight," Jennifer completed the sentence for him, a note of shame in her voice. "That was the first time I'd ever drunk beer. Ever drunk anything alcoholic, for that matter. I got light-headed on the first few sips. Not that I'm using that as an excuse for my behavior." She avoided his eyes.

"You were out of high school and hadn't sneaked a drink?" Cliff demanded, incredulous rather than doubtful. "No wonder you were still a virgin if you were that straitlaced."

Before she could reply, the waitress interrupted, serving their drinks. Then she took their food order after listing again the specials that weren't on the menu. He and Jennifer both selected one of them, the grilled fish of the day, grouper. Cliff could not care less what he ate.

"Back to our conversation," he prompted after the waitress had left. He sipped his beer from the frosted mug.

Jennifer hadn't lost the threads of the conversation, either. "I don't blame you for being skeptical," she said. "But I hadn't sneaked a drink before. Or had sex. I was very straitlaced. My uncle and aunt had impressed it upon me that I had to live by their rules. And I was grateful to them for giving me a home."

"I didn't mean to sound skeptical. But, of course, I'm wondering why you broke the rules that day with me."

She sipped her tonic. "Obviously the temptations were stronger than they'd ever been before."

He waited, but she didn't elaborate, much to his disappointment. "You said you were dating a guy at the time?"

She nodded. "Frank Jennings. He worked in the same accounting firm with my uncle. My uncle and aunt approved highly of him. They pressured me into dating him, in the first place, and were set on my marrying him, if he proposed."

"Didn't you like him?"

"Yes, I liked him, but I didn't love him or want to marry him. He was a very nice, dull man." She turned her glass in circles. "Before Frank, I'd only dated a couple of other guys no more exciting than he was. My uncle and aunt were very strict about dating, too. You were so good-looking and so much fun. I was flattered that you were interested in me. I thought it would be perfectly innocent to go along on the sailing lesson."

"There was a sailing lesson, I swear."

"I'm sure there was. What's your family background?" she asked, changing the subject.

Their salads were served. Between bites, Cliff followed up on a general reply that his family was about as normal as you could get. "My father's a postal worker. My mother's a housewife. I have two sisters, one older, one younger than me, both married with children."

Jennifer put down her fork, her expression strange. "So your parents are grandparents."

"Typical grandparents. They dote on my sisters' kids."

"Will you tell your parents about Andy?"

Cliff shrugged. "In time I probably will. The problem is that it's not news that they would sit on. Before the shock wore off, they would be making plans for him to visit them and meet all his aunts and uncles and cousins."

She picked up her fork again and speared a small piece of lettuce, the odd look still on her face.

"I'll bet you're thinking that you hadn't bargained for surrogate in-laws," he said lightly.

"Your family sounds very nice," she replied almost wistfully.

"Have you kept in close touch with your uncle and aunt? I'm assuming they're still living and still make their home in Florida."

Jennifer shook her head. "I have no communication with them. They washed their hands of me when I left Alabama and came here to Louisiana and had Andy."

Cliff blinked. "Washed their hands of you?"

"I disappointed them terribly and embarrassed them, getting myself into trouble."

"They've never seen Andy?"

"I sent them a baby picture of him. I wrote letters and sent cards the first few years. Once or twice I called them long-distance, but they wouldn't talk to me. Finally I did the kindest thing I could do for them, leave them in peace."

Her uncle and aunt sounded like a couple of cold fish to him. Cliff couldn't relate to the idea of close family cutting a member off, especially not in Jennifer's circumstances.

"What about other relatives?" he asked.

"I don't have any other relatives that I know about."

She'd truly been alone, without any support, pregnant with his child. No wonder she was self-sufficient. She'd had to be. Cliff could understand better now why she'd reacted the way she had to his paying child support. His insight made him want all the more to make things up to her as best he could, to give her some of the support he hadn't been around to give her when Andy was younger.

Their waitress had come to their table to clear away the salad plates and serve their entrées. Cliff waited impatiently for her to leave, wanting to express some of his feelings to Jennifer

Before he could, she steered the conversation in another direction. "Tell me about your adventures. Did you travel as far and wide as you'd planned?"

Cliff reluctantly began outlining his travels. When he saw how she visibly relaxed and seemed to be enjoying her meal as she listened with interest, he went on at more length. He'd left Fort Lauderdale and gone down to the U.S. Virgin Islands, where he'd worked in the charter-boat trade for a year. Next he'd hired on as crew member of a large private yacht owned by a billionaire and sailed to the Mediterranean and back. After that he'd sailed on oceanographic-research yachts owned by Johns Hopkins University. Then he'd gotten an opportunity to join the crew of a super-racing yacht and race in the SORC, or Southern Oceans Racing Circuit to the novice.

During this phase, he explained, he'd met a lot of important businessmen who were boating enthusiasts, among them the CEO of International Marine Hardware. The man had told Cliff that there was a place for him in his company. Cliff had decided about six months later that it was time to start a career. He was twenty-six, by then, and had spent four years seeing the world. He'd contacted the CEO, gotten a job as a sales rep, and had been with the company now for six years.

"So you're still on the move," she said, laying down her dinner fork. He'd talked them through the whole meal. "And you like all the travel, I'll bet."

"Only because my job takes me to boatyards and marinas and marine-supply stores and yacht clubs. It requires me to do business with sailing and boating people. I wouldn't enjoy being a sales rep and traveling from city to city calling on doctors or pharmacists."

A busboy came up to their table and took away their empty plates. Then their waitress promptly appeared to ask whether they wanted coffee and dessert. They both ordered coffee.

Cliff couldn't remember when he'd had better service at a restaurant or appreciated it less. Tonight, service was equated with interruption. And he would have been perfectly content to occupy the table for another hour or two.

"I didn't mean to talk your ear off about myself," he said apologetically, as they stirred cream into their coffee.

"I found your experiences fascinating," she answered. "I'm sure Andy will, too."

Cliff hadn't given Andy a thought since they'd dropped the subject of family backgrounds. He'd been totally engrossed in her company.

Forgotten had been the fact that she was off-limits to him as a woman. They could be *friends,* nothing more. He needed to keep sight of that, to give off nothing but friendly signals.

"Is Andy busy tomorrow?" he asked, leaning back in his chair. The next day was Saturday.

"He doesn't have any plans that he wouldn't gladly change if you wanted to do something with him."

"I'd like to take him sailing."

Her eyes widened with surprise. "Sailing? Have you arranged to borrow or rent a sailboat?"

Cliff grinned. "Neither. You're looking at the new owner of a thirty-foot sloop."

She questioned him, seeming anything but thrilled at learning that he'd bought a sailboat and would be keeping it in a Mandeville marina.

"I'll call Andy first thing in the morning," she said. "What time would you want him to be ready?"

"Say about nine o'clock. Unless that's too early for you."

"No. Nine isn't too early."

"How about coming along, too?" he suggested casually.

The invitation caught her completely off guard. "Me? Oh, I have too many things to do on a Saturday."

"How can you pass up Andy's first sailing trip?" Cliff cajoled. "Somebody needs to be on hand with a camera to snap a few pictures of him."

That was the right tack to take with her. He'd known that instinctively. Her struggle showed on her face.

"I'll lend you my camera," she offered.

"I'm going to have my hands full sailing the boat and being an instructor."

"I don't know...."

Her wavering filled him with elation. His own reaction disturbed Cliff. It shouldn't be this important that he talk her into coming along.

"You don't have to decide this minute," he said, backing off. "There'll be other sailing trips, if you're too busy tomorrow."

"I would hate not to get pictures."

The salesman in Cliff recognized that the moment was ripe to press for a commitment. He managed somehow not to.

"Speaking of pictures, I wonder if you have an extra one of Andy that you could give me. A school picture, perhaps."

"Why, certainly."

He'd scored points with her by the request, and, damn it, that honestly hadn't been his motivation. Cliff downed the rest of his coffee and looked around for their waitress. She was headed their way with a coffeepot.

Jennifer placed her hand over her cup and smiled at the woman. "No more coffee for me."

"What about you, sir?"

"None for me, either. Just the check, please."

"Remind me when you come for Andy tomorrow, and I'll give you the picture," Jennifer said.

Just as easily, he could get Andy's picture tonight when he took her home. It was the perfect excuse for going inside her house with her. But Cliff *didn't* need to be alone with her in her house with Andy not there.

He might make a wrong move. The man in him might take over and ruin his friendship with Jennifer before it got off the ground. *Friends,* he repeated to himself as he used a credit card to pay the check.

"Thank you for dinner," she said as they were leaving the restaurant. "I enjoyed the meal. And the company."

"Same here," Cliff replied heartily. They crossed the street, with him refraining from taking her arm or resting his hand on the small of her back.

"The bridge is opening," Jennifer noted as they reached the car.

"A boat must have radioed ahead to the bridge tender. Shall we walk off some of our dinner while we wait, rather than sit in the car?"

His suggestion met with a brief pause, as though she were weighing the alternative. "I suppose we might as well."

"Watch your step," Cliff cautioned as she stubbed her toe on a root. He took her arm. After they'd reached smoother ground and were strolling parallel to the concrete dock along the grass, he released his hold and loosely clasped her hand. *Friendly* hand-holding should be all right.

The lights of the approaching boat came into sight downriver, accompanied by the hum of a motor. It was a tugboat pushing a barge. As it got closer and more visible, the noise increased. Cliff could see that the barge was loaded with gravel.

"Andy would be waving his arms and shouting at the captain to blow his horn," Jennifer remarked fondly.

Her hand felt soft and warm in his. The natural thing to do was give it a little friendly squeeze.

"He's never very far away from your thoughts, is he?"

He hadn't necessarily meant it to be a rhetorical question, but she didn't answer.

By the time the tugboat had passed them and gone under the bridge, they'd reached the end of the town riverfront. If this had been a normal date, it would have been a perfect spot for Cliff to stop and steal a kiss.

But, of course, this wasn't a normal date.

He felt frustrated as hell as they turned around and started back. She pulled her hand free, and he realized he'd tightened his hold. He thrust both his hands in his slacks pockets, deciding that maybe he should just square with her and clear the air.

"You probably don't realize that I'm having a problem tonight," he commented.

"A problem?" she repeated, giving him a little encouragement with her tone.

"In a nutshell, I want us to be good friends and yet I'm strongly attracted to you. Back there, if you hadn't been Andy's mom, I would have tried to kiss you." She didn't say a word during the short pause he gave her, so he went on. "I realize I probably wouldn't have gotten to first base. The point is that I'm in conflict with myself. Maybe it's better for you to know that."

"Surely you realize that I'm attracted to you," she stunned him by saying. "You're much too experienced with women not to have a sixth sense about such things."

Cliff had stopped dead in his tracks and had to hurry to catch up with her. "I haven't realized any such thing," he insisted. "You probably have me typecast as a womanizer because I've stayed single. I'm really not. The women I date are usually career women with a lot on the ball."

"All I ask is that you keep your life-style as a bachelor separate from entertaining Andy and spending time with him. I would definitely object to his being included in your dates with women."

Cliff protested, "I have no intention of bringing a string of women into Andy's life. As for my bachelor's life-style, that's gone completely to hell since I learned about him. The few dates I've had have been total duds."

"I'm sorry that you had to learn about him. It was just bad luck for you."

Her words cut into him. "I'd like to think that it wasn't bad luck, damn it. That it might turn out to be a fortunate occurrence. For Andy. For me. And even for you."

"I'm sorry," she apologized quickly. "I shouldn't have said that. It was a thoughtless, unkind remark."

Her sincerity didn't help matters. She might regret offending him, but she'd spoken her true feelings. If it killed him, Cliff was going to earn her respect and admiration.

"In case you're worried about my language around Andy," he said gruffly, "I'll clean up my vocabulary and won't use any four-letter words." He'd let loose with a couple of heated expletives during the past five minutes.

"I wasn't worried," she assured him. "I only hope Andy's as well spoken as you are when he grows up."

They were almost abreast of the car now and headed toward it. Reaching the drip line of the live oak tree, Cliff walked more cautiously, mindful of the unevenness of the ground beneath the tree's branches. He started to take Jennifer's arm, then didn't. She had slowed down and was picking her way with care over the exposed roots.

"In Louisiana the root systems of most of our trees are very shallow—"

On the last word, she gasped, one leg buckling and spinning her sideways facing Cliff. He quickly put out his hands and grabbed her shoulders to steady her, but she'd lost her balance. As she grabbed onto the lapels of his jacket to keep from falling, he slid his arms around her body and held her tightly, supporting her weight.

"I twisted my ankle," she explained unsteadily, gazing up at him.

Cliff's heart was pounding, the adrenaline rushing through his bloodstream. "Does it hurt badly?" he asked in a husky voice, looking down into her face.

She didn't answer but sucked in a breath, closing her eyes. He couldn't help himself. Her lips were just inches away, soft and slightly parted. He lowered his head and kissed her, brushing his lips against hers.

"Forgive me," he murmured against her mouth, feeling her warm breath on his face. "I didn't mean to do this."

Her arms slid up around his neck and she didn't pull back, didn't do anything to stop him. For the life of him, Cliff couldn't raise his head. He kissed her again, a sweet, hungry kiss. Her lips clung. She was kissing him back. He moaned in his throat as though to say, *Stop me*. Then he gently parted her mouth with his and found the tip of her tongue.

The sound of a car door slamming and voices and laughter penetrated his fog. Even in the gloom underneath the tree, this was hardly a private place, outside a popular restaurant. With that realization, Cliff still couldn't lift his head, not before he tasted her passion. He deepened the kiss and coupled his tongue urgently with hers for a few brief, glorious seconds.

Jennifer turned her face aside, sucking in a deep breath. "I hope those people didn't know me," she whispered. "I'm so embarrassed."

She'd heard the voices, too, and hadn't pulled away. Cliff was disturbed by how much that pleased him, considering that he'd counted on her to keep anything from happening between them.

"Now maybe we've gotten that out of our systems," he said, sucking in his own oxygen supply. "I just hope my hotel has lots of cold water."

"Cold water? Oh." She comprehended his reference to the cold-shower remedy.

It wasn't entirely a joke. Cliff was in a half-aroused state. What he wanted was to go somewhere with her and make love. He didn't dare think about it, or he'd be more than half aroused.

"How's your ankle?" he inquired, loosening his embrace. She immediately pulled away from him.

"It seems to be okay. I don't think I sprained it, thank goodness."

He kept a firm hold on her arm as she took a few experimental steps and then walked the remaining few steps to the car without noticeably limping. Neither of them made any attempt at conversation. Cliff could sense that she was agitated beneath her calm, and he was more furious with himself by the moment for his lack of control.

His main concern was undoing whatever damage had been done. Getting into the car, he turned sideways in his seat. "You're upset, aren't you?" he asked gently.

She was clipping on her seat belt. "I'm upset at myself, not at you."

"But I'm the one at fault. I kissed you."

"I let you kiss me. I kissed you back. You must think I haven't changed. That I'm still . . . 'easy.'"

"No, I don't think anything of the kind." God, he wanted to touch her, to take her into his arms again, but he didn't dare. "Let's just put it behind us and be on our guard. Okay?"

She looked at him. "I don't want to get involved with you, Cliff."

"Same here," he said. "But I do want to be friends, Jennifer. Good friends." He held out his hand to her, palm up.

After a long moment, she gave him her hand. He squeezed it gently and then turned forward in his seat, buckling his seat belt.

Starting the car, he was aware of dissatisfaction gnawing at him.

"Do you go out on dates?" he asked when they'd crossed back over the bridge. The silence had been starting to get to him. Riverfront condos with boat slips were over on their left. Marshland crowded the two-lane highway on their right-hand side.

"Very seldom."

"I'm sure you get asked out. You must run into single men at the club."

"I occasionally get asked out," she replied. "But I don't accept, because I'm not open to a relationship right now. That's what dates are all about, as you know. Andy is my number-one priority. No man is going to be happy for long being number two."

"You've learned that from experience?"

"Yes, I have." She didn't elaborate.

"You go by your maiden name," Cliff noted. "I'm assuming that you haven't married and divorced."

"No, I never married. I came close to it when Andy was three. There was a period when I dated with the purpose of finding a good stepfather for him," she admitted. "Eventually I gave up on the idea. Could we talk about something else besides me?"

"Sure." He didn't want to change the subject, but it was probably a good idea. Sooner or later, he would get around to asking her how she managed without sex.

Sex wasn't a topic he should bring up, not until he could discuss it objectively, like a friend. The memory of kissing her was going to have to fade first, however long that took.

"Would you like for me to make sandwiches for your and Andy's sailing trip?" she offered.

"Thanks, but I couldn't let you go to that trouble. I thought I would buy sandwich makings and snack food at a supermarket."

"I could ice down some soft drinks. We have a cooler."

"The boat has an icebox. I'll buy soft drinks and ice."

"It sounds like you've thought of everything. Andy's going to be so excited."

"Better plan to come along and bring your camera," he urged lightly. "Bring your swimsuit, too. Or wear it. We'll drop the anchor and go for a swim. If you're worried about too much sun, the boat has a sailing awning to shade the cockpit."

"I like the sun. I would use sunscreen to protect my skin, of course."

"I have sunscreen on the boat."

Cliff left the matter there, feeling there was at least a fifty-fifty chance that she would come.

Reaching her subdivision, he again felt as if he were visiting a foreign land. Here and there a garage door was open, with the light left on. Exposed to view was the usual family paraphernalia—kids' bicycles, shelves with paint cans, a workbench with tools, lawnmowers and gardening implements. Some yards had swing sets dimly visible. More than one tricycle had been abandoned on a lawn or paved walkway.

In most of the houses, windows glowed with light. Undoubtedly televisions were tuned to programs in living rooms and dens. Younger kids would be snuggled in bed by this time, fast asleep. Husbands and wives would be staying up later on a Friday night than on a weekday. What were they doing? Maybe watching a rented video, maybe playing a trivia game with the next-door neighbors.

Cliff couldn't imagine what it felt like to be one of those husbands, chained to a domestic routine. Maybe he'd waited too long to settle down and have a family, he thought, as he pulled into Jennifer's driveway.

"Would you like a cup of coffee before you drive back across the causeway?" she asked hesitantly. He sensed that she'd probably been debating with herself whether to invite him in.

His passion had been cooled by the ride through her subdivision, but he'd still better not go inside. "Actually I'm not driving back to New Orleans tonight. I'm staying in a motel on this side of the lake."

"Oh." She glanced surreptitiously at her watch. It wasn't quite ten o'clock, Cliff knew. "Then I'll say goodnight. Thank you again for dinner."

"My pleasure."

He got out and walked with her to her front door. Jennifer held out her hand to shake hands with him. Cliff took her hand and, holding it, bent and kissed her on the cheek.

"Tomorrow morning about nine o'clock," he reminded over his shoulder on his way to his rental car, which was just like the Johnsons' new car.

Inside her foyer, Jennifer raised her hand to touch her cheek. Closing her eyes, she let herself remember the kiss on the riverfront. Cliff's lips on hers. His tongue touching her tongue. The harder, more demanding pressure. The deeper intimacy of their tongues coupling. His arms tightening around her.

Jennifer moaned softly in her throat, sweet desire melting her bones. Abruptly she opened her eyes, hearing her voice and Cliff's.

I don't want to get involved with you, Cliff.
Same here. But I want us to be friends.

How on earth could she be friends with him when the sound of his voice made pleasure wash through her? Her whole body responded when he looked at her, when he came near.

Jennifer wouldn't stand a chance of keeping up her defenses, if he wanted to get through them. For his own reasons, he didn't want to. She knew she should be glad. Falling for him would only end in heartache.

Andy's mom didn't need a broken heart.

Now, more than before, she had to forget about herself and think only of being the best possible mother to him.

He was so vulnerable, not having had a father. It wouldn't take much for him to get very attached to Cliff, who sincerely wanted to be a part of Andy's life now. Jennifer didn't doubt that. What she did doubt was Cliff's staying power.

How long before his interest in Andy waned?

Whenever it happened—six months from now, a year from now, two years from now—Jennifer was going to have to help Andy through his hurt and rejection. No, she definitely couldn't afford the luxury of a broken heart.

Andy still had only one parent that he could count on.

Remembering Cliff's request for a picture of Andy, she got together a small collection of wallet-size school pictures from different years. After a moment's deliberation, she included a five-by-seven of this year's picture. What he did with it was his business, but just in case he might want a framed photograph of his son for the world to see, she was giving him the option.

Cliff wasn't sleepy. He could go back to his motel room and get caught up on some paperwork, but he really wasn't in the mood. He'd brought the latest copy of *Sail* magazine along with him on this trip, but he didn't feel like reading either, or watching TV.

The commodore at the yacht club had presented him with an honorary membership card. Maybe he would drop by the yacht-club bar and have a beer. The idea had more appeal than any of his other options, so he drove to the lakefront and followed the street to where it curved sharply, hugging the corner of the yacht-club property.

On previous visits Cliff had admired the casual southern charm of the clubhouse, a one-story building painted blue and trimmed in white, with a wraparound porch. Tonight, as on those other occasions, tables out on the porch were occupied. Stepping out of his car, he caught snatches of boating conversation that made him feel right at home.

"...damned halyard broke on me."

"Wind died down and we put up the spinnaker...."

This was his world, the world of sailing and boating. Could Jennifer fit in? Impatient with himself, Cliff slammed the car door harder than necessary. The main reason he'd come here was not to have a beer or find some company, but to put Jennifer out of his mind for the night.

He stood there for a moment, filling his lungs with the brackish lake air, before he went inside. Glancing around, he saw that the crowd was made up mostly of couples, the majority of them probably married couples, gathered into groups around tables in the lounge area. Cliff was immediately recognized and hailed by several people.

He made the rounds, speaking to acquaintances. Then he stood at the bar, drinking a draft beer. The bar seemed to be the favored spot for those who dropped in singly, like himself, male and female, married or unmarried. Not surprisingly, there was some interplay between the sexes.

Cliff consciously gave out no signals, but a vivacious brunette he heard addressed as Kay introduced herself and engaged him in conversation. He divulged that he was a new boat owner, and in answer to her questions he explained how he'd happened to buy a boat in Mandeville.

"Are you going to take your boat back to Georgia?" she asked.

"No, I'll come here on weekends."

"Need a crew? If you do, I'm available."

"Actually, I have a crew. A good friend of mine and her son."

This being a small town, he wasn't free to say that his crew was his son, and his son's mother. Cliff might run into Kay some time when he was with Andy. It bothered him that he couldn't claim Andy as his flesh and blood.

"Good friend as in 'significant other'?" Kay inquired.

"Something along those lines," Cliff replied.

She chatted with him a couple of minutes longer and then went to talk to someone else. He finished his beer and left.

There wasn't any reason he couldn't have been friendlier to Kay. Jennifer *wasn't* his "significant other."

It didn't make sense that on a Friday night he was headed to his motel room when he still wasn't sleepy, wasn't in the mood for reading or watching TV. But what was the use of going to another bar and striking up another dead-end conversation?

He might as well have a "significant other," for all the difference it made. He had to stop dwelling on Jennifer. She'd made it crystal clear they had no future. This celibate life was starting to get to him, and there was just no reason for living like a monk. He hadn't taken any vows, religious or marital.

Come Monday, Cliff vowed to get his social life back on track.

Chapter Seven

Andy was grinning from ear to ear and his face was lit up like a beacon as he ran to the car the next morning, tossed his duffle bag into the backseat and jumped into the passenger seat. "Mr. King is really going to take me out sailing! Why didn't he tell me last night?"

"Maybe because he wanted you to sleep," Jennifer replied indulgently.

He plied her with questions on the way to their house and hardly gave her a chance to answer them. It was the most excited he'd ever been about anything. She supposed that some women in her shoes might have been jealous, but how could she be when he was this thrilled and happy?

"Are you going sailing too, Mom?" he asked eagerly.

"Mr. King invited me," she replied. This morning she was still undecided.

"I wish you'd come."

"You do?"

"Maybe you might have fun and start liking sail-boats."

"I think I probably would have fun, just watching you having your first sailing lesson."

"Then *come.*"

It was settled, and she could feel her own excitement bubbling up.

They were ready and waiting when Cliff arrived, wearing old shorts and a T-shirt and leather boating mocca-sins. One look at him and Jennifer admitted to herself that watching him today was going to hold its own pleasure.

Maybe she would get her fill of looking at him, she thought. Maybe her pulse would settle down to normal when she was around him for an extended period. Maybe her heart would stop leaping when she made eye contact with him. Maybe she would get used to the sound of his voice. If so, then friendship with him could be a real pos-sibility.

"So you decided to come along. That's great," he said to her, seeming sincere but not overly glad. His routine male inspection of her appearance was casual and quick. "Bringing your swimsuit?"

"Mom and I are both wearing our swimsuits under-neath our clothes," Andy explained.

"Good," Cliff said, and his eyes ran quickly over her shorts and blouse again.

Jennifer could feel her nipples hardening and tingling against the spandex of her one-piece. She lifted the cam-era hanging by its cord around her neck and remarked, "I'm the official photographer."

"So I noticed. Are we ready?"

Andy answered for himself and her, and the three of them trooped to Cliff's rental car. Across the street and next door, neighbors were out in their yards, and they waved and called friendly greetings to Jennifer and Andy.

Cliff had all the windows in the car rolled down, Jennifer noted as she got into the car. The sailor in him probably liked fresh air blowing in.

"Your subdivision is a tricycle derby this morning," he commented, driving along at a crawl.

"Saturday morning. The working moms are home," Jennifer pointed out. "It's a young neighborhood."

She followed his glance out of his window. A man about his age and dressed similarly in old shorts and a T-shirt was pushing a lawnmower out of his garage, obviously about to begin mowing his grass.

In the backseat, Andy noticed him, too, and made his own thought connection. "I mow our grass, Mr. King. I used to pick up the sticks, but my mom has that job now. She still won't let me use the weed-eater, not until I'm a little older."

Cliff looked over at her. "You operate the weed-eater?"

Jennifer nodded. "We don't have a very big yard. There isn't much trimming to do. I can reach everything with a long electric cord." The gas weed-eaters were heavier than the electric models, as she was sure he knew.

"Do you have a riding lawnmower, Mr. King?" Andy inquired. From his tone of voice, he'd discounted the idea of Cliff's having any other kind.

"I don't own a lawnmower, Andy. I live in a condo and pay a monthly fee that includes the upkeep of the lawn and the landscaping."

"That's neat."

"I did my share of mowing grass when I was growing up," Cliff told him. "You see, I was the only boy in the family. I have two sisters, and they didn't do yardwork. They helped my mother in the house."

"Did your parents have a large yard?" Jennifer asked. It was so easy to visualize him when he was Andy's age.

"They have an acre lot. It seemed like ten acres to me. After I moved out on my own, my father bought a riding lawnmower."

"It would be *fun* mowing grass with a riding mower," Andy declared.

"If you ever visited my father, I'm sure he would let you ride his," Cliff said. "His grandkids all love to help him mow his lawn."

"Let's talk about something more interesting than mowing grass," Jennifer suggested, before Andy could make some innocent response.

Cliff looked at her and she met his gaze reproachfully. It wasn't fair to Andy to discuss his grandparents with him when he had no inkling that they were his grandparents.

Oblivious to the undercurrents, Andy cheerfully went along with changing the subject. "Yeah. Let's talk about sailing."

Father and son carried on a two-way conversation during the rest of the ten-minute ride. Jennifer couldn't help noticing that Cliff seemed more relaxed after he'd pulled out onto the highway, leaving their subdivision behind.

At the marina they all carried supplies from the car to Cliff's sailboat, which was named *Windsong*. To her surprise, Cliff beamed in response to Andy's boyishly enthusiastic praise and her own compliments on his new acquisition. It was as though their approval really mattered.

The three of them went aboard and Andy was in heaven, finally realizing his dream of actually being on a sailboat. For Jennifer, there was some sense of déjà vu, setting out on this, her second sailing trip, but not much. The whole situation was so totally different.

Eleven years ago, when she'd met Cliff in that much larger marina in Fort Lauderdale, she'd been focused on herself, full of guilt and romantic yearnings. Today, she just wanted Andy to have a marvelous time and for Cliff's first outing with him to be successful.

Cliff took charge as host, unlocking the hatch and going down inside the cabin. Jennifer and Andy handed him bagged ice, the grocery sacks and their tote bag through the open hatchway.

"Come on down, and I'll give you two the tour," he said, just as she was about to sit down in the cockpit, out of the way.

Andy didn't need a second invitation. He scampered nimbly down the companionway ladder, following Cliff's example and descending with his body turned sideways.

Jennifer had gotten a glimpse of the close quarters inside. "Is there room for all three of us?" she asked.

"It's cozy, but there's room," Cliff assured her.

"Here I come, then."

"You can back down, if that feels more natural. I won't let you fall."

He stood near the foot of the ladder. If she took his suggestion, she would be giving him a close-up view of her backside.

"I won't fall. I've been down one of these ladders before," Jennifer reminded him, flustered. The words were out before she remembered Andy was listening.

"You've been on a sailboat before, Mom? You never told me that."

"No, I guess I haven't," she said.

"You're stepping down into the galley. On your right, the starboard side, is the icebox set into the counter. Just lift the lids, as so." Cliff demonstrated as Jennifer reached the last step, standing almost on a level with him. He'd begun his guided tour, heading off any further interrogation from Andy.

"On the port side is a gimballed two-burner stove that will be great for heating up soup during cool-weather sailing or for cooking meals on a short cruise over to the Gulf Coast."

"You mean *sleep* on the boat?" Andy inquired delightedly.

"Sure. She sleeps five people. There're two bunks up forward in the forecastle. These long settees in the main cabin can be made up into bunks. One of them pulls out into a double."

"So that two people can sleep on it. They'd have to sleep close together, huh?"

"They'd have to be compatible sleeping partners," Cliff agreed. He hadn't moved from his station near the companionway, where Jennifer was still poised on the bottom step, not participating in the conversation.

"Like me and Kevin."

Jennifer didn't correct her son's grammar. "Mr. King will probably want to explain to us how to flush a boat toilet," she said, stepping down to the cabin floor and easing as far away from Cliff as the limited space in the galley allowed.

Andy was all interest. "A boat toilet doesn't flush like a house toilet?"

Cliff took him into the head and showed him how the toilet operated. After hearing enough of the instructions to refresh her memory, Jennifer climbed the ladder without an audience.

Sitting in the cockpit, she thought about her blunder minutes earlier. Sooner or later Andy would question her about her previous sailing experience. She guessed she would have to make up a lie.

Cliff saved the day just now, sidetracking Andy by pointing out the features of the sailboat's interior. He had his own reasons, so different from Jennifer's, for wanting to keep Andy in the dark about their past relationship. He was content to be Mr. King, a recent acquaintance.

Jennifer sighed, half wishing she hadn't come along. This incident, combined with the one in the car, had put a damper on the day for her.

"Can I help you put stuff away?" Andy was asking Cliff down in the main cabin.

"Sure thing. You can ice down these soft drinks."

They talked companionably as they worked. The sound of their voices soothed and cheered Jennifer. She looked around, taking in the activity in the marina. Several boats away, a man was washing his deck, using a bucket of soapy water and a hose. A large sailboat had a whole party of people aboard. Jennifer watched as they proceeded to untie the mooring lines and back out of the slip with a considerable amount of shouting back and forth. The owner and captain, she surmised, was the man who shouted the loudest.

Cliff and Andy came up on deck, having finished stowing things down below, and they both watched, too. Cliff frowned and winced as though in pain when the big sailboat scraped loudly against a piling. Andy noted his reaction, just as Jennifer did.

"I hope we don't scrape a piling like that, Mr. King." His young voice was faintly apprehensive.

"We won't." Cliff laid a hand on his shoulder. "I have a first-class crew. The trick is to back out slow and easy and not gun the engine. You don't drive a sailboat like a car. An engine in a sailboat is only auxiliary power." He gave Andy's shoulder a squeeze. "How about giving me a hand taking off the sail covers? We'll get ready to put up the sails today right here in the slip.''

''Okay.''

Jennifer remembered her camera and snapped several pictures of father and son as they moved around the deck, a blond duo, Andy all eagerness and Cliff all patience. Andy repeated words like *halyard* and *cotter pin* and *winch,* committing to memory what was obviously to him the fascinating vocabulary of sailing.

Cliff was a marvelous teacher, giving very simple explanations and letting Andy do each step in the process. Andy was an apt student, catching on quickly. He glowed at Cliff's praise.

Largely ignored, Jennifer looked on, a smile on her lips.

''Now we're all set. We can start the engine and get under way,'' Cliff announced, and the cockpit got pleasantly crowded as they both joined her.

The departure from the slip went smoothly, with Cliff never raising his voice from a conversational level. Jennifer was pressed into service, assigned to untie a mooring line, loop it over a cleat on the nearest piling, and then stand by up on the foredeck to push off gently against the piling as the sailboat slid near to it.

They motored along a channel to the lake. Cliff turned the wheel over to Andy, whose expression left no doubt that he was experiencing the biggest thrill of his life.

''Be sure and get a good picture, Mom,'' he said. ''Kevin won't believe this.''

''We'll have to bring Kevin along with us sometime,'' Cliff remarked indulgently.

If possible, Andy's grin got wider and his blue eyes sparkled brighter at the clear implication that there would be more sailing trips and one of them would possibly include his best friend.

Once they'd passed the buoys at the mouth of the channel, they were in Lake Pontchartrain, with the causeway over on their right. Cliff waited until they'd motored a short distance farther. Then he stood up.

"Let's get those sails up so we can turn that engine off, Andy. Jennifer, you take the wheel."

"Me?"

"Just head for that sailboat out there, and you'll be holding us into the wind." He pointed.

"Into the wind," she repeated nervously.

Cliff's eyes met hers, recollection flashing between them. With similar reluctance, she'd steered when he put up the sails on their sailing trip eleven years ago.

"You can do it, Mom," Andy encouraged.

"Thanks for the vote of confidence," she said lightly, jolted by the few seconds of shared reminiscence. Was it possible that Cliff remembered that day as clearly as she did? She'd assumed that he didn't, that it had blended into a hundred other sailing trips with girls.

Jennifer had never fooled herself into believing that she was in any way special to him. As he had been special to her, standing out among all the men she'd known.

Left alone in the cockpit, she gripped the stainless-steel wheel, feeling the anxiety of the novice sailor.

"You're doing just fine," Cliff called back to her as he and Andy raised the mainsail. It fluttered in the breeze. "Now fall off a little," he instructed. "Turn the wheel a quarter turn to port."

"That's the left side, Mom," Andy shouted.

Jennifer did as she was bade. The sail billowed and the boat heeled gracefully and surged forward with increased speed. Andy's and Cliff's voices blew back to her from where they stood, near the mast, side by side. Cliff had his arm around Andy's shoulder, probably helping to brace him.

"Wow! This is great, Mr. King!"

"You like it, Andy?"

"I *love* it!"

"So do I. Let's go unroll the jenny." He tightened his arm and hugged Andy's shoulders. Watching, Jennifer swallowed a lump in her throat.

They joined her again in the cockpit. With the engine out of gear but still running, Cliff showed Andy how to unfurl the headsail and let him crank the winch, using a winch handle. Watching the procedure, she recalled that Cliff had raised the front sail differently in Fort Lauderdale, from on deck. He seemed to read her mind.

Glancing around at her, he said, "Not all boats are equipped with roller-furling equipment. But it's more common now than it once was."

Was there some déjà vu for him, too, today? she wondered, and blushed at the thought.

With both sails taut, the boat was skimming along. Cliff turned off the engine, and suddenly it was quiet enough to hear the water gurgling against the hull.

"Isn't this neat, Mom?" Andy demanded. "Don't you like sailing?"

"I'm having a good time," she assured him. It wasn't a relaxed enjoyment, but it was enjoyment nonetheless.

"Are you tired of steering?" he asked hopefully.

"Why don't you take over the wheel, Andy?" Cliff directed.

"Okay."

During the transfer, Cliff and Jennifer exchanged a smiling glance. He sat across from her, on the side of the cockpit that was higher, his legs sprawled open comfortably. They sailed along for several minutes in tranquil silence, with Jennifer trying to look elsewhere, not at him. Suddenly the sails made a fluttering noise.

Andy tensed, looking at Cliff for direction. "Which way should I turn the wheel?"

"Try turning it a little one way and see what happens," Cliff suggested, unperturbed.

On Andy's first attempt, the fluttering got worse. Then he corrected it.

"You were turning into the wind and losing the wind in the sails," Cliff explained and gave him a simple lesson on sailing technology, which Andy eagerly absorbed.

Jennifer tilted her head back and closed her eyes, enjoying the delightful combination of warm sunshine and cool breeze on her skin. By now she knew she could relax her mother's vigilance and put Andy in Cliff's hands.

"I think I'll take my shirt off too, Mr. King."

Andy's words brought her eyes open. Cliff had stripped off his T-shirt and sat with his lean, muscular upper torso bared to view.

"Go ahead, Andy. I'll keep her on course for you." He stretched out one long arm to the wheel, making a slight adjustment, Jennifer noticed, while Andy stripped off his T-shirt. His sleek, young body was tanned the same golden brown hue as his father's.

Cliff looked at Jennifer questioningly. Didn't she want to shed some clothes?

"I guess I'll go inside and take off my blouse," she said lightly. "Otherwise I'm going to feel overdressed around you two."

"If you don't mind, you can take our shirts down with you," Cliff said, not making an issue of her modesty.

Jennifer's one-piece swimsuit was a vivid print with bright yellow and fuchsia and green. The bodice wasn't daringly low cut to show a lot of cleavage. But she felt self-conscious as she reclaimed her spot in the cockpit minus her blouse.

Cliff didn't whistle or stare, naturally, but there was definitely male approval in his gaze, which strayed to her breasts. Her self-consciousness subtly changed character and she felt sexy and alluring, feelings that were entirely inappropriate in Andy's presence.

Jennifer wasn't at all comfortable with the role of sexy mom. She sensed that Cliff wasn't nearly as much at ease, either, since she'd taken off her blouse. He left the cockpit and walked around on deck, inspecting the rigging and fittings.

"Okay, Andy, let's tack," he said when he returned. He explained exactly what was involved in tacking. They would "come about," the bow of the boat pointing into the wind and then passing through it so that the breeze was blowing from the opposite side. The sails would respond and need to be released and retrimmed, the winches on the opposite side of the cockpit coming into play.

Jennifer remembered the flurry of excitement in changing direction. "Where shall I go to be out of the way?" she asked.

"You can change places with me. Then you'll be on the leeward side again after we've tacked."

They changed sides. He signaled Andy to turn the wheel. The sails flapped frantically. Cliff freed the lines from the drum-shaped winches near him. Then he crossed over to Jennifer's side and with easy expertise made the sails taut again.

She held her breath, the drama of the moment heightened by the fact that he was so close his bare shoulder brushed against hers. Eventually she had to breathe, though, because Cliff stayed there, coiling the loose ends of the lines he'd wound tightly around the winches.

When he'd finished, instead of crossing back over and sitting across from her, he settled himself on the leeward side, too. Jennifer was conscious that she could have reached out her hand and laid it on his tanned, muscular thigh.

So far on this sailing trip, proximity wasn't doing anything to lessen her physical awareness of Cliff, as she'd hoped.

"That was pretty exciting, Andy, wasn't it?" She turned her head and smiled at her son, whose blond hair ruffled in the breeze.

"Yeah, Mom, real exciting." He answered her absently, his eager attention all for his father. "Did I do okay, Mr. King?"

"That was perfect, Andy. You're going to be an expert sailor before the day's over."

Andy beamed with pleasure. Hero worship was written all over his young face.

When the time came to tack again, Jennifer had every intention of keeping her seat and having Cliff end up on the opposite side of the cockpit. But he asked her to take the wheel and let Andy "pull the strings," with his help.

Jennifer managed to snap some more pictures while she played helmsperson.

The sun climbed higher into the sky. At noon they dropped the sails and anchored. Cliff put up an awning to shade the cockpit, then got out a swimming ladder and hung it over the side of the hull.

"Everybody ready to cool off with a swim before lunch?" he inquired.

Andy was already shucking his shorts, revealing his abbreviated nylon racing trunks. Without any ado, Cliff undid his shorts and dropped them. He was wearing nylon racing trunks, too, only his were black, whereas

Andy's were bright blue. About to go down inside and remove her shorts and rubber-soled canvas shoes, Jennifer sucked in her breath and tried not to stare at Cliff.

"Don't dive in headfirst, Andy," she admonished weakly.

"I'm not that stupid, Mom!" he protested. He balanced himself on the raised edge of the deck and hopped off gracefully, feet first.

"He's some athletic kid, isn't he?" Cliff said, sounding not just admiring but *proud*. Before she could find her voice and answer, he called to Andy, "How's the water?"

"The water's *great!* You and Mom come on in!"

Cliff looked at Jennifer inquiringly.

"You go ahead," she said. "Don't wait for me."

He stepped to the edge of the deck and dropped over the side, feet first, with the same athletic grace he'd passed along in his genes to his son.

Jennifer pressed a hand to her middle, weak in all her joints. She couldn't be friends with Cliff! Not when the sight of him in a swimsuit did this to her!

He and Andy were swimming away from the boat, side by side, when Jennifer returned from inside the cabin, suffering a new attack of self-consciousness. Relieved to postpone modeling her swimsuit for him, she backed down the ladder into the water, which felt delightfully cool on her sun-heated skin.

The exercise of swimming helped to ease her tension. By the time Cliff and Andy had swum back, she'd circled the boat twice and was prepared to participate in some water games with them, the usual ducking and splashing. But Cliff headed straight for the swimming ladder.

"You two enjoy the water. I'll fix some sandwiches for us," he announced, climbing aboard. Rivulets of water streamed down his tautly muscled back and legs, and the wet black nylon trunks were molded to his tight buttocks. Treading water, Jennifer watched his ascent; she kept watching when he stood on deck and turned around, the front of his body molded by the wet nylon, too.

"Can I help you fix the sandwiches?" Andy offered.

"Sure. I'd be glad of some help."

Andy displayed the same agility getting up the ladder. They disappeared down inside the boat. Jennifer swam around a few minutes more, working off new tension. Then she climbed the ladder herself.

After toweling off, she sat in the cockpit under the shade of the awning. Cliff handed her an ice-cold soft drink. He also gave her a quick once-over that made her aware of her wet swimsuit, clinging to her body like a second skin. Jennifer was back to feeling sexy and alluring.

"We're not putting mustard on your sandwich, Mom," Andy called up to her. "I told Mr. King you don't like mustard."

"Thank you, dear."

Jennifer folded her arms across her waist, sitting very straight and prim. Today was her last sailing trip. Her last outing with Cliff and Andy. She couldn't handle feeling like a mother and a vamp at the same time. A mother— that was her role in life until Andy was grown-up.

"Why don't you serve your mother, Andy? I'm going to change into dry clothes."

"You are?"

"Yes. Sitting around in a wet swimsuit isn't very comfortable."

The conversation down in the galley brought Jennifer alert. They'd evidently finished making sandwiches.

"I guess I'll change too, then."

"You don't have to. Your swimsuit will dry pretty quickly."

So would his. Was he uncomfortable with the thought of being so scantily clothed around her? Had she made him self-conscious, ogling his body? Jennifer wondered with embarrassment.

Whether she had or not, she was relieved that he was putting on more clothes, as she herself intended to do as soon as the cabin was clear.

After less than five minutes, Cliff and Andy came up, both wearing their T-shirts as well as their shorts. Cliff had probably donned his shirt first, and Andy had followed his example. They'd combed their hair and looked vital and healthy.

Jennifer had brought underwear for herself and Andy, and obviously he had dug his briefs out of their tote bag, pulling out her bra in the process, she discovered when she went down to change. It dangled over the side of the bag, which gaped open. If Cliff had cared to look, he would have gotten a glimpse of her purple panties, too.

She took her time getting dressed, letting her flushed cheeks cool.

The lunch tasted delicious. They ate hungrily, munching chips along with their sandwiches and deli potato salad and cold soft drinks. Cliff evidently hadn't brought beer along to drink.

After lunch, they applied sunscreen, took down the awning, pulled up the anchor and set sail again. Jennifer got out her sunglasses and a magazine she'd stuck into the tote bag and found a comfortable spot up on the foredeck. Cliff didn't visit her up there. He stayed in the cockpit with Andy and sent Andy to deliver her a cold drink when they got thirsty and assumed rightly that she might be thirsty, too.

She wasn't being hostile toward him, and she sensed that he understood that and wasn't being hostile toward her. They'd just both given up on the idea of friendly camaraderie. There was simply too strong a physical attraction between them for them to be companionable.

And for Jennifer the attraction went deeper. That was the real problem, the real danger.

He and Andy were going to have to spend time together without her.

In the late afternoon, they returned to the marina. Andy, hating to call it a day, suggested washing down the boat. Cliff looked to Jennifer for her response to the idea.

"Maybe you two could take me home and come back," she suggested. "I have things to do, and you don't really need my help."

Cliff didn't put up any argument. She wondered if he hadn't been thinking the same thing. Evidently he'd come to the same conclusion she had, that family-style togetherness wasn't going to work.

At her house, he suggested going out for supper that night and once again didn't try to persuade her when she declined for herself but was open to his taking Andy out to a restaurant.

Nor did Andy try to persuade her. That hurt a little.

"Take your key with you. If I'm not here later, you and Mr. King can let yourselves into the house so that you can shower and change clothes before you go out to eat," she told her son.

"Why doesn't Andy get his clothes now?" Cliff said. "He can shower and change in my motel room. That way we won't have to barge in on you, if you are here."

"It's fine with me."

It was definitely fine with Andy. He bounded ahead of Jennifer to the front door. Cliff, declining to come inside, waited for him in the car.

Alone in the house after they'd driven away, Jennifer suddenly felt wind battered and weary, her emotions close to the surface. She was glad the day had gone so well. Truly glad. And yet this was going to be hard, much harder than she'd realized, sharing Andy's affection with Cliff.

Jennifer didn't want to be jealous. But she was.

Certainly she didn't want to envy her own son, either. But she was envious, much to her shame.

It wouldn't do to mope around and feel sorry for herself when Andy was with his father. It wasn't fair to Andy.

Cliff had mentioned seeing him every other weekend. Jennifer would have to wait and see if those intentions materialized. If they did materialize and she found herself with free weekends, then maybe she should start going out on dates.

Not in the least cheered by the prospect of a social life, she went into her bedroom and stripped off her clothes. In her bathroom she turned on the shower.

Then she turned it off, ran water in the tub and took a long soak instead. The dozen things she could be doing could wait.

Chapter Eight

Cliff pulled into Jennifer's driveway and shifted into neutral, letting the motor run while Andy unbuckled his seat belt.

"I had a great time today, Mr. King. Thanks for taking me out sailing on *Windsong*. And for buying me supper."

"The pleasure was all mine, Andy. I had a great day, too." Cliff held out his hand to his son and squeezed his smaller, callused little hand when Andy placed it trustingly in his. "If things work out for me with my schedule and your mom doesn't object, I'll see you next weekend."

He'd explained that tomorrow morning he was catching a flight back to Atlanta. After taking Friday and Saturday off, he needed to get home.

"You mean you and her will be going on a date?"

"Oh, I don't know about that," Cliff evaded. "I was thinking about you and me going out sailing again."

"I'd like that!" He grinned happily, wiggling in his seat with that youthful excitement Cliff remembered.

"As I said, I'll have to check with your mom."

"She probably won't mind. She always lets me do stuff to have fun." He swung open the door. "Bye, Mr. King. And thanks again."

"Bye, Andy. You be careful now."

"I will."

Cliff watched him make a dash for the front door, swinging his duffle bag. He stopped at the porch and waved exuberantly. Cliff lightly tooted the horn. Andy disappeared inside the house.

You be careful now. Cliff had meant those words. He couldn't stand the thought of some harm befalling Andy. During the course of the day, he'd developed paternal anxiety.

He was beginning to *feel* like a father.

Unfortunately, his hope of being friends with Jennifer wasn't panning out. It was too much for Cliff to handle, being in her company and Andy's. Adjusting to being a father was enough in itself, without also having to fight his attraction to his son's mother.

Cliff *wanted* Jennifer, but he couldn't have her, not unless he was ready to make a commitment. And he wasn't ready.

If Cliff had any doubts about that, all he had to do was cruise the neighborhood and watch all the domestic activity going on.

Cliff had no choice but to exercise iron self-control.

Jennifer had given Cliff their unlisted phone number so that he could call Andy and chat with him. Cliff had in mind calling maybe once or twice a week. But on Sunday night, he found himself picking up the phone and punching out the digits.

All day he'd been thinking about Andy. And Jennifer. He wanted to hear their voices and make sure everything was okay with them.

Andy answered the phone and sounded thrilled that the caller was Cliff. "Mr. King! Hi!"

"What've you been up to today, Andy?"

"Mom and me went to church this morning. This afternoon we took Kevin to the club to swim." He chattered on eagerly, outlining his busy day.

Cliff settled back and listened, an indulgent smile on his lips. Maybe on a steady basis that youthful enthusiasm would be wearing, but not so far. Instead, it infused him with energy and optimism.

"What did you do today, Mr. King?" Andy asked with interest.

"Mostly I did paperwork connected with my job. But I also went out and played a game of tennis. I thought I would bring my racket along next weekend and hit some tennis balls with you."

That suggestion met with overwhelming favor. They talked tennis for a while, discussing brands of rackets among other things.

Glancing at his watch, Cliff saw that he'd been on the phone thirty minutes. "How's your mom?" he inquired.

"She's fine. Did you want to talk to her?"

"Yes, why don't you put her on?"

"Just a minute."

Obviously she wasn't in the same room. Cliff's heartbeat quickened as he waited. His impatience was marked by anticipation.

"Hello, Cliff."

Her voice came over the line, filling him with a different pleasure than Andy's voice had evoked.

"Hi, Jennifer. I hope you didn't get a sunburn yesterday."

"No, the sunscreen did its job. I got some tan, but no burn."

Cliff had a vision of her in the wet one-piece swimsuit. The alluring picture made desire stir in his groin.

"Well, that's good. You have such pretty skin."

"Thank you for the compliment." She sounded flustered. "Andy mentioned that you were tentatively planning to come to Mandeville again this weekend."

"Yes. I didn't want to be more definite with him until I'd consulted you."

"It's fine with me. In fact, I'll go ahead and make plans for myself, if you are coming."

"Do that," Cliff forced himself to say, instead of inquiring what kinds of plans she intended making. "Count on me for Saturday and Sunday until early afternoon." He went on, "I'm thinking of driving to Louisiana in my car. I should arrive late Friday night, and I'll leave Sunday afternoon."

"What about Saturday night? Should I assume you and Andy will be going out for supper?"

"Sure." He fought with his better judgment, which lost the battle. "Maybe you might want to join us."

"I wasn't hinting to be included," she said. "I just need to know whether to depend on you, in case I'm invited out somewhere."

"By all means, depend on Andy's being with me Saturday night. We'll touch base during the week."

"Very well. I'll let you go, Cliff. You take care."

"You, too, Jennifer. Could I say good-night to Andy?"

"Of course. Hold on."

He needed to hear Andy's voice again before he hung up. The conversation with her had him in upheaval. Damn it, he couldn't even manage friendly chats with her on the phone.

"Come in." Jennifer looked up with a smile at the man standing in the open door of the office. He'd tapped lightly on the door frame to alert her to his presence.

"Hi, Jennifer. I needed to check something on my bill for last month."

"Certainly."

He looked familiar, but she couldn't put a name to his face. Taking the bill from him, she glanced and saw that his name was Richard Mackey. That rang a bell. Probably she'd checked his ID at the entrance desk.

"What's the problem, Richard?" she inquired.

"It's a minor thing, really." He leaned over her desk, pointing to an item. "I was charged for a meal in the snack bar and, as it happens, I've never eaten in there."

"You haven't? You should give the snack bar a try. The food is really very good." She turned her attention to the bill, jotting down his account number and the amount of the charge. "I'll see that your next month's bill is credited. Sorry for the inconvenience. We have more mix-ups during the summer when a lot of members' children make charges to their parents' accounts. Some youngster may have mistakenly written down your account number."

Richard smiled ruefully. "Frankly, I wouldn't mind next month's bill having a similar error. Not if it meant an excuse to talk to you."

Jennifer started to make one of her typical polite, tactful remarks that she used to discourage the interest of male club members. Instead she smiled back at Richard, who was quite an attractive man. About six feet tall, he was broad shouldered and well built, with brown hair and brown eyes.

"I'm flattered," she said and motioned to a chair. "Would you like to sit a moment? Things have been hectic this morning, so I haven't taken a break yet."

He didn't need any urging. They had a brief get-acquainted conversation, and Jennifer learned that he was the co-owner of an appliance store in the Mandeville area. He was divorced and had two children. His ex-wife, who lived in Jackson, Mississippi, had custody of them. Richard made points with Jennifer when he took out his wallet to show her pictures of two little girls, aged five and seven.

Before he left her office, he asked her to go out to dinner with him, and she made a date for the coming Saturday night.

There wasn't any reason not to. Andy would be with Cliff. The best thing for all three of them, Andy and herself and Cliff, was for Jennifer to get out of the house and have a pleasant evening.

Cliff learned about the date on Saturday morning when he picked Andy up. No sooner had he parked in Jennifer's driveway than Andy came dashing out of the house, full of admiration for Cliff's sporty car.

Jennifer came out, carrying Andy's duffle bag. She greeted Cliff with a smile and looked his car over admiringly, too. She also gave him a key to her house and said, "I'll plan to be home tonight no later than eleven o'clock, possibly a little earlier than that. I'm going out for dinner."

Andy piped up with the specifics. "Mom has a date with a man named Richard. He's a member of the club. He works out with weights."

"Mr. King isn't interested in knowing all the details, Andy," Jennifer reproved.

She couldn't have been more wrong. Cliff wondered what the guy looked like, what he did for a living, whether she had dated him before.

"Don't feel as if you have a curfew," he said. "Andy and I may take in a movie."

"Yeah, Mom, stay out later than eleven o'clock, if you want," Andy encouraged.

She waved as they drove off with the sunroof open. For Cliff the brightness of the day had dimmed. It made him angry that during the week he'd worried over how she was going to deal with Andy's spending so much time with him. Meanwhile, she was busy taking advantage of her new freedom.

Was this Richard a muscle-bound weight-lifter type? Had he just recently joined Northshore? Or was he someone she'd known for a while and come to like?

These questions plagued Cliff intermittently throughout the day. Jealousy gnawed at him.

Last weekend it had been her presence that had given him problems. This weekend it was her absence that kept him from enjoying Andy's company one hundred percent. Damn it, Cliff couldn't seem to win, no matter what he did.

Jennifer's date set off a whole disturbing train of thought regarding Andy. What if she married, and Andy had a stepdad? Would Andy call the guy Dad and continue to refer to Cliff as Mr. King? *No way*, Cliff said grimly to himself.

Fortunately, Andy's Saturday wasn't spoiled by Cliff's mental agitation; nor was Cliff's fun entirely spoiled, for that matter. He enjoyed the sailing trip, the supper, the movie, but his enjoyment wasn't as wholehearted as it should have been, and Jennifer was the reason.

He and Andy left the movie theater about ten-fifteen. Now what? Cliff thought. Were he and Andy supposed to delay going back to the house? Not be there when this Richard fellow brought her home?

To hell with that, Cliff decided.

At the house he accompanied Andy to the door and waited outside while Andy checked to see if his mom was home yet. She wasn't.

"You don't have to stay, Mr. King," he said. "I'm not scared. Mom probably won't be long."

"I'd better stick around until she comes, Andy."

That decision suited Andy fine. He showed Cliff into the living room and went to change into his pajamas, at Cliff's suggestion. With the TV turned to a movie, Cliff sprawled on the long sofa and Andy took the love seat. In no time Andy was yawning, and then he was out like a light, sound asleep.

Cliff gently shook his shoulder to rouse him and sent him off to bed.

About ten minutes later, eleven o'clock on the dot, a car pulled into the driveway. Cliff flicked off the TV and sat up straight, waiting for Jennifer to come in.

Another five minutes passed. She must be sitting in the car with Richard. What was taking her so long? Cliff sure as hell wasn't going to sit here all night while they carried on out there.

"Nice car," Richard said to Jennifer, sounding surprised and curious as well as admiring. His car's headlights spotlighted Cliff's sleek, expensive, little automobile.

"Yes, it's very sporty."

"Is that your sitter's transportation?"

Jennifer hadn't gone into explanations about her arrangements for Andy tonight. It hadn't seemed necessary.

"My unpaid sitter, so to speak. He's sort of a family friend, an avid sailor. He treats Andy like a son. They went sailing today and probably to a movie tonight." All true, if somewhat vague and not the whole story.

Richard clicked off his headlights and tilted the steering wheel up out of his way. "How old is he?"

"Thirties."

"Not married, I take it."

"No, he's single."

He removed his seat belt and turned toward her. "He isn't an old boyfriend, is he?"

Jennifer didn't know exactly how to answer. Finally she just nodded.

"Still carrying a torch for you?" he queried.

"Nothing like that."

"Glad to hear it. Because I like you a lot." He'd released her seat belt. Now he leaned closer, his voice softening. "Can I kiss you good-night?"

Before Jennifer could answer, Richard brought his lips to hers. His kiss was gentle and seeking, asking her for a warm response. But all she could think about was that Cliff was waiting inside her house.

She pulled back and smiled at him. "I had an enjoyable evening tonight." It wasn't his fault that she hadn't had a better time. He was a nice man—he just wasn't Cliff.

"I enjoyed your company very much," he said.

They got out of the car, and he accompanied her to the front door.

Jennifer inserted her key. "Good night," she told him. The thought of going inside and seeing Cliff had her much more jittery than she'd been hours earlier, awaiting Richard's arrival.

"Good night, I'll see you around the club—" He broke off in surprise as the door abruptly opened.

Cliff stood there, glowering at them, a frown on his face.

"Cliff...you did say not to worry about being home at eleven on the dot." In her surprise, Jennifer sounded like a guilty teenager who'd broken her curfew. A sixth sense kept her from getting alarmed about Andy. Cliff was irritated, not wrought up over some grave situation.

Richard stepped forward. "We haven't met," he stated. "I'm Richard Mackey."

"Cliff King." Cliff shook hands with Richard, his expression hardly any less grim.

"Good night, Richard. And thanks again for a lovely evening," Jennifer said with a note of apology.

Richard hesitated. "Maybe I will have that cup of coffee, after all." *Would she rather that he didn't leave?* he was asking her.

She was touched and embarrassed by his concern and gallantry. "Perhaps another night."

Richard nodded and touched her shoulder in a parting supportive gesture. "Good night," he said and left.

Jennifer stepped inside her foyer and extracted her key ring, dangling from the lock. She stood to one side while Cliff closed the door. A glance into the living room told her that Andy must have gone to bed.

"How dare you create a scene like that?" she demanded, still befuddled, but also indignant. "You might have been an irate husband from the way you acted!"

Cliff shrugged, looking sheepish. His tone was defensive as he replied, "I didn't create a scene. I was on my way out, heard you unlocking the door and opened it. What was I to do? Stand there and eavesdrop?"

"You were leaving?"

"Yes, I was leaving. You'd gotten home. I saw the headlights."

Evidently he wasn't leaving now, Jennifer surmised. She trailed after him into the living room, where he sat down at one end of the full-size sofa. There was a dent in the throw pillow. Had he been lying down? she wondered. Seeing him here in her living room took some getting used to.

"Andy's asleep?"

Cliff nodded. "He crashed almost as soon as we got back here tonight."

"What time was that?"

"About ten-thirty."

Jennifer glanced at her watch. He hadn't been waiting for hours, not long enough to get so impatient. Maybe the day with Andy hadn't gone well. Suddenly anxious, she perched on the arm of the love seat.

"How was the sail?" she asked tentatively.

"Great. Andy can practically sail the boat by himself."

In response to her questions, Cliff described what had apparently been a leisurely, fun-filled Saturday for both himself and Andy.

So why had he acted that way just now at the door? He'd acted . . . *jealous.*

"You got some tan last weekend on our sailing trip," he observed. His gaze moved over her shoulders and arms and neck, bared by her sundress. She felt about ten times more provocative and sexy than she'd felt all evening with

Richard, who'd been very complimentary on her dress and her tan.

"I tan easily," she said, folding her arms self-consciously.

His face and arms were bronzed in the lamplight, which cast a sheen on his blond hair. Underneath his shirt, his broad shoulders and chest and back would be bronzed, too.

Jennifer sucked in air.

"Would you like some coffee?" she asked.

"Sure. A cup of coffee would be good."

She stood up, relieved for some excuse to leave the room. "I have decaf, if you'd prefer."

"Whatever."

He rose, too, and followed after her to the kitchen.

"I'll bring the coffee into the living room," Jennifer protested over her shoulder, but he ignored her words.

Conscious that he was watching her every move from only a couple of yards away, she poured water into her small coffeemaker, her hands unusually clumsy. Measuring coffee grounds, she spilled some on the counter. In her exasperation, she muttered an expletive under her breath.

"I'm not used to making coffee with an audience!"

"You must be planning to get more used to it. You invited Richard in for coffee."

"No, I didn't. I might have, but you were here." With the coffeemaker turned on, she faced him. He leaned against the counter, his hands thrust into his pockets. "And Richard probably would have taken my hint and stayed in the living room and given me a little space to breathe."

"Richard could sit on the sofa and expect you to come back and sit next to him," Cliff said, dislike in his voice. "The situation's not quite the same."

Jennifer's mouth gaped. "What am I supposed to say to that, Cliff?"

He shrugged impatiently. "How the hell can I put words into your mouth?" Before she could find her own words, he blurted out, "Do you like the guy?"

"Yes, I like him."

"You intend to go out with him again?"

"I doubt he'll ask me. You probably scared him off."

"Of course, he'll ask you. Damn it, Jennifer, I'm having a real problem with all this!"

"All what?" she cried.

"You and other men."

Jennifer stared, totally nonplussed.

Cliff jammed his hands deeper into his pockets. "When I opened the door tonight, I wanted to take a swing at that guy. It made me crazy knowing that he'd been kissing you in the car."

She murmured foolishly, "You looked furious. I was afraid for a moment that you might do something violent."

"It's not necessary to tell me that I'm reacting completely irrationally. I know that."

"Yes, you are reacting irrationally," Jennifer agreed with him, trying to collect her wits. She *shouldn't* be thrilled over his admission that he was jealous of Richard. "You don't want to date me yourself. Nor do I think it's wise for us to date. We both agree that getting involved with each other wouldn't be wise."

"The question is whether our wisdom will prevail," he said soberly, taking his hands out of his pockets and straightening to his full height.

Her heart was beating wildly. She turned around in a state of panic and opened an upper cabinet door, taking down two mugs with hands that shook. The mugs clanked together noisily as she set them down. "The coffee should be ready soon. Do you take cream and sugar?"

Cliff had stepped up close behind her. His hands lightly cupped her bare shoulders and slid down her arms. She shivered, her whole body going weak at his possessive touch.

"I *want* you, Jennifer," he said, aching need in his voice.

"Please don't, Cliff," she whispered.

"Please don't what? Tell you what you already know? How are we going to deal with the problem?" He was grasping her waist and turning her around to face him.

She raised her hands, bracing them on his chest. Beneath her palms, she could feel the thud of his heartbeat, feel his hard, pulsing masculine warmth. "Like responsible adults," she said breathlessly. "Like conscientious single parents who can't carry on an affair in front of their ten-year-old son."

"It's asking too much for me to sit on the sidelines while you get involved with some other guy, like Richard." Cliff was touching her hair with that same possessiveness that threatened all her defenses.

"What am I supposed to do?" she asked. "Sit around and pine for you and be miserable? You wouldn't want that, I'm sure."

"I don't have any solution. I wish I did." He framed her face and caressed her bottom lip with his thumb. "You let Richard kiss you?"

"I didn't let him—he kissed me. It was a chaste good-night kiss. Nothing passionate. I was very distracted by the thought of your waiting inside."

"I guess I should apologize for opening the door like that."

"You're forgiven. We'll avoid anything similar happening in the future."

"Probably we should have that coffee now and discuss how we're going to avoid it," he said huskily.

His tone melted away what little resistance to him remained. "We really should," she concurred without conviction.

Cliff's arms went around her, and he lowered his head to kiss her, his expression intent. Jennifer had plenty of time to turn her face aside, to protest, to push against him. Instead, she closed her eyes and whispered his name.

When his lips met hers, her arms reached up around his neck and his arms immediately tightened, gathering her close against him in a glorious, strong embrace. Sweet, hot sensations exploded inside her as he kissed her with pent-up hunger and need. She kissed him back, answering the pressure of his mouth and the ardor of his tongue.

Cliff groaned her name like a plea for sanity, turning aside his head and hugging her even tighter, tremors of passion running through his body. Through their layers of clothing, Jennifer could feel his hard, aroused condition and knew that she was just as ready to make love.

"I know we have to stop," he said, his voice full of frustration. "But I don't want to stop."

"We *have* to—Andy might wake up."

"Do you see what I mean about the power of wisdom, Jennifer? It's no match for how much I need to take you to bed."

"Especially not if you can't depend on me to keep my head. We'll both just have to show more self-control, Cliff."

He sighed deeply, not answering, but his arms loosened. Jennifer reluctantly lifted her head and brought her arms down from around his neck. They moved apart, a mutual dissatisfaction almost a tangible presence in the kitchen.

"I guess I'd better go," Cliff said. "That's probably my best form of self-control tonight."

Jennifer smiled wanly at his rueful note. "And I should show you to the door, not remind you that I made this pot of coffee at your request."

He shook his head slightly. "You know what? I *like* you a hell of a lot, more than I've ever liked any other woman."

"I like you a lot, too."

"It's a damned shame that we can't go sit on the sofa and have coffee and enjoy each other's company. There're a hundred questions I'd like to ask you about yourself."

Jennifer nodded. "It is a shame."

"But you couldn't kick back and feel comfortable, either, could you?"

"No, I never feel *comfortable* with you, Cliff, not like I felt with Richard tonight. I'm too attracted to you and too busy fighting the attraction," she admitted honestly.

He'd scowled at the mention of Richard's name. "Let's work this thing out between us before you make any more dates with Richard. Is that a fair proposition?" he urged.

She sighed. "Probably I shouldn't involve any man in my life without explaining at the outset exactly who you are. Under the circumstances, I don't feel free to do that." Because he didn't choose to openly declare himself Andy's dad.

"So we have an understanding?"

"I suppose we do."

Jennifer picked up the mugs and put them back on the shelf in the upper cabinet. "Are you also restricting yourself from dating?" she asked.

"I haven't been able to muster any interest in dating other women in months, not since the Sunday I ran into you and Andy on the lakefront."

His blunt reply seemed to end the conversation. Jennifer simply didn't have nerve enough to pose the question in her mind: was his problem simply that he needed a woman? Any woman? In silence they left the kitchen, their pact having done nothing to lessen the currents of awareness between them.

"Well, good night," Cliff said at the door. "Be sure and lock up."

"I will. I always do," she added. "What time will you pick up Andy in the morning?"

"About nine. We're planning to hit some tennis balls. I brought my racket."

"He'll enjoy that."

"So will I. Afterward I'd like to take you both out to brunch."

"You're always springing for meals in restaurants. Why don't I fix brunch?" Jennifer suggested impulsively.

"That's too much trouble for you." His refusal came quickly.

Obviously he wasn't in the least tempted by the offer of a home-cooked meal, as some men would be. "Are you afraid I'm a rotten cook?"

"No, but you work all week at a job. Let's go to a restaurant." He leaned over and kissed her on the cheek, opened the door and was gone, calling back, "See you tomorrow."

Jennifer closed the door, convinced that Cliff had his own reasons for preferring to take them out rather than eat at her house. Probably it came as second nature to him to act the wary bachelor, she reflected, her cheeks burning at the thought that he might have construed her invitation as arising from misguided hopes of domesticating him.

Cliff wasn't husband material. She didn't have any illusions on that score.

Chapter Nine

Andy came to the door of the laundry room, where Jennifer was transferring a load of wet clothes from the washer to the dryer.

"Looking for me?" she inquired with forced cheer.

"Mom, Kevin just called."

"I heard the phone ring. What did Kevin have to say?"

"He invited me to go camping with him and his dad this coming weekend. They're going to a state park in Alabama. I told him I would ask you." Andy sighed. "I want to go, but Mr. King might be coming for the weekend again."

"Mr. King isn't likely to come every weekend, and he's been here for two in a row," Jennifer pointed out, empathizing with her son's dilemma. "Why don't you make plans to go camping? You enjoyed the last trip very much. When Mr. King calls during the week and finds out you'll be gone, I bet he'll wait until another weekend to come."

"You really think so?"

"I'm almost positive." She was certain that Cliff's plans would revolve around him, but, of course, she couldn't tell Andy that Mr. King came to Mandeville specifically to spend time with him.

"Then I'll call Kevin back and tell him I'm going."

He dashed straight to the phone in the kitchen. Jennifer could hear him talking. She sighed, straightening and twirling the dial of the dryer to the right setting.

It was Sunday afternoon. Cliff had been gone about four hours and was en route to Atlanta. She'd been doing housework, trying not to think about him.

The brunch today with him and Andy had only proved once more that she and Cliff couldn't be friends. The three of them had ridden in his car, Andy in the small backseat. Cliff had seemed more virile and masculine than ever behind the wheel. When he'd looked over at her, Jennifer had felt as sexy as a model in a bikini in one of those sexist auto commercials. The interior of the car had been much too cozy and intimate, even with the sunroof open and blue sky above.

She could use a couple of weeks to recover from this weekend and let the memory of last night and today fade. Even more important, it would be good for Andy to have other recreation besides sailing with Mr. King.

Jennifer's first concern was still Andy.

Cliff was home by eleven o'clock Sunday night. He considered calling Jennifer, but decided against it. She hadn't suggested he call and let her know he'd made the trip without mishap. And by now she was probably asleep in bed.

If she didn't hear from him all next week, would she be worried about him? He doubted it. Cliff could stop any further communication and, more than likely, she wouldn't make any effort to contact him and find out why.

Knowing that bothered the hell out of him, but it didn't stop him from thinking about her when he got into the shower to wash off grit and fatigue.

God, he wanted her.

The next morning Cliff went to his office and attended a sales meeting, where he received the usual gratifying accolades. An economic recession throughout the country had adversely affected the whole boating industry for several years, but Cliff's sales figures were still impressive. When he gave his report, he repeated his formula for success, a high-quality product and personalized service to the customer.

After the meeting he had an appointment with his boss, Jim Regis, the regional sales manager for the southeastern states in Cliff's territory. Jim dropped a bombshell: he was taking early retirement in three months. Cliff could count on being offered his job.

"This will give you time to think through the pros and cons," Jim said. "I know you like being on the road, but it's not a life for a family man, being gone from home most of the time. You might take that into consideration, Cliff, if marriage and family figure into your plans for yourself in the near future."

"Filling your shoes wouldn't be easy, Jim." Cliff didn't comment either way on marital plans. He was thoroughly shaken up by this unexpected development.

"You can do my job without any problem and do it with your own style. No one doubts that."

"Thanks for the vote of confidence. May I ask what led to your decision?"

A shadow crossed the other man's face. "Mary has been diagnosed with cancer." Mary was his wife. "She's going to have chemotherapy, but the prognosis isn't very optimistic for a long-term recovery. I want to make the most of what time we have left together."

"I'm terribly sorry," Cliff said somberly.

"I appreciate your sympathy."

As he left the company headquarters, Cliff's mind was on Jim. He thought about how tragedy changed priorities. Suddenly Jim's job meant little to him, as he faced losing his wife. She was so much more important than a successful career.

What kind of personal tragedy could occur in Cliff's life to make his job meaningless? He would grieve over the death of his mother or his father or any family member, but he wouldn't lose all ambition. How would it affect him, though, if he had to cope with the death of Andy or Jennifer? Or the death of both of them? They could both be killed in a car accident or other catastrophe. Cliff couldn't bear to contemplate any of those tragic possibilities. It was too painful.

In a short amount of time, his son and his son's mother had become extremely important to him. It came as a sobering revelation that the two of them might be crucial to his happiness.

He turned his thoughts to the promotion he was going to be offered. Did he want to move up to management or remain a sales rep?

Cliff had some serious soul-searching to do about his future. In order to gain a little perspective, he decided he would stay away from Louisiana this coming weekend.

That night in his motel room in Saint Petersburg, he decided to call Andy and Jennifer before going out to eat. Andy answered the phone.

"Hi, Andy."

"Hi, Mr. King!"

The eagerness and gladness in his son's voice gave Cliff a warm, good feeling. He had trouble keeping his voice light as he inquired, "How are things with you and your mom?"

"We're fine. I'm glad you called so early in the week. I've been invited to go camping with Kevin and his dad. They're leaving on Friday and coming back Sunday night. Mom didn't think you'd be coming to Mandeville for a third weekend in a row. So I told Kevin I'd go. But I can call him tonight and tell him I'm going sailing with you instead. That is, if you want me to," he added.

Andy would choose sailing with Cliff over camping with Kevin and his dad. That gave Cliff a deep, humbling satisfaction.

"No, stick with your plans, Andy," he instructed his son. "I'll just count on seeing you the following Saturday, if that arrangement is agreeable with your mom."

"She's taking a shower, or you could ask her now. I'm sure it'll be all right with her," Andy declared confidently. "How long did it take you to drive back to Atlanta?"

"About nine hours."

Cliff chatted with him for ten or fifteen minutes and hung up without talking to Jennifer. She'd obviously encouraged Andy to accept the camping invitation.

It was silly of Cliff to feel hurt. Probably she really had been operating under the reasonable—and accurate—assumption that he wouldn't be coming to Mandeville three weekends in a row. He shouldn't conclude that she would rather Andy went camping with his best friend and his best friend's father than go sailing with his own father.

But, damn it, she didn't have to second-guess Cliff's intentions and wait for him to mention his plans. She could take the initiative and communicate with him, like amicable separated parents did all the time.

He *was* Andy's father.

He might have liked to be consulted about this camping trip. No *might* about it, Cliff amended. He wanted to be consulted on decisions affecting his son's safety and well-being. Camping could be hazardous. Was Kevin's father an experienced outdoor type? Cliff certainly hoped so.

Later, when he got back to the motel room, he would call Jennifer and tell her how he felt. By then, maybe he would have a better grip on his emotions.

But Cliff was still churned up after he'd gone out to a restaurant and returned. He picked up the phone and put it back down.

He needed to talk to her in person. This was too important a matter for a phone conversation. And too urgent to postpone for a couple of weeks.

With Andy off camping, this weekend was the ideal opportunity for a conference between his parents. It obviously was also the ideal opportunity for them to go to bed together.

Realistically, that was probably going to happen sooner or later—if not this weekend, then some other time, Cliff reflected. Why fight the inevitable? Let it happen. Maybe once they'd been lovers, the attraction would cool, and they could be friends. Maybe.

The house was very quiet and empty with Andy gone. Jennifer glanced inside his room. Not surprisingly, in the process of packing for his camping trip, he'd left his room messier than usual. Tomorrow she would put clean sheets on his bed and straighten up, a chore she did not mind in the least.

The main reason she held Andy responsible for keeping his room fairly neat was to teach him to pick up after himself, not to save herself work.

The several phones in the house pealed to life, startling Jennifer out of her reverie. Hurrying down the hallway to her bedroom, she felt a little pang of loneliness. Andy usually rushed to answer the phone, calling out, *I'll* get it, Mom!

Sitting down on the side of her bed, she picked up the phone on her bedside table and said a quick "Hello" into the mouthpiece.

"I was starting to wonder if I would get your answering machine," Cliff said.

"*Cliff.*" She blurted out his name in her surprise. He'd talked to Andy the previous night and knew their son wouldn't be home. Why was he calling her, when he hadn't asked to speak to her on any of the evenings he'd called this week?

"I'll be arriving in New Orleans tomorrow afternoon. Would you have dinner with me tomorrow night? We need to talk about Andy," he explained before she could answer.

"But you weren't coming this weekend," Jennifer objected, trying to sound calm, not panicky the way she felt.

"I intended to come. I just didn't mention it to Andy because I didn't want him to have mixed feelings about going on his camping trip."

"He would have had mixed feelings, if he'd known. What is there to talk about concerning him? I'm letting you see him as often as you please." Jennifer's heartbeat was settling down a little closer to normal. The mother in her was pushing the woman into the background.

"I'd rather discuss it tomorrow night, if you don't mind."

"Can't we discuss whatever is bothering you on the phone and save you a trip to Louisiana?"

"I'm due to call on my New Orleans customers soon anyway. I plan to see them on Monday. So how about dinner? I'll pick you up about seven, if that's okay."

His usual pattern with her and Andy. Pick them up and take them somewhere and play the generous host. Jennifer balked. "It's not necessary for you to take me to dinner. You can come here to my house from the airport and we can talk."

"Very well," he agreed quietly. "This is on the up-and-up, Jennifer. I promise I won't invite you to my motel room tomorrow night."

"I didn't mean to imply that you had ulterior motives," she denied, her cheeks hot with embarrassment, but also hot with shame. The idea of going with him to his motel room was so titillating.

"I knew that I preferred having dinner with you rather than eating alone." Maybe she felt differently, he silently added with his wounded tone.

Jennifer couldn't think of anything she'd rather do than be with him tomorrow night. That was her whole problem.

"Of course, it would be silly for both of us to eat alone if you're in town," she said. "But rather than have you pick up another restaurant tab, if you have no objection to home-cooked food, I'll fix dinner for us. Without candlelight and music."

"Of course, I have no objection to home cooking," he replied.

"Then come about seven o'clock. Don't bring wine or flowers. This isn't a date. We'll discuss what's on your mind first and then sit down at the table. After dinner, if you're interested in seeing some picture albums of Andy, I'll bring them out and show them to you.''

''I would love to see them.''

Hearing the earnestness in his voice, Jennifer allowed herself faint new hope that she and Cliff might develop a companionable, comfortable relationship. Maybe looking at pictures of Andy together would put them on the right footing tomorrow night.

In view of the discussion she assumed that they would have about Andy, it was all the more necessary to defuse the sexual tension between them and become friends. Jennifer's guess was that Cliff had reached the state of mind where he wanted Andy to know who his real father was.

She still had reservations. She still had fears on Andy's behalf, but she had to agree to telling him the truth, or part of the truth. How could she not agree? After the initial shock faded, Andy was going to be thrilled to learn that his hero, Mr. King, was actually his dad.

By now, Jennifer had more faith in Cliff's capability of being a good father than she'd had initially. His wanting to acknowledge Andy would be proof in itself that Cliff's interest in his son wasn't a passing whim.

But Jennifer still couldn't go along with telling Andy that he was illegitimate. She just *couldn't*. A partial truth would have to do, at least until he was older. She and Cliff could say they'd been married and divorced. That was a story Andy could relate to his friends without shame. Surely Cliff would agree to that.

The rest of Friday evening and all the next day, Jennifer's thoughts were too much on the talk with Cliff to allow for much apprehension about being alone with him in her house, with no sleeping Andy who might wake up and interrupt a passionate love scene.

Cliff had taken her at her word, she saw, when she opened the door to him at seven o'clock on the dot. He was empty-handed. He was also solemn and tense. Jennifer could feel herself tensing up in response.

"You're right on time," she declared with a bright smile.

"I've learned by now to allow an extra fifteen minutes to drive through your subdivision to your house," he replied, stepping over the threshold.

"You mean because of the children playing in the streets. I guess it is nerve-racking for someone who's not used to living in a family neighborhood."

"Very nerve-racking."

Jennifer led him into her living room. "Would you like a cold beer or a glass of wine?"

"A beer sounds good," he said in the same sober voice.

When she returned, he was standing in front of the fireplace, looking at the pictures of Andy on the mantel, his expression serious.

"Here you are." Jennifer handed him the beer in a frosted glass and sat on the long sofa with her own glass of sparkling mineral water. After a moment of seeming indecision, he came over and sat at the other end.

"I think it's time I should start being more up-front," he said, taking a gulp of his beer. "About everything. For starters, driving through your subdivision gives me the willies."

Jennifer nearly choked on her mineral water. She'd assumed they were through with the discussion of her neighborhood and about to discuss Andy. "It's a neat, well-kept subdivision," she protested. "My neighbors are nice people."

"There's nothing wrong with it. I'm only telling you my reaction."

"What about it bothers you so much? The children?"

He shook his head. "The kids are cute. It's the general atmosphere that bothers me, I guess. Maybe the knowledge that most of the husbands and fathers are probably in my age range, late twenties to mid-thirties."

"And you could be in their shoes, if you hadn't avoided getting married," she elaborated for him, trying to sound matter-of-fact.

Cliff gazed down into his beer. "I guess I have avoided marriage," he admitted. "Why, I can't explain. My parents are certainly happily married."

"You obviously enjoy the life-style of a single man."

He looked at her. "I did, until May of this year. Since then, I haven't."

Jennifer took a nervous sip of her mineral water and had trouble swallowing it. "I'm sure you will again."

"I'm *not* sure. But, then, neither am I sure that I'm ready to settle down."

"*Why* do you feel obligated to tell me that?" she demanded, the blood rushing to her cheeks. "Because I invited you to dinner? Believe me, it has *never* entered my head to try to trap you into marriage!"

"I didn't mean to imply any such thing," he quickly assured her. "I'm just trying to be completely honest with you."

"Shall we talk about Andy? Then, you're welcome to leave and go have dinner somewhere else, where you might enjoy your food."

Cliff sighed. "I want to stay and have dinner with you. And that's being honest, too."

"Then, stay." Nothing he'd said changed the fact that she wanted him to stay. There had been no revelations that truly surprised her.

"About Andy." He set his half-finished glass of beer on a coaster on the coffee table. Jennifer's fingers tightened on her glass. "I know I'm Mr. King to him, but he's still my kid. I'd like to have some input when you're making decisions affecting him that aren't everyday decisions. Take this camping trip, for example. It worried me to think of his going off with Kevin's father when I had no inkling whether the man was an experienced outdoorsman or a novice."

"I guess I assumed he was experienced," Jennifer said, beginning to be worried herself. "He has all the equipment. Is there that much danger in camping?"

"There're safety precautions to follow, as in any form of recreation. I don't mean to alarm you," Cliff said. "Rather I'm requesting that from now on you discuss the matter with me when Andy gets a similar sort of invitation.

"I'll provide you with my itinerary so that you can contact me seven days a week. And, of course, I'll be calling frequently. My theory is that two concerned parents are better than one." His expression anxious, he paused for Jennifer to respond.

"I certainly wouldn't argue with your theory," she said. "Not in principle, anyway. There have been plenty of times when I've wished I had someone to help me make decisions regarding Andy."

"Well, now you have someone. From here on out," Cliff declared earnestly. "I can't promise that I'll be a wise parent, but I can promise that I'll be an interested one." He moved closer, reached out his hand and ran his knuckles lightly across her cheek. His voice softened.

"You're a remarkably fine person, Jennifer. I wouldn't have blamed you if you'd told me just now to take my theory and stick it."

"I'm not so remarkable," she denied. "Just a typical mother, who wants the best for her child."

"You're anything but typical." He leaned forward to pick up his beer, sat back, visibly relaxing, and raised the glass to his lips.

"Is that all you wanted to talk about in regard to Andy?" Jennifer asked.

"For now, that's all. Is there anything you wanted to bring up?"

"No. If you'll excuse me, I'll go and toss the salad." She escaped to the kitchen, devastated by her disappointment.

He was satisfied to go on being "Mr. King" to Andy.

Jennifer composed herself as she put the finishing touches on the meal she'd prepared: baked chicken breasts, steamed asparagus and green salad.

It was still daylight outside when she summoned Cliff to the table in the dining alcove adjacent to the kitchen. The house she rented didn't have a formal dining room. She and Andy ate all their meals at this same table, which seated six and served also as a worktable for his school projects.

"This looks delicious," Cliff said as he sat down. "And also healthy."

"I probably should have warned you that I believe in eating healthy, for the most part."

"So do I. I feel so much better when I don't make a steady diet of heavy, fatty foods." He sampled his chicken breast and chewed with relish.

Jennifer tried not to beam like a pleased housewife. "Isn't it difficult watching your diet when you eat primarily in restaurants?"

"Not nearly so difficult as eating in people's homes," Cliff replied. "Actually, I associate an unhealthy diet with home cooking. After a holiday visit to my parents' house, I'm sluggish for a week afterward. My mother's feelings get hurt if I don't overeat."

"Is she a good cook?"

"She's a marvelous cook in the old-fashioned mold. Sometime I'll have to tak—" He broke off with a cough and took a big swallow from his glass of water. Picking up his fork again, he stabbed a bite of salad and didn't finish his sentence.

What had he been about to say? *Sometime I'll have to take you and Andy home with me for a visit?* He'd suddenly caught himself and stopped.

"What about your aunt? What kind of cook was she?" he asked.

"My uncle was diabetic and she had high blood pressure. So our meals were bland and pretty tasteless. But they were well balanced," Jennifer added in fairness.

"I get the impression from what you've told me about your background that you had a joyless childhood," he remarked, his tone disconcertingly gentle.

"I've been much happier as an adult than as a child or teenager," she admitted. "Maybe not having a happy childhood made it that much more important to me that Andy grow up happy and secure. Perhaps I've enjoyed his childhood vicariously."

"If it's not too painful a subject, what happened to your parents? They'd both died by the time you were seven, hadn't they?"

Jennifer's fingers gripped her fork tightly. "Actually, only my mother had died. My father was alive. But I never knew him."

"Not at all?"

"No. He and my mother were only common-law man and wife. They'd split up by the time I was born, and he took no interest in me. He died when I was fifteen." Jennifer picked up her knife and cut into her chicken.

"I'm sorry. I didn't mean to pry. I see that talking about your parents upsets you," Cliff apologized in the same gentle tone of voice.

"I've always been ashamed to talk about my background. It's not a very pleasant story to tell." For some reason, she wanted to tell him the sordid facts.

"Sometime I'd like to hear it."

"Only if you promise not to make a slip around Andy. I don't want him to know the truth about his grandparents on my side."

He nodded, not seeming surprised at the restriction.

Jennifer laid down her knife and fork, deciding not to wait until another time but go ahead and tell him now. "I think you'll agree that he's better off not knowing that his grandfather was a convicted felon, sent to prison for armed robbery and second-degree murder." Cliff put down his knife and fork. His shock showed on his face. She continued, "While he was serving his term, he was killed in a prison riot. It was reported in the newspaper, which is how I learned about it."

"My God, Jennifer," he said, compassion in his voice.

"My mother didn't die violently—she merely drank herself to death."

Cliff shook his head. "Poor kid. You did come from a rough background." With those sympathetic words, he resumed eating. Her appalling true story hadn't killed his appetite.

Jennifer picked up her fork and took a bite of her salad. To her surprise, it tasted good. She began to eat her food with real enjoyment. Cliff casually brought up another topic of conversation, and they finished their dinner.

When she got up to serve dessert and coffee, he rose and picked up his dinner plate and carried it into the kitchen. While she dished up fresh fruit and sherbet, he poured the coffee.

Jennifer had wanted to establish a companionable relationship tonight. This was undeniably companionable. But wonderfully so.

Her state of relaxation with him was dangerous, she knew. It made her that much more vulnerable. She felt brimming over with pleasure in his company. All her being was opened up to his looks, his personality, his character.

For Cliff wasn't a shallow man. Her attraction to him wasn't superficial. She could love him so easily.

Jennifer was fully conscious of the perils as she and Cliff returned to her living room.

Chapter Ten

Seated next to Cliff on the sofa, Jennifer narrated while he slowly turned the pages of photo albums, studying the pictures of their son in his various stages of infancy and childhood.

It was impossible for her not to make the comments of an adoring mother. "Isn't that a darling picture!" she exclaimed with some frequency. And "Look how cute he was in that little outfit!"

From time to time Cliff's gaze lifted and rested on her face. In his blue eyes, which were so like Andy's, she read an emotion that tugged at her heartstrings: regret.

Closing the last album, he put it on the coffee table and remarked quietly, "I hate that I missed the first ten years of his life. I also hate that I wasn't around to lend some support to you."

"You shouldn't blame yourself. It wasn't your fault you didn't know that Andy existed."

Jennifer laid her hand lightly on his forearm in a gesture of sympathy. Before she could draw it away, he immediately placed his other hand over hers, keeping it there. She could feel the corded muscles beneath his warm bronzed skin.

Her voice came out breathless as she added, "You shouldn't feel guilty about me."

"But I do. Any man would." His voice was low and husky.

"No, not any man," Jennifer denied.

She knew that she should pull her hand away, break the mood of intimacy, but her whole body had gone weak. Cliff shifted sideways and his knee touched hers.

"I'll put those albums away," she said, not making a move.

He didn't answer as he leaned toward her, his intention to kiss her evident in his face. Jennifer whispered his name as much in invitation as protest, tilting back her head. He released her imprisoned hand, using that arm to circle her waist and pull her close. Now was her last chance to push him away before his mouth claimed hers. Instead, she closed her eyes, put her arms around his neck and kissed him back with a hunger that matched his.

As their tongues coupled urgently, Cliff's free hand found one of her breasts. He captured it and squeezed with strong, possessive fingers. Pleasure exploded in Jennifer. She arched her back, hot desire rising like lava.

He pulled back and looked into her face, raw need and desire in his eyes. "We *have* to make love," he said. "It's more than I can handle, wanting you this much."

His hand still cupped her breast. Glancing down, he stroked the hard peak with his fingertips, then gently pinched it through the layers of her clothes. Jennifer closed her eyes, moaning in response to the pleasure shocks rocketing through her.

"You want me, too. That's what makes our situation so impossible," he said, kissing the side of her neck. His warm breath and the low resonance of his voice sent shivers of delight all along the surface of her skin. "I fantasize about being naked with you, touching you everywhere, kissing you everywhere, satisfying you."

He was unzipping her dress. Jennifer didn't make any attempt to stop him. There wasn't any stopping, not when his need for her was so great. She could feel the tremor of passion in his fingers as he caressed her bare back, running into the obstruction of her bra.

"Wait, Cliff," she said, and his hand went still. He groaned and gazed at her with mute pleading. Jennifer smiled at him, tenderness welling up. "I was only going to say, 'Let's go into my bedroom.'"

He hugged her tightly, then stood, drawing her up with him.

In her bedroom he stripped down to navy briefs, flinging aside his clothes, in the amount of time it took her to step out of her dress and lay it over a chair. Wearing her bra and panties, Jennifer gazed at his body with blatant feminine appreciation, the way she'd wanted to look at him in his racing trunks on the Saturday two weeks ago when she and Andy had gone sailing with him.

"You're so sexy," he said softly, coming toward her, tall and lean and bronzed in the lamplight. His cotton briefs fit snugly, revealing that he was fully aroused.

Jennifer sucked in her breath with the raw impact of his masculinity. "Cliff, I'm not on birth-control pills."

"Don't worry. I came prepared."

He bent and kissed her on the mouth, his hands roving over her shoulders and arms, her back, her waist and hips, her thighs. Jennifer tingled from head to toe with his caressing touch. Her breasts jutted out as though to tempt him, and finally he came to them, squeezed their aching fullness. Finally he slid one palm down her stomach, slid lower to her pelvis and then slipped between her legs to cup and possess her womanhood.

Jennifer's knees buckled with her total surrender to feminine pleasure. She grasped his shoulders for support. Feeling the ridged muscles beneath his warm, smooth skin, she stroked him, exploring the expanse of his shoulders and his back, all the while returning his deep kisses. Her hands had reached the elastic waist of his briefs, when he unfastened her bra and began caressing her bare breasts. The sensations were so exquisite that she paused.

"Don't be shy," Cliff implored against her mouth. "Touch me down there."

She did as he urged and acquainted herself with his lower body, fondling his hard buttocks, his tumescent manhood, straining to be free of the restriction of his briefs, the vulnerable softness between his muscular thighs. Groaning her name, Cliff reached down and imprisoned her hand against his groin. Through the cloth, she could feel the pulsing heat of his arousal.

"I want you so much," he said in a pained voice.

"Make love to me," Jennifer replied, wanting him inside her.

He picked her up in his arms and carried her to the bed. Bending over her, he removed her panties, exposing her to his view. She gasped when he stroked between her legs, delving into her molten desire, then leaned down to kiss her inner thighs, his breath warm on her skin, his mouth incredibly close to the most intimate part of her.

Jennifer cried out in sheer ecstasy, her thighs coming apart for him when he kissed her *there*, in the volcanic center of sensation, and made love to her with his tongue. Spasms of unbearable pleasure erupted and burst, one after another, until she lay weak and languid. Cliff planted one more gentle kiss before he straightened and peeled off his briefs. Jennifer opened her eyes and gazed at him as, nude, he retrieved his slacks, got a condom from his wallet and joined her on the bed.

Her languor fast dissipated and new sensual excitement was reborn as she helped him sheathe himself. His fingers trembled with his sexual urgency.

But still he delayed his satisfaction, kissing her and fondling her breasts and caressing her until she was aroused all over again, wanting him inside her.

"I may last five seconds, sweetheart," he warned her apologetically. The casual endearment made the moment very sweet for Jennifer.

"It's okay," she reassured him.

Cliff thrust deep inside her and filled her with joyous sensation. The same joy was in his voice as he said, "We're so *good* together. *Too* good."

He stroked deep again and again, taking them both to a cataclysmic peak of shared pleasure and beyond it to a boundless satisfaction that they also shared. Jennifer reveled in being merged with him, body and spirit.

In a moment of calm, profound insight, she knew why she hadn't been able to love another man during the past eleven years. That day when Andy was conceived, she'd given herself to Cliff. All he'd had to do was come along and claim her, and she was his.

But what would he do with her? How long would he want her? In her state of happy lassitude, Jennifer postponed those questions until later.

"It's no wonder we made Andy in a day." Cliff raised his head as he spoke and looked down at her, his expression tenderly bemused. "We've got some powerful chemistry between us."

"You can take the credit." She stroked his cheek lovingly. "You're a marvelous lover."

"You're a very passionate sex partner."

"With you."

He didn't reply to that admission, but levered himself up and carefully withdrew. "Be right back. Don't move." He kissed her lightly on the mouth as though to underline his instructions and climbed out of bed.

Jennifer did move, but only to throw back the bedspread and cover herself with the sheet while he went into her bathroom and returned. Before he slid under the sheet, he got a second condom and placed it on the nightstand.

"Just to be on the safe side," he said.

"Cliff, you can't spend the night. I have to be careful of my reputation."

"I know that." He lay alongside her, propped up on his elbow, caressing her beneath the sheet. "But I'm not sleepy yet. Are you?" He flipped back the sheet and bent to nuzzle her breast with his mouth. Jennifer arched her back in response, lifting her chest to him, as he laved her nipple with his wet, rough tongue.

"How can I feel sleepy when you do that?" She stroked his shoulders and back, delighting in touching him.

They made love again, prolonging the arousing stages of kissing and touching. Jennifer was bolder this time, exploring his body intimately with her mouth and tongue. When they were both hot with desire and could wait no longer, Cliff lay on his back, drew Jennifer astride him and let her couple their bodies and set the pace and rhythm for another joyous trip together to the pinnacle of pleasure.

Afterward she lay collapsed on top of him, his arms wrapped around her and holding her close. If Jennifer had been capable of words, she couldn't have kept from saying *I love you, Cliff.*

"You're wonderful," he murmured with a deep intake of breath that swelled his chest.

She raised her head and looked down at him tenderly. If he'd opened his eyes, he would undoubtedly have been able to read the love on her face, but he kept his eyes closed until Jennifer had pressed her lips to his forehead and sat up.

Then all his attention seemed focused on safely disengaging their bodies.

"We probably can't be too careful," he remarked, sitting on the side of the bed. "Something tells me that you and I could easily give Andy a sibling."

"We certainly don't want that to happen," Jennifer replied, walking over to her closet to get the caftan that she used for a robe.

"If it did happen, I wouldn't leave you in the lurch this time. We would get married," he stated soberly, the prospect obviously a grim one for him.

It was anything but grim for her. She slipped the caftan over her head, trying not to entertain the idea of Cliff as her husband and herself pregnant with a little brother or sister for Andy.

Cliff had made no move to get up and get dressed. Jennifer sensed that he was expecting some answer from her. "You didn't knowingly leave me in the lurch before," she said. "And we were careful tonight. I wouldn't feel anxious if I were you."

"I don't feel anxious." He sounded faintly annoyed. "I thought you might be."

He gathered up his clothes and began putting them on. Jennifer watched him in the dresser mirror as she ran a comb through her mussed hair.

"Andy will be home tomorrow night. Would you like to see him?" she asked. "You could have supper with us. I'm planning to barbecue some ribs. That's one of his favorite meals."

He was tucking his shirt into his slacks. "I do want to see him. But why don't I take you both out to supper? You cooked for me tonight."

Jennifer sighed, turning around. "Cliff, if you're going to be a regular part of Andy's life, you'll have to resign yourself to accepting our hospitality. There are no strings attached. I have no thoughts about trapping you."

He had sat down on the side of her bed again to don his socks and shoes. "I know you don't, but—" He broke off, shrugging his broad shoulders.

"But what?" she demanded. "Go ahead and finish."

"Damn it, Jennifer. Here you are, single and the mother of my kid. I'm not married. I couldn't hope to do any better than you in finding myself a wife."

"If you wanted a wife, you mean. And you don't. Cliff, don't you realize that I've known from the very beginning that you weren't cut out to be a husband? Why do you think I accepted the fact that it was just as well you'd left Fort Lauderdale and I didn't know how to contact you? I didn't want a reluctant bridegroom then, and I don't want one now. You're *not* under any pressure," she assured him.

He looked more offended than relieved to have cleared the air. "I was twenty-two years old when you met me.

The majority of guys that age aren't ready to settle down."

"You're thirty-three now. Have you ever asked a woman to marry you?"

"No."

Jennifer rested her case. "The supper invitation is open. Just come, if you decide you want to."

"I definitely want to have supper with you and Andy. What are you doing tomorrow?" he asked. "I was hoping you might go sailing with me."

"Sailing. Just the two of us?" Jennifer was taken completely by surprise. He hadn't mentioned any plans for the next day.

"Just the two of us," he confirmed. "It's supposed to be a nice day. I'll pick up some food and drinks in the morning."

She shook her head, mustering her willpower. "I really shouldn't take the day off tomorrow. I have yardwork to do. The grass needs mowing. I didn't get around to it today."

"How about we go sailing in the morning and get back early enough in the afternoon for me to mow your grass?"

"You don't want to mow grass, Cliff," she protested.

"Some honest labor won't kill me."

They'd carried on the discussion with him sitting on her bed and her standing in front of the dresser. Now he stood up as if the matter were settled.

"Do you really think a sailing trip tomorrow is a good idea?" Jennifer asked hesitantly. "Considering what happened here tonight?"

"You mean because we would be alone and might be tempted to make love out on the water?"

"That's exactly my point. Am I wrong in assuming that you feel as I do, that tonight wasn't the beginning of an affair, but just a one-time occurrence?"

"This weekend isn't the norm, with Andy not in the picture," he hedged.

"You do agree that we can't have an affair," she pressed him.

"Sure, I *agree*. Whatever that's worth. All along, my judgment has ruled out getting sexually involved with you. You saw how well my judgment held up tonight. I can't promise you that we won't make love again after tomorrow. I think we're going to have to deal with our relationship as we go along." He held out his hand. "Walk me to the door?"

She accompanied him in troubled silence, carrying on a debate with her conscience. Her conscience had won by the time they'd reached the foyer.

"I'm going to back out on sailing tomorrow," she told him regretfully.

"No, don't. Please." He took both her hands. "I'm looking forward to it. If you don't come along, I won't have a helmsman."

"Play fair, Cliff. You know you don't need me along to be your helmsman."

"Okay, scratch that argument. I mainly want you to come along and keep me company." He squeezed her hands and implored, "Please come."

"You're worse than Andy. He takes a no more easily than you do," Jennifer said, giving in to his persuasion.

"I'll pick you up at nine. Is that too early?"

"No, but why don't I meet you at the marina and save you from an unnecessary trip through our subdivision?"

"The trip is always worth it," he said, his tone apologetic. "But if you don't mind meeting me at the boat, it would give me a little extra time to do my shopping at the grocery store.''

''I don't mind.''

''Don't forget your swimsuit.'' He bent and kissed her lingeringly on the mouth. ''Good night. And thanks for dinner.''

With another warm kiss, he left.

So much for willpower, Jennifer thought, touching her fingers to her lips.

It was a little late for willpower, anyway. She supposed they might as well throw out judgment tomorrow, too. That was apparently what he'd decided. *This weekend isn't the norm,* he'd said.

Of course, they would make love tomorrow on his sailboat. Just visualizing him in his abbreviated swimsuit quickened Jennifer's pulse.

Her love for Cliff wasn't going to lessen or grow, based on the number of times they had sex. Her only defense mechanism at this point was to remain clear-sighted and not build foolish hopes.

A woman couldn't ask a man to be more honest than Cliff had been with her. Being a married man didn't appeal to him at all.

Cliff drove slowly back to his motel, the windows in the car rolled down. His mood was strange, totally unfamiliar to him, a mixture of exhilaration and cold fear.

He felt like a fish who'd taken the bait and was being reeled in. It wasn't an accurate simile. Jennifer wasn't out to land him. In fact, he wasn't sure she wouldn't throw him back very gently, if he were flopping at her feet.

She didn't have the first manipulative instinct. She accepted him exactly as he was, or exactly as she'd sized him up to be—a confirmed bachelor.

Cliff was trying hard to be completely honest with her, but how could he, when he couldn't get a grip on his own feelings? Tonight, he could have told her that making love with a woman had never been like that for him before. But how could he have articulated the difference?

Was the sex more meaningful because he cared for her? Or was that just romantic nonsense?

He could also have confided that it had thrilled his ego when she confided that he brought out her passionate nature more than any other man had. Except that Cliff wasn't certain that mere ego was involved. And along with the thrill, he'd felt jealous as hell because there had been other men—though he doubted there had been many.

He'd had a lot of experience with women. After all, he'd been dating since high school. None of that experience seemed relevant now. With Jennifer, he'd ventured into the unknown. He was operating on instinct, taking careful steps, part of him wanting to avoid pitfalls and part of him wanting to abandon all caution.

Was he in love with Jennifer? He'd never felt such tender emotion for a woman before. He'd never felt this protective, this possessive.

Just for the sake of argument, say he *was* in love with her. Did being in love pave the way for adapting to married life? Cliff had no way of knowing whether he would be happy as a husband and head of a household.

He did know that he wouldn't be happy now without Jennifer and Andy in his life.

The thought of going sailing with her tomorrow, of having supper with them tomorrow night, filled him with anticipation. Sandwiched between was the chore of mowing her lawn, but even that prospect wasn't repugnant. He liked the idea of saving her from having to do Andy's job.

Best of all, he had an excuse to be with her at her house in the afternoon. Maybe he would bring a change of clean clothes, so that he could shower there. Maybe she could be persuaded to join him in the shower.

Cliff drifted into male fantasy. After the satisfying sex, he arrived at his motel in a state of arousal. Lying in bed, he felt not only dissatisfied but lonely.

He wished Jennifer were sleeping with him tonight.

Jennifer felt shy and self-conscious as she approached Cliff's sailboat. He was apparently inside. The hatch was open.

How would he behave toward her today?

"Hello," she called, standing on the dock and holding her tote bag. In it was a long-sleeved blouse and also her one-piece swimsuit, which she'd stuck in at the last moment. Under her denim shorts and summery blouse, she wore a red bikini that she'd bought on sale five or six years ago and worn only a few times for sunbathing in privacy. Something had possessed her to put it on this morning.

On the way here, she'd decided definitely to change into the one-piece. She was ashamed of herself for wanting to be sexy. What kind of message would that send?

"Hello there," she called out louder.

Immediately, Cliff's blond head popped up in the open hatchway. Next, his bare upper torso emerged, and he sprang out with a lithe, muscular ease, wearing burgundy shorts, with boating moccasins on his feet.

"Hi. Come aboard," he invited warmly, extending his hand to her. His blue eyes spoke male compliments about her appearance.

Flustered and even more self-conscious, Jennifer grasped his hand and stepped onto the deck of the sailboat. He helped her solicitously down into the cockpit.

"If I can do something to help, just tell me," she said.

"We're just about ready to get underway. Can I take your bag and put it below for you?"

Jennifer handed him her tote bag.

"How are you?" Cliff asked gently. "Did you sleep well?"

"Much better than I should have slept," she admitted.

He touched her cheek. "You look pretty and well-rested."

"How are you?" Jennifer asked. "Did you sleep well?"

"Not especially. But I had some terrific dreams about you." He bent and kissed her on the lips. "We're almost ready to get underway."

Neither one of them had answered the question, *How are you?* What could Jennifer have said to describe her state of mind? Adjectives like happy, pessimistic, eager, anxious, glad, ashamed, hopeful and afraid all applied.

The good emotions had to do with the joys of the present, with being with him. The darker emotions were linked to the future.

Feeling his lips on hers, Jennifer felt gladness swell inside her.

Cliff started the engine. He managed to handle the wheel and also help to cast off lines as they backed the boat out of the slip. As they motored out to the lake, Jennifer steered while he removed the sail covers and moved about on deck surefootedly, uncoiling lines and readying the boat for sailing. He performed each task with easy expertise. It was sheer delight for her, watching him.

Then came the drama of raising and trimming the sails. Cliff turned off the engine, and they could hear the quiet ripple of water along the hull, the peaceful creaking of the rigging. He sprawled back in the cockpit with a contented sigh. Jennifer was absurdly pleased that he didn't relieve her at the wheel.

They sailed along in comfortable silence for a minute or two. Suddenly, Cliff snapped his fingers and cursed mildly.

"Damn. I forgot my father's birthday."

"When was it?"

"Yesterday. I'll have to call him tonight."

What had made him think of his father? Jennifer wondered. "How old is he?" she asked.

"Fifty-nine."

"He's still relatively young."

Cliff nodded, his expression rueful. "He's eligible for retirement from the post office. He has over thirty-five years of employment under his belt. But he'll probably work until they force him to retire, because after that he'll be under my mother's thumb twenty-four hours a day."

"Your mother's bossy?"

"She pretends that she doesn't wear the pants in the family, but she does. I think poor Dad learned a long time ago to go along with whatever she wanted because she would eventually wear him down and get her way." Cliff shook his head, a faraway expression on his face. "My sisters and I had to go to him when we needed parental permission to do something. And yet we knew Dad was only the figurehead. 'Your mother and I will talk it over,' he'd say. I can't recall an instance when he gave me a yes or no, acting on his own authority."

"Did that cause you to lose respect for him?"

"I suppose it did. I guess I've always felt a little sorry for him. He was kind of in the same boat with us kids. Don't let me give you the wrong impression," he added. "My father's a man who's happy with his lot in life."

"But you never wanted to grow up and be like him?"

"No. I love my father and admire some of his good qualities, but he wasn't my role model."

Jennifer hesitated. "Has it occurred to you that your attitude toward being a husband might stem from your feelings about your father?"

"It occurred to me just now, as we were having this conversation," Cliff replied. He shifted positions, angling his body closer to her, and reached to stroke his palm along her forearm. "Want me to take over the wheel now?"

"If you'd like."

Much to Jennifer's regret, he apparently didn't wish to continue the discussion.

After a while, they tacked. The sun grew warmer. Jennifer was wishing she could take off her blouse, when Cliff inquired, "How about a cold beer? Since Andy isn't along today, I bought beer and soft drinks."

She went inside and handed him an ice-cold beer, plunged her hand back into the icebox and came up with another can that also happened to be beer. On impulse, Jennifer popped the top and took a sip. The taste was cold and refreshing.

Beer in hand, she rejoined Cliff in the cockpit.

"I thought you might have shed some clothes down there," he remarked with a note of disappointment.

"That was silly of me. I should have," Jennifer replied, realizing that she'd overlooked the opportunity to change swimsuits while she was getting the drinks.

"Now's the perfect time to get some sun, before noon."

"You're right."

She briefly considered going back inside the cabin, but instead unbuttoned the top button of her blouse. Cliff had seen hundreds of women in bikinis. Hers wasn't even a string bikini. She might as well go ahead and wear it since she'd put it on that morning, wanting to look sexy.

Cliff whistled appreciatively when Jennifer slipped out of her blouse. "Hey, I like that swimsuit, too," he said.

"I've only worn it in my backyard," she confessed.

"Thank heaven you didn't wear it on our sailing trip with Andy a couple of weeks ago. I had problems enough as it was." His gaze rested intimately on her breasts, curving out of the red cups of the bikini top.

Her self-consciousness faded. Enjoying the sensation of being womanly and alluring in his eyes, Jennifer relaxed, sipped her beer and delighted in feeling the breeze against her bare skin.

When their cans were empty, she took them down to place them in a separate trash bag for recyclable garbage. While she was in the cabin, she also shed her shorts and found sunscreen in a locker.

"Wow," Cliff said when she climbed up the companionway steps. His gaze had a possessive quality as he admiringly inspected her from the waist down, the bikini bottom a bright triangle of red.

He shed his shorts, beneath which he wore the same black racing trunks. Jennifer subjected him to her own feminine inspection. In a haze of sensual pleasure, she applied sunscreen and handed the bottle to him, watching as he smoothed the creamy liquid over his face and shoulders and chest and thighs.

"Want me to do your back?" she offered, itching to feel her moistened palm on his taut, tanned body.

"Would you?" He shifted sideways.

Jennifer massaged the lotion onto his sun-warmed skin, taking her time. When she'd finished, she gave him a little pat. He shifted forward again and put his arm around her, keeping her there beside him.

"Will you come along on sailing trips with Andy and me?" he asked.

"When I'm invited," she replied.

"You can count on being invited." He tightened his arm around her.

Jennifer thought about those future sailing trips, when she would be Andy's mom and Cliff would be Mr. King. The two of them would continue the pretence that he was simply a nice man who'd taken a big interest in Andy. The prospect dimmed some of her pleasure in today.

"What is it?" Cliff asked with quick perception.

"Oh, just the whole business about keeping the truth from Andy."

"Don't worry. I swear to you I won't ever tell him the real story without first getting your permission." His arm tightened around her in a hug of reassurance.

But will you ever want my permission? That was the question she wanted to blurt out, but didn't. He would answer her honestly, and she could guess what he would say: he didn't know at this point when, or if, he would ever be ready to publicly claim Andy as his son.

Chapter Eleven

"I'll pick up the sticks and pinecones," Jennifer said.

"You don't have to," Cliff objected. "Why don't you stay inside where it's cool?"

"I would feel guilty, leaving you out in this sweltering heat, doing my yardwork," she insisted.

He relented, since he selfishly preferred having her outside with him, even if she sat in the shade. She donned her gardening gloves, but stayed there in the garage near him while Cliff checked the oil level on the lawnmower, added motor oil and filled the gas tank. The thought occurred to him that more than guilt might be keeping her from staying inside in the air-conditioning. Maybe she was willing to put up with discomfort to be outside with him.

"All set," he declared, straightening up and glancing over at her. Any time she was in kissing range, he felt the urge to indulge. Giving in to it now, he leaned over and pressed his mouth to hers.

"Cliff!" she protested when he'd pulled back reluctantly. "The garage door is open!"

He turned his head and looked out toward the street. "No one saw us, and if they had, they'd just think you were giving your yardman some incentive pay." With these teasing words, he stole another kiss. For all her worry about being seen, her lips clung to his, he noticed with an inner satisfaction.

"Let me get to work," she announced, turning to get the wheelbarrow.

Cliff followed her out, pushing the lawnmower and enjoying the view of her rounded bottom in a pair of khaki shorts. After last night and today, he knew every inch of her slim, curvaceous body.

They'd anchored the boat at noon, and taken a swim, which had turned into foreplay in the water. Instead of cooling off, they'd both heated up to the melting point. If it hadn't been for the necessity of birth control, he would have taken her right there in Lake Pontchartrain.

On the boat, he'd peeled the wet red bikini off her. She'd skinned off his racing trunks, freeing his jutting manhood. Together they'd coupled their bodies. He'd buried himself between her open thighs, sinking into the velvety heat of her, not wanting ever to withdraw. They'd both reached an explosive climax almost immediately. The memory made Cliff sweat.

He couldn't get enough of making love to her.

Unless he wanted to mow the grass in an aroused state, he would do well to get his mind on something else, Cliff reflected as he started up the lawnmower.

The neighborhood offered distractions even on a hot Sunday afternoon. School-age children rode their bicycles up and down the street. Minivans passed, the majority of them with an infant seat and at least two child passengers. Several houses down, one of the minivans pulled into a driveway and a family of five spilled out with plastic bags from a discount store. From this distance, Cliff could read the bold print naming the store.

He stopped, mopping his brow, and watched while the husband and father, a man in his thirties, played referee in a dispute between a little girl with pigtails and her older brother, who looked to be about Andy's age. Meanwhile, the mother and wife, a petite redheaded woman, scooped up a chubby child from a car seat and carried him inside.

Resuming his mowing, Cliff tried to put himself in the man's shoes and imagine what it would be like to make Sunday-afternoon family shopping excursions to discount stores. He rarely shopped in such stores, which always seemed to be swarming with masses of people, especially on weekends. On his few trips to that particular store where Jennifer's neighbors had just been, he'd observed parents with children in tow.

Had he ever felt a twinge of envy at the sight of a father in the auto department or the sports department with a son fidgeting beside him, asking questions or pleading with his dad to buy him some item that was being hyped on children's commercials?

No, he hadn't.

On the other hand, Cliff reacted very positively to the idea of taking Andy along shopping with him, to any kind of store. He didn't think he would mind answering Andy's questions. But then, Andy wasn't just any kid. He was bright and fun to be around. A great kid.

Cliff's kid.

He hadn't dreamed that being a father could bring so much pleasure, could be such an enriching experience. Maybe the same was true about being a husband.

Cliff hadn't ever felt envious seeing a husband and wife together, but maybe he would like being tied down. To Jennifer.

But what if he didn't?

There was no way to tell, without first speaking marriage vows and wearing a wedding ring.

He would definitely like the honeymoon period, though. No doubt about that. Her presence out in her yard made pushing a lawnmower on a sweltering afternoon pleasurable for Cliff.

When she caught his eye, he smiled at her, infused with energy. After she'd finished her job, she returned the wheelbarrow to the garage and disappeared. A few minutes later, she reappeared with an oversize glass of lemonade.

Cliff drained it thirstily.

He was almost finished himself by this time, his T-shirt soaking wet and plastered to him. Under her soft brown gaze, full of feminine interest, his sweaty condition wasn't repugnant. Cliff felt male and vigorous.

"I hope you don't get heatstroke," she said, raising her voice over the noise of the mower.

He grinned and assured her, "I feel great."

And he did.

She got out her electric weed-eater. Cliff started to stop her, but selfishly didn't. He didn't want her to go inside before he did and take her shower and change. After he'd mowed the last strip of grass, he took the weed-eater from her and made short work of the edging and trimming, while she trailed along, making sure the electric cord didn't get tangled.

If he were doing this chore on a regular basis, he would buy a gas weed-eater, Cliff thought. The light electric model felt like a thistle and didn't have much power.

"Thank you," Jennifer said gratefully, as Cliff coiled the long cord on his way to the garage. She walked along beside him. "I can do that. You've done enough. Why don't you go ahead inside and shower and change clothes?"

"Actually, I was hoping to have you wash my back," he replied. She blushed, and didn't insist that he go in without her.

They put everything back in place in the garage, the yardwork having taken less than two hours. With the garage door lowered, Cliff stripped off his shirt and wadded it into a sodden ball. "Got a plastic grocery bag I can use?" he asked.

Jennifer held out her hand for the shirt. "I'll just wash your clothes for you."

"You don't need to go to that trouble."

"It's no trouble, and your clothes will mildew, wadded up in a bag."

"They're old, anyway," Cliff protested.

He lost the argument, but hung on to the shirt, dropping it into the washing machine himself on their way through the laundry room. A round wicker hamper for soiled clothes sat next to the washer. On top of the dryer was a laundry basket, three-quarters full of neatly folded clean laundry. Cliff was reminded that he had washer and dryer hookups in his condo, but hadn't bothered to buy either appliance, preferring not to do his own laundry.

His whole life-style, which suited him so well, was that of a single man.

Throughout this subdivision, every house undoubtedly had a laundry room similar to Jennifer's, with some sort of clothes hamper where the family members' discarded clothes ended up together. It was certainly a novel idea for Cliff, but not at all unpleasant to contemplate his socks and underwear and washable things being jumbled up with hers and Andy's.

"You can shower first," she offered graciously, when they'd reached her bedroom with its adjacent bath.

"Why don't we both shower first?"

It didn't require a great deal of persuasion on his part, to get her to agree to his suggestion. They shared the pelting spray of warm water, the soap, the washcloth, her bottle of shampoo. He washed her and she washed him, both of them ending up squeaky clean and wildly aroused. Cliff had a condom within arm's reach in the bathroom and he made love to her right there in the shower.

Afterward he wrapped her in a towel and carried her to the bed, where he kissed and fondled her, and she kissed and fondled him, the two of them getting aroused again. This time he made love to her slowly and deeply, mindful that his satisfaction was going to have to last him until next weekend.

The previous night, she'd pressed him to agree with her that they couldn't have an affair. But it was going to be impossible for them to be around each other and not have an intimate physical relationship.

And they *would* be around each other a lot from now on. There wasn't any going back to the status quo before this weekend, not in his mind.

His trips to Mandeville would be to see Andy *and* her.

"Mind if I use your phone?"

"No, of course not."

"I want to call my father and wish him a belated happy birthday." Cliff tossed aside the section of the Sunday newspaper he'd been perusing and went over to sit on the smaller sofa, close to the phone.

He and Jennifer were relaxing in her living room, awaiting Andy's arrival. Kevin's mother had called a half hour earlier to say that the campers were on their way home and that Kevin's dad would drop Andy off at his house.

"I'll go check on your clothes in the dryer," Jennifer said, making a move to rise.

Cliff motioned for her to stay seated, and she sank back on the cushions again. Apparently he didn't mind her overhearing his phone conversation.

"Hi, Mom." He greeted his mother warmly and then for the next five minutes mainly listened to her, getting in an occasional phrase or sentence in response to what she was telling him. Jennifer turned the pages of the section of newspaper on her lap, covertly observing him. His expression mirrored patient indulgence. "I'm doing great," he declared, evidently answering his mother's inquiry. "No, I'm not at my condo. I'm in Louisiana.... Yes, I'm staying at a motel.... No, for the time being I'll keep my sailboat here, near New Orleans.... Mandeville's the name of the town.... Why, yes, of course, I've made some friends here."

Jennifer pretended to be reading an article. She wished she'd left the room. It made her feel cheap and insignificant to hear him evading mentioning her name. She was a "friend" who'd been in and out of bed with him this weekend.

"Mom, could I speak to Dad and wish him a happy birthday?"

His father came on the line. Cliff apologized for forgetting his birthday. Obviously those apologies were brushed aside. The whole tenor of the conversation changed, with Cliff doing most of the talking, asking questions and getting brief answers. Jennifer surmised that his father wasn't as talkative as his mother.

"My job? Everything's fine. I'm having a good year."

Some new note in Cliff's voice caught Jennifer's attention. She could feel his gaze on her during a short pause in which his father must have been responding.

"As a matter of fact, I have been offered a promotion. Regional sales manager. It would cut out most of the travel. I'd be pretty much stuck in Atlanta. Between salary and bonuses, I would earn more income. I'm giving serious consideration to the pros and cons."

The chance of promotion was news to Jennifer. He hadn't seen fit to mention something that important all weekend. Obviously she and Andy didn't figure into those pros and cons he was weighing in making a major career decision.

A faint buzz from the laundry room signaled that the dryer had finished its cycle. The familiar domestic summons seemed to trigger her emotions. Swallowing a huge lump in her throat, she got up from the sofa and went to fold Cliff's clothes.

Waves of humiliation washed through her as she thought about how he'd objected to having her launder his soiled outfit for him and how she'd overruled his protests and insisted.

What did he have to do to get it through to her that he was a wary bachelor always on his guard? He didn't want his women performing wifely acts for him.

Jennifer *wasn't* going to be one of his women, despite the way she'd behaved this weekend. Her self-respect wouldn't stand for it. Her sense of right and wrong wouldn't allow it.

Most importantly, her judgment as a mother advised against having an affair with Andy's father, an affair that could only end unhappily and adversely affect all three of them. She could and *would* find the strength of character to do what was best for her son.

The sound of the doorbell ringing several times in succession seemed to punctuate Jennifer's resolve. As though on cue, Andy had gotten home. His dear young voice floated through the house.

"Mr. King! You're here!"

"Hi, Andy. How was the camping trip?" Cliff's deeper man's voice was warm with affection. The sound of it tightened a band around Jennifer's heart.

"It was great!"

"You'll have to tell your mom and me all about it over supper."

"Where is Mom? In the kitchen?"

"Let's go find her."

They came looking for her, father and son, both of whom she loved. As she bent down and hugged Andy, Cliff looked on. For all her turbulent emotions, Jennifer was happy that he was there, making up the threesome of Mr. King and Mom and Andy.

It was as near to a traditional family threesome as Andy was ever likely to have. From now on, she wouldn't lose sight of preserving the all-important relationship that bound them together, that of parents and son.

"Is anybody hungry?" she inquired cheerfully and got two affirmative responses.

That morning she'd made coleslaw, precooked the ribs in the microwave and assembled the ingredients in a casserole dish for Boston baked beans. For the last hour the beans had been cooking in the oven. All that remained to be done was to barbecue the ribs on her gas grill, out on the small cement patio, and set the table.

The latter job she assigned to Andy, meaning to tend to the barbecuing herself. When Cliff volunteered to play chef, she handed the platter of ribs over to him and took care of last-minute details in the kitchen. As soon as Andy had finished setting the table, he deserted Jennifer and went out on the patio with Cliff. She got the beans out of the oven and the coleslaw out of the refrigerator. With everything done, she went outside, too, and sat in a patio chair and joined in the conversation.

In a few minutes Cliff loaded the platter, and the three of them trooped inside into the cooler air.

"That's your place, Mr. King," Andy said, pointing to the place mat at the head of the table. "Mom sits over there, and I always sit here, across from her."

Cliff took his seat. "How on earth did you put together a meal like this?" he marveled, addressing her. "You were busy doing other things all day."

"There wasn't that much preparation involved," she replied. "The trick is planning the menu ahead of time and being organized. I don't spend hours slaving in the kitchen in order to make meals for Andy and me."

"Except at Thanksgiving and Christmas, huh, Mom?" Andy said. "Mr. King will have to have dinner with us on Thanksgiving and Christmas this year, won't he?"

"If he doesn't have other plans when the time comes. Remember that Mr. King has a family, and most people visit their families on holidays."

"Do you, Mr. King?"

"Usually I have, in the past," Cliff said, obviously not comfortable with the whole discussion. Jennifer's guess was that he was hating to be pressed into acknowledging that this year he would also spend the important holidays with his parents and sisters and their husbands and children. His legitimate family.

They'd been passing the food and filling their plates. "Don't the ribs look delicious?" she inquired, picking up a rib in her fingers. "What did you have to eat on your camping trip, Andy?"

Cliff gave her a swift look, whether in gratitude for the change of subject, she didn't know. It was impossible not to feel reproachful on Andy's behalf. When the holidays rolled around, Andy was sure to lament Mr. King's absence.

This year, more than in other years, she would be put to the test to make Thanksgiving and Christmas festive events in a household of two. But Thanksgiving was months away. When the time came nearer, she would worry about it.

Andy did most of the talking through supper, regaling them with anecdotes about his weekend, some of which were humorous. Jennifer and Cliff gave him their fond attention, occasionally exchanging smiling, indulgent glances. Her earlier sense of happiness in Cliff's presence returned.

He ate heartily, once he'd relaxed after the holiday conversation. She and Andy consumed their fair share, and there weren't any leftovers.

While Jennifer spooned frozen yogurt into dessert dishes, father and son loaded the dishwasher. The three of them sat down at the table again for the final course. When they'd finished, she sent Andy to his bedroom to unpack his duffle bag. Cliff went along with him, at Andy's invitation. Jennifer hummed a tune as she tidied up the kitchen and started the dishwasher.

She felt serene and content in the moment. Her glass was half full, not half empty. Rather than be unhappy that evenings like this one would never be routine, she would enjoy such evenings when they occurred.

The important thing was that Andy's glass was brimming full with both her and Mr. King in his life.

"Mom cleaned up my room while I was gone," Andy observed guiltily. "I left it kind of messy, packing for my camping trip. But she probably won't fuss."

"Your mom's pretty terrific, isn't she?"

Andy nodded. "I'm real lucky. Except for my dad dying before I was born." He dropped his duffle bag onto the carpet and walked over to the table beside his bed. "This is a picture of him."

Cliff reluctantly took the small framed photograph of a man his son held out to him. What the hell was he supposed to say? He knew what he wished he could say: *Your dad's not dead, Andy. I'm your dad.*

"Him and Mom had only been married less than a year. She moved here and had me after he was killed in a car accident. I guess she was too sad to stay in Florida."

"That would be understandable," Cliff managed to get out. He studied the photograph of Frank Jennings. When it was taken, Jennings must have been in his early thirties, much too old for the eighteen-year-old Jennifer. His hair was combed precisely. He wore a conservative suit and tie and smiled with self-conscious dignity into the camera.

Jennifer had said she hadn't loved Jennings. So why had she kept his picture? And why had she passed him off as Andy's dad? Did he have qualities she admired, qualities she found missing in Cliff? These speculations added jealousy to Cliff's other emotions. Guarding his expression, he handed the photograph back.

"You can sit on my bed, Mr. King," Andy urged.

"That's okay. I'll sit over here on this chair by your desk."

He didn't want to sit where he could see Jennings's face, turned toward his son's pillow.

Cliff could understand why Jennifer had lied to Andy. It had been terribly important to her for Andy to believe he was conceived in wedlock. But, damn it, the boy had a real father. Him. Cliff might not be named Father of the Year, but he sure as hell could do a better job of being a dad to Andy than a photograph.

Why hadn't she come to that conclusion by now? Surely she realized how much Andy had come to mean to him. What did Cliff have to do to prove himself to her?

How long was he going to have to play along with being Mr. King? He *wasn't* Mr. King. He was . . . Dad.

"Want to play a video game when I'm through unpacking?" Andy inquired.

"Sure."

They stayed in his room, sitting side by side in chairs in front of his small TV, until finally Jennifer came to the door and announced good-naturedly, "Hey, guys, it's ten o'clock. Tomorrow's a work day."

"As soon as we finish this game, Mom, we'll quit," Andy promised, his concentration unbroken.

Cliff, however, wasn't so single-minded. He was aware that she lingered in the doorway a few moments, watching father and son. Once again he was also conscious of the photograph of Frank Jennings, which he'd managed to put out of his mind in the thick of competition.

Andy accompanied him out into the living room, where Jennifer was watching the ten o'clock local news.

"Who won?" she inquired.

"Andy did," Cliff replied, sitting down beside her on the long sofa.

Andy sat down next to him. "Mr. King won one game. He's pretty good, for a grown-up."

All three of them gave their attention to the screen as the anchorwoman gave the lead-in for the weather report: "Now stay tuned for information about a tropical storm gathering force in the Caribbean."

After a commercial break, the meteorologist came on and showed the location of the storm on a weather map and gave the stats, such as wind speed and current direction. The atmospheric conditions all pointed toward the storm's gaining force and becoming a full-fledged hurricane within the next twenty-four hours, he warned. If so, it would be the first hurricane of the current hurricane season—which started in June and lasted through October—that might threaten the Louisiana-Texas coast.

"Tomorrow there'll be a big rush to buy batteries and candles and bottled water," Jennifer predicted with a sigh. "Remind me to fill up the car with gasoline, Andy."

"What do you usually do when there's a hurricane headed for New Orleans?" Cliff asked somberly. "You don't stay here in Mandeville, do you?"

"We always have. When I first moved to Louisiana, I would go to a shelter. Certain schools and public buildings are always turned into storm shelters for people who are evacuated or are afraid to stay in their homes," she explained. "Then I got braver and would go to a friend or neighbor's house, for moral support. The last couple of years, Andy and I have just ridden out hurricanes right here at our house."

Cliff didn't like the sound of that at all. "The last couple of years there hasn't been a really dangerous hurricane to hit this area, has there?"

"No, we've been fortunate," Jennifer admitted.

"The roof could blow off your house. A tree could fall on it. A tornado could reduce it to rubble. Why risk your lives when you can drive north for five or six hours and rent a motel room?"

"You have to make an advance reservation, and it's never a sure thing when or where a hurricane is going to hit. Hurricane Juan, for instance, wandered up and down the coast from Florida to Louisiana. Hurricanes are just one of the hazards of living here close to the Gulf of Mexico."

"What about *Windsong,* Mr. King?" Andy spoke up worriedly. "Will she be safe in a hurricane?"

"*Windsong*'s insured, Andy. She's replaceable, but you and your mom aren't."

The newscast ended. Jennifer picked up the remote control and turned off the TV set. Cliff rose to leave. She and Andy both walked him to the door.

"Bye, Mr. King. See you next weekend." Andy stuck out his hand in farewell.

Cliff took it and squeezed it, remembering that a few weeks ago a handshake had sufficed. Now he longed for a bear hug from his ten-year-old son. "Bye, Andy. Have a good week. I'll call you."

"Take care of yourself," Jennifer said as he looked at her. She opened the door, stepping back and drawing Andy with her, her arm around his small shoulders. "Good night."

"Thanks for supper."

"Thank you for having supper with us."

Cliff ached to put his arms around her and hold her close a moment, ached to kiss her goodbye. "Walk out with me to the car?" he asked.

"It's late," she said regretfully, with a little shake of her head.

"Good night, then."

Feeling more rejected, more dissatisfied than he'd ever felt before in his life, he made his exit.

Cliff had forgotten to take his clean clothes, Jennifer realized as she closed the door. It took every ounce of willpower not to jerk the door open and call his name, stopping him.

"Mom, I think you hurt Mr. King's feelings," Andy said reproachfully. "It wouldn't have taken all that long to walk out to his car with him."

"I certainly didn't mean to hurt his feelings." Jennifer locked the deadbolt, hearing the sound of Cliff's car starting up. "Mr. King isn't going to get insulted by anything I say and not have anything more to do with us, if that's what's worrying you. He's very fond of you. You're his main reason for coming to Mandeville on weekends."

"He came this weekend when I wasn't going to be here. He took you out sailing with him and mowed the grass for you."

"Tonight he stayed in your room with you while I watched TV alone," she reminded.

"I know he likes me. But I think he likes you just as much," he insisted.

"Is that okay with you if he does?" Jennifer inquired uncertainly. Was he jealous?

"Sure, it's okay."

She ruffled his hair, walking with him toward his bedroom. "You didn't let him win that one game, like you let me win once in a while?"

His grin was halfhearted and his denial earnest. Obviously, he was still troubled by the parting scene with Cliff.

After she'd changed into her nightgown and slipped on her caftan, Jennifer went to his room to say good-night and tuck him in. He'd donned his pajamas and gotten into bed. Lying on his side, he was gazing at the picture he believed to be a picture of his father. He turned over on his back as she sat on the edge of his bed.

"I'm sorry that I ever showed you that picture," she said with aching regret. "It makes me feel bad to see you looking at it with a sad expression."

He patted her arm. "I wasn't feeling sad, Mom. I was thinking about Mr. King. He acted real funny tonight when I showed him Dad's picture."

"Did he?"

"Almost like he was mad or something."

"I doubt he was mad at you."

"He was fine after we started playing one of my video games. I just wonder what was wrong."

Jennifer bit her lip. "You'll have to ask Mr. King to explain his own reactions. Now you'd better go to sleep." She tucked his sheet around his waist and kissed him tenderly on the cheek. "Good night. I love you very much."

His strong, young arms hugged her around the neck. "Good night, Mom. I love you."

She rose to her feet and gazed down at him, her heart overflowing with maternal adoration. He lay there, his expression deeply thoughtful.

"Is something else bothering you?" she inquired.

"Sort of. This weekend I talked about Mr. King to Kevin and his dad. You know what Mr. Pritchard said?"

"What?"

"That it sounded to him like Mr. King would make an awfully good stepfather for me. Mom, if you were nicer to Mr. King, maybe he might want to marry you."

Jennifer sank back down on the edge of the bed again. "Andy, Mr. King *isn't* going to marry me, no matter how nice I am," she told him gently, her own words causing a painful constriction in her chest.

"How do you know?" he protested.

"I just *know*. Women have a sixth sense about these things. Put such thoughts out of your mind, think about all the fun you had on your camping trip and try to get to sleep."

"Okay, Mom." He sighed and turned on his side, facing away from his bedside table and the photograph of the nice, dull man she hadn't loved, but might have married if she hadn't met an adventurous sailor named Cliff King.

Chapter Twelve

Cliff stayed up until midnight doing paperwork and organizing his work week ahead. Thoughts of Jennifer and Andy kept intruding. The scene in her foyer flashed into his mind over and over, hurting anew each time, until he felt flayed and raw.

How could Jennifer say goodbye to him and send him away without so much as a kiss on the cheek, when they'd been about as intimate as a man and woman could be?

There was a sense of déjà vu. Eleven years ago she'd responded just as passionately to his lovemaking on that one day they'd spent together and then driven away without a word.

Was she hot and cold where he was concerned?

It was frustrating as hell for him to be sitting there in a motel puzzling over her behavior, when he was just fifteen minutes away from her house.

Cliff went to bed, knowing that he was too worked up to sleep. After tossing and turning, he finally dropped off, but had disturbing, disjointed dreams. He was up at quarter of six, fifteen minutes earlier than his wake-up call, feeling lousy.

Some of his confusion and hurt had hardened into resentment. He was tempted to pick up the phone and call Jennifer, but in his wounded, hostile state, he would probably pick a fight with her. And what would that accomplish?

Cliff realized that he was reacting very emotionally. He needed to sort out those emotions before he could deal maturely with their relationship.

She wasn't petty or mean. She wasn't manipulative. Whatever her reasons for being standoffish the previous night, they rose from her conscience and convictions.

It wasn't as simple as outright asking her, *Why did you act that way?* The real question, the one Cliff wasn't ready to ask or have answered, was *What do you feel for me?*

Needing some mental relief, he flipped on the TV. A New Orleans station came on the air. The morning weather report was in progress, with an update on the tropical storm in the Caribbean. Cliff listened soberly to what was essentially a repetition of the previous night's report. The storm was in the Caribbean Sea, gathering force and heading slowly in a southwesterly direction toward Cuba.

Unless it turned more to the west, toward the Yucatan, it would hit Cuba and probably pass over it into the Gulf of Mexico, where it was likely to build up force again and pose a threat to all the coastal areas in the entire Gulf, including the Texas-Louisiana coast.

Cliff would keep himself posted on the storm. If it did head toward New Orleans, he would see to Jennifer and

Andy's safety. They could always catch a flight to wherever he was, if it happened to be midweek.

The idea appealed to him so much that Cliff's anxiety ebbed and his mood improved. While he showered and shaved and got dressed, as he'd done countless mornings on the road, he thought about Jennifer and Andy getting up in their house and going through their morning routine.

What would it be like to wake up with them, share that routine? Cliff's speculation made him surprisingly wistful. His motel accommodations seemed sterile and lonely as he visualized himself shaving at one of the sinks in Jennifer's bathroom, while she brushed her teeth and applied makeup. Andy might come to the bedroom door with some typical emergency of a ten-year-old. Cliff could hear him say, "Mom, I can't find my U. S. Open T-shirt. I wanted to wear it today."

The three of them would assemble at the breakfast table, where he would have his first cup of coffee of the day with Jennifer while they both scanned the newspaper and carried on conversation with each other and with Andy. The three of them would have a light, healthy breakfast before they left the house.

If the reality was as nice as he imagined it, he didn't doubt that he could get used to it pretty quickly. The only way to find out, though, was to marry Jennifer. He couldn't move in with her.

Cliff's solitary breakfast in the motel restaurant wasn't very satisfactory. His coffee was bitter. His cereal and fruit were tasteless. He read the newspaper while he ate, conscious of the impersonal surroundings.

His rental car was packed and ready to go. After he'd paid at the cash register, he drove to the causeway, joining the horde of southbound commuters who lived on the Northshore and worked in New Orleans.

It promised to be another bright summer day in July. Early morning sunshine burnished the calm surface of Lake Pontchartrain. Cliff looked to left and right, seeing miles of water in either direction extending to the horizon. He rolled down the windows partway to let in the fresh air, turned on the radio and set the cruise control so that he was rolling along with traffic.

It was the start of a new day, a new week. He had people to see, places to go. Life was good. He was single and free. Cliff waited for the rush of exhilaration that he should be feeling.

In the car ahead of him, a man was talking on his car phone. In the left lane, a woman passing him was carrying on an animated phone conversation. Normally Cliff put car phones in the same category with beepers. He detested the very notion of someone being able to contact him every minute of the day.

But today he sensed a whole new isolation, riding along in his car by himself. He would give almost anything to have a car phone right now, put it to his ear and hear Jennifer's voice.

How nice it would be for her to call him for a change.

Cliff's day had been busy. He'd called on customers and had lunch at West End with Southern Yacht Club sailing cronies. In the late afternoon, he'd driven to Gulfport, Mississippi, and checked into a motel overlooking the white sand beach. Tomorrow, he would call on customers along the Mississippi Gulf coast and drive on to Mobile, Alabama.

This evening he was having dinner with some Gulfport and Biloxi boating friends, one of them a big customer.

Before he left the motel, he called Jennifer's number, got her answering machine and left a message. Rather than promising to call again later, he impulsively requested, "Please call me after nine-thirty."

The talk at dinner was mainly about boating and sailing. Cliff's companions were interested in hearing all about his having recently become a sailboat owner.

"Why are you keeping your boat over in Mandeville?" his big customer, Hank Collier, wanted to know. Hank owned a boatyard in Biloxi with a marine-supply store on the premises. "Come over here on the Gulf Coast, where the sailing's a hell of a lot better than in Lake Pontchartrain."

The others at the table heartily seconded the suggestion.

"The sailing's been pretty good," Cliff replied evasively.

"Are you sure it isn't a female crew member who's keeping you in Mandeville?" Marge Collier, Hank's wife, inquired with an arch smile.

"Actually, my crew is a mother and son."

His indirect admission that Marge had hit on the truth caused a buzz of reaction. Was it serious? his friends wanted to know.

Cliff nodded. "Pretty serious from my viewpoint."

He wanted to mention Jennifer's name, tell them about her. He wanted to take out his wallet, show them a picture of Andy and claim him as his son. But Gulfport wasn't that far away from Mandeville. Before he could go public with the news that he was a father, Andy himself needed to be told. That couldn't happen until Jennifer agreed.

Until this point in his life, Cliff hadn't understood the urge that made men carry wallet-size photos of their wives and children and proudly show them at the least opportunity.

It pained him to steer the conversation away from Jennifer and Andy and bring up the hurricane brewing in the Caribbean. Everyone at the table had been watching the weather reports as closely as he had. They well remembered the devastation to the Mississippi Gulf Coast from past hurricanes.

For all his enjoyment of the evening, Cliff kept an eye on his watch. At nine-fifteen he announced he had to get back to his motel. He was expecting an important phone call. A personal call from a special someone in Mandeville? they wanted to know. He let his grin suffice as a confession.

From *two* special someones, he amended privately as he drove along the beach highway, more eager than he'd ever been to return to a motel early in the evening by himself.

In his room, he resisted the strong temptation not to wait for the phone to ring, but to go ahead and call. No, he would let Jennifer take the initiative to communicate with him.

"Mom, it's nine-thirty."

Jennifer knew very well what time it was. "Why don't you wait another five or ten minutes, and then you can call Mr. King."

"You want me to call him? Why don't you? He left the message for both of us."

"It will be good practice for you, placing a long-distance call." Jennifer wanted to place the call herself, but she was afraid of the messages her voice might send.

"Aren't you going to talk to him, too?"

"If he asks to speak to me."

Andy sighed, turning his attention back to the TV. Jennifer flipped through the pages of her fitness magazine, counting the minutes until she would hear Cliff's voice.

Cliff grabbed the phone on the first ring. His tone was expectant as he said, "Hello."

"Hi, Mr. King. It's me, Andy."

"Hi, Andy." As glad as he was to hear his son's voice, Cliff felt a stab of disappointment. Damn it, why couldn't Jennifer have put forth the effort to call him? Her message was plain: she didn't care if she talked to him.

He and Andy chatted for about fifteen or twenty minutes, with Cliff mostly asking questions and listening. When they'd caught up with the day's happenings, Andy asked with a note of uncertainty, "Did you have anything to say to Mom?"

Lots of things, one of them *I miss you.* But was she interested in hearing that or anything else he had to say to her?

"Did she tell you that she wished to speak to me before you hung up?" Cliff asked.

"No, sir," Andy admitted apologetically.

"In that case, I guess I won't bother her."

"It was sure great talking to you, Mr. King."

"It was great talking to you, Andy. I'll give you a call tomorrow night from Mobile, Alabama."

"Mom teaches her step class at the club from seven to eight. We should be home by eight-thirty. Huh, Mom?"

Jennifer was obviously right there in the room with him. They were probably in their living room. Cliff strained to hear any reply she might make, but she must have nodded, cheating him even of the sound of her voice in the background.

"We'll be home by eight-thirty," Andy affirmed.

"Why don't I plan to call you about nine-thirty?"

"I'll be waiting near the phone," he promised, his childlike eagerness warming Cliff's heart and easing a little of the hurt caused by Jennifer's coolness.

Back off, she was telling him. Well, he would back off, way off, until she gave some indication that she was open to a relationship with him. It couldn't be all one-sided.

"Mom, I told you that you hurt Mr. King's feelings last night."

"Andy, I doubt that Mr. King gets his feelings hurt that easily. He sounded like his normal self on the recording on our answering machine."

Jennifer played the message in her mind, thrilling to his deep, attractive voice. *Andy and Jennifer, I'm in Gulfport. Tonight I'm going out to dinner with some friends. I'll be back by nine-thirty. Please call me.*

Were his friends a married couple? A group of people? Was one of them a single woman he saw when he visited the Mississippi Gulf Coast? Jealousy gnawed at Jennifer.

Evidently, he hadn't asked Andy to talk to her. She'd been sitting there on pins and needles, waiting for her turn.

Probably he'd had time to think things over and was regretting this weekend. Probably he was relieved to be putting distance between them.

Had her feelings for him been transparent? Did he know that she was in love with him? If so, he was probably trying to figure out how to keep from hurting her.

"You could have said hi to him, Mom." Andy broke into her dispirited speculation. He'd gone to his room to change into his pajamas and returned, still dwelling on his conversation with his father. "I think he would have liked that."

"Tomorrow night you can tell Mr. King 'hi' for me."

He nodded resignedly. "Okay, Mom."

The next night in Mobile, Cliff switched on the weather channel before he went out to dinner. The tropical storm, which had been upgraded to a hurricane status and dubbed Freda, was over Cuba and wreaking havoc with hundred-mile-an-hour winds. By tomorrow morning she was expected to clear land and move into the open waters of the Gulf of Mexico, where chances were good that she would regain her fury and build greater strength.

The update on the weather news didn't bring any new information to him. All day he'd heard bulletins on the radio. The storm had come up in practically every conversation he'd had. Everyone along the coastal U.S., and undoubtedly along the Mexican coast, was keeping track of Freda.

In his phone conversation with Andy a couple of hours later, Andy divulged that Jennifer was taking her usual storm precautions, stocking up on canned foods and bottled water, buying extra batteries and candles. When a hurricane hit, losing electrical power was almost inevitable, and it could be days before electrical service was restored, depending on how much damage was done to power lines and conductors.

"Mom's keeping the gas tank in the car full," Andy said matter-of-factly.

"Does your mom seem to be worried about Freda?" Cliff had resolved ahead of time *not* to ask to speak to her. He *wasn't* going to force a phone conversation on her, as he'd done numerous times prior to this past weekend.

"No, not too worried. She said to say 'hi' to you."

"Say 'hi' to her for me, will you?"

"She's right here, sewing a button on one of my shirts. Mom, Mr. King said 'hi.' "

Cliff's pride couldn't keep him from pressing the receiver hard to his ear and straining to hear any reply she made, but he heard none. The need to hear her voice was like an ache inside him.

"Tomorrow night I'll be in Pensacola, Florida. I'll call you earlier in the evening, Andy." By calling earlier, he would have more time to recuperate from the inevitable disappointment of Jennifer's staying off the line.

"I'm not going to be home tomorrow night, Mr. King," Andy informed him regretfully. "I'm spending the night with Kevin. We're going to a movie." He told Cliff the name of the movie, a big box-office hit about dinosaurs.

"Well, have a good time. I'll give you a call on Thursday night, from Saint Petersburg."

"Mom's going to be home tomorrow night. Aren't you, Mom?"

Cliff heard her answer in the background: "As far as I know, I will." By being indefinite, she was giving herself an out for not answering the phone.

Andy dutifully conveyed his mother's reply.

"I probably won't bother your mom," Cliff said, trying his best not to sound bitter. "If you have a pen and paper handy, I'll give you the name and number of the motel where I'll be staying. In case of emergency, you'll be able to reach me."

"Mom, would you get a pen and paper? She's going to get it," Cliff's son informed him. They chatted until Jennifer had returned. "Now you can tell me, and I'll tell Mom so she can write it down," Andy prompted.

Why don't I tell her myself? Cliff had never wanted to utter any words as much as he wanted to utter those. His restraint cost him all his self-control.

Tomorrow night he was going to need it and more to keep from calling her house in the hope that she would pick up.

"How did Mr. King sound tonight?" Jennifer asked after Andy had hung up.

"He sounded good."

"Had he gone out to dinner with friends again?"

"He said he ran into some people he knew at the restaurant where he went to eat." Andy yawned and stretched. "I'm gonna go and get ready for bed, Mom."

"Here. You can take this shirt with you and hang it in your closet."

Jennifer sighed downheartedly as he left the room. She was still holding the notepad on which she'd jotted down the name and telephone number of the motel in Pensacola. No wonder Cliff liked his sales-rep job so much. Travel throughout his territory was anything but lonely for him, with friends in every city he visited.

He didn't just have married friends, either. She didn't doubt that he could have female companionship in any one of those cities, whenever he wanted it.

Again, tonight, he hadn't asked to talk to her, although Andy had made it known to him that she was right there. Jennifer had cringed at her son's reporting that she was sewing on a button. Cliff's mental picture of her, needle in hand, had probably reinforced all his qualms about being sucked into a domestic trap.

He was putting distance between them this week and not just miles. His silence told her that.

* * *

Hurricane Freda had completed her stormy passage over Cuba by noon Wednesday. Stalled just off the southern coast of the island, she dealt it a vicious back-lash before inching farther out into the open water of the Gulf in the afternoon. Cliff kept himself updated as he tended to business in Mobile and then drove on to Pensacola. Everywhere he went, radios and TVs were tuned to weather reports.

There was no predicting Freda's path once she started on the move again. She could continue her former south-southwesterly direction or she could head due south and veer southeast. At this stage, there was no reliable time frame. She might reach her next destination as early as the weekend or she might dawdle. Cliff heard at least a dozen different meteorologists elaborate on the uncertainties. They all agreed that Freda had the potential for turning into a major hurricane.

Cliff hadn't changed his resolve to look after Jennifer and Andy's safety, in the event that a hurricane developed and targeted the New Orleans area. But now he was skeptical about his plan to have them catch a flight and join him somewhere. He seriously doubted Jennifer would want to do that.

If she insisted on staying put, then he would go to Mandeville and ride out the storm with them.

By Friday, Cliff should be able to make better plans.

He was meeting friends for drinks at the Pensacola Yacht Club, then going out to dinner with them. He'd decided in advance that he wouldn't come back to his motel room until it was too late to call Jennifer.

On Thursday night, Cliff weakened during his phone conversation with Andy. "Is your mom close by?" he asked. During the day, Freda had resumed a slow, steady southwesterly course that could take her on a beeline to Louisiana, if she didn't deviate. At her current rate of forward momentum, she wouldn't reach land until Tuesday. Cliff had discussed the hurricane with countless other people today. Surely it provided a good excuse to speak to Jennifer.

"No, she's in the kitchen, making her special dip for a baby shower tomorrow afternoon at the club. The shower's for Rita. She's one of the other aerobics instructors."

Cliff didn't know that Jennifer had a special recipe for dip. Although it was a minor fact, his ignorance made him feel very peripheral in her life.

"Did you want me to see if Mom can pick up the phone?"

"No, it's not important."

"Are you still coming this weekend, Mr. King?"

"I don't think so, Andy. I need to go to Atlanta and check in at my office and also take care of some personal business." Cliff was looking ahead to possibly spending most of the coming week in Mandeville, depending on Freda's impact.

"The weather probably won't be good, anyway," Andy said, disappointment in his voice.

"I'm keeping a close eye on the weather situation, Andy. I'll see to it that you and your mom are safe, so don't worry, son."

"I won't," he promised.

Cliff didn't go into more detail about his contingency plans since he hadn't discussed them with Jennifer yet.

"Mom, Mr. King isn't coming for the weekend. He needs to go to Atlanta."

Jennifer pretended to be concentrating on snapping a cover over her plastic bowl of dip. When she'd finished, she put the bowl in the refrigerator, hiding her expression. "I'm not surprised," she said. "After all, Mr. King has his own life to live. He can't spend every weekend in Mandeville."

"He could if he moved here," Andy pointed out glumly.

Her son's faint note of accusation added to Jennifer's pain. She turned to face him. "You think it's my fault that Mr. King isn't coming?"

He shrugged. "I guess you can't help it if you don't like him as much as he likes you."

Jennifer swallowed hard. "Andy, I like Mr. King a lot, more than I've ever liked any other man."

"Then why don't you smile at him and let him hold your hand and kiss you, like grown-up people do on television shows, and all?"

"Because despite what you would like to believe, holding hands with him and kissing him isn't going to make Mr. King want to marry me."

She could tell that he was unconvinced. Suddenly, Jennifer decided that she was going to tell him a portion of the truth.

"Andy, do you remember that first Sunday we ran into Mr. King on the lakefront, that he thought I looked familiar?"

"Sure, I remember. He asked if you'd lived in Fort Lauderdale, Florida."

"Well, I did live in Fort Lauderdale at one time. I met Mr. King there and went out on a date with him. When I saw him on the lakefront, I recognized him, but it had been such a long time ago. I had become a different person and didn't see any point in getting reacquainted with him." Jennifer had Andy's rapt attention. She continued, "Later that same day he came here to our house. He'd found out our address. You were at Kevin's. Mr. King had remembered who I was. We talked a few minutes and then he left. So you see, I do know Mr. King very well as a person."

"Why didn't you tell me before that you knew him in Florida, Mom?"

"I've never liked talking about my life prior to the time I moved to Louisiana and had you. Most of my memories aren't particularly good ones."

"Not even your memories of my dad? You've never talked about him much."

"No, I haven't. Actually, I didn't know him very well. But I do have some happy memories of him that I'll share with you when you're older and can relate to them." Memories of his real father, of course. Memories of Cliff at twenty-two.

Andy nodded solemnly.

Jennifer held out her arms. "Can I have a hug?"

He came and wrapped his strong, young arms around her waist and hugged her hard.

Andy had changed into his pajamas and gotten into bed, but he didn't look sleepy when Jennifer went to his room to tell him good-night. A thoughtful frown knit his smooth young forehead. Was he puzzling over her earlier disclosure that she'd lied to him about being acquainted with Cliff years earlier? Was he figuring out the truth for himself? she wondered anxiously.

"Mom?" he said with reluctance as she sat on the edge of his bed.

"Yes, Andy."

"You said you didn't have good memories of when you were a kid." He hesitated and then went on, dread in his voice. "Your mother and father weren't mean to you, were they?"

He'd been lying there worrying about whether she'd been abused as a child. "Nobody was deliberately mean to me," she assured him, a big lump in her throat. "Actually I never knew my father at all. He and my mother were separated when I was born. She died when I was seven years old, and my aunt and uncle raised me. They were very strict, but not cruel. I've shown you their pictures," Jennifer reminded him.

He nodded, his expression showing relief. But obviously she'd raised more questions than she'd answered.

"You like pictures, don't you, Mom? You have lots and lots of pictures of me. Didn't you have a camera before you came to Louisiana?"

If she did, he was asking, why was her collection of photographs taken in Florida so small?

"I had little use for a camera before you were born. People use cameras to capture happy events. The first truly happy event in my life was having you placed in my arms at the hospital." Jennifer smiled at him, her eyes glazed with tears of remembrance. "I don't have a picture of that, either, but I'll never forget the moment."

Andy wrinkled his nose. "There is a picture of me when I was first born. I'm all red and wrinkled and ugly."

"You looked beautiful to me," she insisted.

"Mom, boys aren't 'beautiful.'" He yawned. "I guess I'd better go to sleep. I have a swim meet tomorrow." His mind made some connection and he glanced at the likeness of Frank Jennings on his bedside table. "Did Mr. King know my dad? He acted real funny when I showed him Dad's picture."

Jennifer was speechless for a second, the mention of Cliff completely unexpected. "No, Mr. King didn't know Frank."

Andy looked satisfied. He yawned again and confided, "I've been practicing real hard on the freestyle. Tomorrow I'm gonna try to break my record." A happy smile curved his lips. "If I do, I'll have some good news to tell Mr. King tomorrow night when he calls me."

"He'll be excited and proud of you."

"Yeah, I know." He settled his head deeper into the pillow.

Jennifer kissed him good-night and left the room, her heart very heavy.

It was harder and harder for her to keep the truth from Andy. And yet she was so afraid of his learning it. So uncertain of his reaction. How would he take the news that she'd lied to him? That Cliff, not Frank, was actually his father? Could he understand that she'd misled him with the best of intentions?

Even if she were more confident that telling him was the right thing to do, the decision wasn't solely hers to make. Cliff had to want to shed his title of "Mr. King" and become "Dad." It wasn't something she could push him into.

Cliff's dilemma, she suspected, was that he saw her and Andy as a package deal. He thought that coming out in the open as Andy's dad meant giving up his bachelorhood and making an "honest woman" of her. He'd admitted in a roundabout way to feeling pressured into marrying her.

He knew how ashamed she was of her background and how strongly opposed she was to Andy's knowing that he was an illegitimate child. Cliff probably had concluded for himself that making her his wife now would cloak the past in respectability and make her look better in Andy's eyes. With his conscience, he was probably having a struggle with himself, wanting to do the right thing and yet not wanting to relinquish his freedom. He'd all but said as much after they'd made love last weekend.

Despite Jennifer's fears about Andy's being told the truth, she couldn't refuse if Cliff came to her and said that he was ready to end the pretense. That he wanted his picture to replace the one of Frank Jennings.

It would mean that Andy had two fully committed parents. She couldn't deny him that.

Nor could she allow herself to stand as an obstacle. She had to ease Cliff's guilty feelings about her, make him realize that he wasn't dealing with entrapment.

To do that, she had to keep another truth carefully hidden—how much she loved him and wished that he wanted her to be his wife.

Chapter Thirteen

Cliff got Jennifer and Andy's answering machine when he called at six o'clock on Friday evening. He left a message saying hello and stating his plan to return to Atlanta the next morning. He also gave the name and telephone number of his motel, but didn't request a return call.

Actually, he'd called early on purpose, figuring that they wouldn't have gotten home. Tonight, he didn't feel up to another phone conversation with Andy that would be spoiled by the knowledge that Jennifer was somewhere in the house, keeping her distance.

On the weather front, Hurricane Freda was steadily bearing down on the Louisiana coast and was projected to blow ashore on Tuesday, with winds possibly as high as a hundred and fifty miles per hour.

On Saturday, Cliff went to his office and wrapped up a lot of business loose ends. He also attended to personal business, including his accumulated mail. By early Saturday evening, his affairs were pretty much in order. He was all set to call Jennifer and discuss hurricane plans.

Expecting Andy to answer the phone or else for the answering machine to click on, he wasn't at all prepared to hear Jennifer's voice when her slightly hesitant hello came over the line.

Cliff had to find his voice. "Hi, Jennifer. How are you?"

A pause. "I'm okay, Cliff. How are you?"

"I'm fine."

"That's good. Andy isn't home right now. He's at a neighbor's house. But he'll be home later tonight, if you want to call again. He has exciting news about his swim meet that I won't spoil for him. He tried to call you at your motel last night," she added.

"He did? I'm sorry I missed him. I was in the motel bar, watching a baseball game." *Nursing a beer and feeling lonely and down in the dumps.*

"Actually, I'm glad for this opportunity to talk to you without Andy here." She didn't sound in the least glad. She sounded troubled and unhappy. Cliff braced himself for the worst as he waited for her to continue. "The other night, I told Andy that you and I had known each other in Florida. By doing so, I've probably opened the door to a lot of questions in his mind."

Cliff recovered a little from his surprise. "What led to your telling him that?"

She didn't answer at once. Again, he waited in suspense.

"I guess because it was the one truth about my relationship with you that I felt I could tell him. You see, Andy's taken into his head that I should marry you and make you his stepfather. When you decided not to come to Mandeville this weekend, he blamed me. He suggested that I should be friendlier to you, let you hold my hand and kiss me. Can you imagine how hypocritical that made me feel?'' Shame and embarrassment burned in her voice. ''You're going to have to talk to him and support me in getting this idea out of his head.''

''First, I would have to get the idea of marrying you out of my head,'' Cliff said.

''You need to stop feeling guilty about me, Cliff. I wouldn't have wanted to force you into marrying me eleven years ago. And I don't now.''

''Who said anything about force being involved?'' he replied, smothering a deep sigh of discouragement. It wasn't something he wanted to discuss on the phone, especially not when he felt so unsure of where he stood with her. ''I'll talk to Andy and take off the heat, I promise. Thanks to Freda, there should be lots of opportunity for the two of us to chat during the week.'' Cliff went on, sensing her startled attention. ''I've been watching the weather reports. It looks like Louisiana is not the place to be on Tuesday. I've taken the liberty of reserving two places on a flight from New Orleans to Atlanta on Monday. I'll pick you and Andy up at the airport and bring you here to my condo. It has two bedrooms, so there's plenty of space. We'll have our own hurricane party.

''On Thursday or Friday, I can drive us back to Mandeville or we can fly, depending on the condition of the New Orleans airport after Freda has hit. I've taken a week of vacation time,'' he added as a concluding point. In some detail, that was plan one.

''Cliff, I have a job. I can't just fly off to Atlanta,'' Jennifer protested. ''Freda may not even hit Louisiana. At the last minute, she could veer off in another direction. You just never know with a hurricane, until it actually reaches land."

"But by then it's too late to catch a plane. The airport's shut down. Why gamble with your and Andy's lives when it's not necessary?" Cliff argued reasonably.

"I'll put Andy on the flight, since you're taking vacation time. That would take a big load off my mind, to have him safe."

"What about the load on his mind? On my mind?"

"I'm sure I'll be all right. I wouldn't stay here in the house by myself."

"The phone lines could be blown down. It might be days before we could communicate with you. We'd be worried to death."

Her troubled sigh came over the line. "Cliff, it's good of you to be concerned, but I can't just pack up and leave. Tuesday could come and go with no worse weather than blustery wind and a few rain showers. Then there I would be, off in Atlanta, missing work. Hurricanes are just a way of life for those of us who live this close to the Gulf of Mexico."

"Then, I'll have to come to Louisiana." Plan two. "There's a flight to New Orleans on Monday that arrives about noon." He already had a seat reserved on it for himself. "I'll drive a rental car over to Mandeville and go to the marina until you and Andy get home. I need to tie extra mooring lines and put out more fenders on the boat, anyway. Monday night, I'll sleep at your house, since I'll be staying overnight Tuesday, anyway."

A shocked silence.

"Cliff, you can't—"

He broke in before she could finish her statement. "When it comes to a matter of life and death, I can't be too worried about what your neighbors think, Jennifer." *Don't you want me there with you and Andy?* he asked her silently.

"Cliff, please, let me send Andy to Atlanta."

She'd given him her answer: *No, I don't want you here.* He felt broadsided by the same rejection he'd felt on Sunday night, but his emotions didn't undermine his resoluteness. "I'm coming to Mandeville. See you on Monday." He cradled the phone and sat there, weighted down with discouragement.

Unhappy with herself, Jennifer gazed at the phone in her hand, hearing the buzz of the disconnected line. She should have stood up to Cliff and not let him override her objections.

But how could she stick to her guns, when she was fighting herself? It had been hard enough to refuse his plan for her and Andy to go to Atlanta and stay with him in his condo.

After six days of separation, she longed to see him, to be with him. Between now and Monday, Jennifer had to shore up her resistance.

Nothing had changed. Cliff might be giving lip service to the idea of marriage, but she knew that was just the product of a guilty conscience. He hadn't said anything about love, or even about telling Andy the truth. All her reasons for not carrying on an affair with Cliff were still just as valid.

Concern was bringing him to Louisiana, concern for Andy and for her. But after the hurricane was over, he

would be gone again. Jennifer couldn't afford to lose sight
of that cold, hard fact, not for a single moment.

"Mom, let's go by the marina. Mr. King said he'd be
there."

"I'll take you to the marina. Then, I'll go home."

"Okay. Mr. King is really going to stay with us?" He
sounded delighted.

"Unless he's changed his mind."

Cliff hadn't called again. It was now two o'clock on
Monday. Jennifer had gotten off work early. When she'd
left the club, a crew of employees had been busy nailing
plywood over the windows, taking down nets on the tennis courts and bringing in outdoor furniture. Freda was
still bearing down on the Louisiana coast. If she didn't
veer, the eye of the storm could pass right over Lake
Pontchartrain.

The sky was overcast and an eerie calm seemed to add
to the tension of the storm preparations. At every gas
station that Jennifer and Andy passed, cars were lined up
at the pumps. The parking lots at the supermarkets were
crowded. Most of the pickup trucks on the highway were
transporting sheets of plywood. The announcer on the
radio station Andy had tuned in repeatedly read long lists
of schools and businesses being closed the following day.

Jennifer reached out and snapped off the radio. Her
nerves were tight. How would Cliff act toward her? A part
of her dreaded their meeting and wanted to postpone it,
much as she eagerly looked forward to it.

At the marina, she pulled into a parking space, leaving
the engine running. "If Mr. King's here and he wants you
to stay with him, you can," she told Andy, who'd already unsnapped his seat belt and swung his door open.

"I'll wait until you come back and give me a signal that it's okay to leave."

"What's the big hurry, Mom?" he asked. "Can't you take the time to say 'hi' to Mr. King?"

"I guess there is no big hurry," Jennifer admitted. She switched off the engine.

"Don't get all nervous about Freda. Mr. King is going to be here."

Andy was too young to understand that Mr. King, more than Hurricane Freda, was the source of her nervousness.

Be friendly and natural, Jennifer coached herself as she walked along the dock beside Andy. The marina was a beehive of activity, with boat owners securing their boats. The same air of preparing for disaster pervaded. She spotted Cliff on the sailboat next to his, obviously giving his neighbor a hand.

Her heart skipped a beat at the sight of him, tall and blond and vitally good-looking in casual cotton slacks and a short-sleeved knit shirt, open at the neck.

Andy had spotted him, too. "Hi, Mr. King!" he hailed him.

Cliff looked around quickly, a spontaneous smile spreading across his face. "Hi, there, Andy!" he called back. His gaze went to her, and unless she was imagining things, his smile dimmed a little. "Hi, Jennifer."

"Hi, Cliff."

"Be right with you both in a minute."

They waited for him at his slip. Jennifer took advantage of the chance to watch him as he moved about surefootedly, his movements those of the coordinated athlete. She tried to blank out the awareness that beneath his shirt, his broad shoulders and back and chest were as bronzed and hard muscled as his arms.

Tonight he would be sleeping in her house.

Jennifer couldn't imagine that she would ever relax enough to get any sleep herself.

Cliff climbed off his neighbor's boat. Jennifer sucked in a breath, tensing as he came toward her and Andy. *Friendly and natural.*

"This is a nice surprise," he declared.

Andy stepped forward, grinning from ear to ear. "Mom got off work early. They're boarding up the club for the hurricane."

Cliff tousled his son's blond hair. Then, bending down, he picked him up bodily, wrapping him in a bear hug. "I missed you, kid," he said gruffly.

"I missed you a lot." Andy's arms were tight around his dad's neck.

Jennifer's eyes had glazed over with tears. She blinked and swallowed hard as Cliff set Andy back on his feet, keeping one big hand on Andy's small shoulder. The urge was strong to hold out her hand to Cliff, to step forward and rise on her tiptoes and kiss him on the cheek to express how meaningful his display of love for their son had been for her.

Instead, Jennifer hung back, clutching her purse in both hands in front of her. She didn't dare make an overture that he might misinterpret. "Andy's going to be wishing for hurricanes," she commented. "He's been so excited that you were coming."

Cliff's eyes searched her face as though seeking some unspoken communication. She could sense his restraint. He had held back from greeting her with a spontaneous display of affection, no doubt fearful of conveying a wrong message, too—not just to her, but to Andy, whose false hopes he'd promised to put to rest during this visit. Jennifer realized that she'd been harboring a tiny false hope, too. Feeling it die, she wondered how she was going to get through the next couple of days.

Andy spoke up, ending the brief awkward moment. "You can have my bed, Mr. King. I'll sleep on the trundle bed. It's already made up with sheets."

Cliff patted Andy's shoulder. "That's very generous of you, Andy." His voice had a forced note, and he avoided Jennifer's eyes. "I'm all through here. Shall we go to your house and batten down the hatches there?"

"I'll ride with you. Mom won't mind. She already said I could stay here with you."

Jennifer turned and led the way to the parking lot, welcoming the arrangement. It was one of the few times since Andy had been born that she would be glad not to have his company. She badly needed a few minutes of solitude, to regain her perspective.

There was too much to be happy about for her to be feeling this overwhelming despair. Any remaining doubts she had had about Cliff's deep commitment to being a father to Andy were gone. He loved Andy. Should something happen to Jennifer, Cliff would take good care of him, see that Andy was educated. What a wonderful relief it was to truly be able to share parenting.

When the three of them arrived at her house, Jennifer resolved, she *would* be friendly and natural toward Cliff. She *wasn't* going to adopt a hangdog attitude because he didn't want to marry her. She *wasn't* going to exclude herself from a threesome that was good for Andy. That would be too selfish on her part.

In another twenty-four hours, the fury of Hurricane Freda might be approaching Mandeville, toppling trees and lifting roofs off houses. In view of that more serious, life-threatening danger, Jennifer's crisis of the heart wasn't so important.

She prayed that no lives would be lost, that no extensive property damage would occur, but she also prayed that when Freda had come and gone, she herself would have weathered her personal emotional storm.

"Aren't you going to bring your suitcase in, Mr. King?"

"I can bring it in later," Cliff said, looking at Jennifer for direction. He'd started to pop open the trunk before he got out of the car, but her neighbors were out next door, the man in the process of nailing a sheet of plywood over their picture window. "Actually I could stay in a motel or on the boat tonight."

"You don't have air-conditioning on your boat," she pointed out. "And it's silly to pay for a motel room."

"Stay with us," Andy implored.

Cliff would have given almost anything to hear her second the sentiment, but at least she hadn't taken advantage of the out he'd given her.

"I think you must have guessed I have a present for you in my suitcase," he said teasingly to his son.

"A present? What is it?"

"I'll give it to you when we get inside."

Cliff unlocked the trunk and lifted out his suitcase. The three of them trooped to the front door.

To his surprise Jennifer accompanied them into Andy's bedroom and looked on while Cliff opened up his suitcase and gave Andy his present, a new video game.

"Oh, wow! Thank you, Mr. King!"

"You're welcome." Cliff smiled wryly at Jennifer. "I thought maybe I might have a better chance of holding my own with a video game he hadn't played before."

She smiled back at him with amusement. He felt warmed through and through.

"Can we play it now?" Andy asked eagerly.

"First, we'd better prepare for Freda," Cliff replied. He looked questioningly at Jennifer. "What needs to be done?"

"Not a lot," she said. "We just need to clear the patio and put the grill and patio furniture in the garage. That won't take much time."

"You don't board up the sliding-glass door?"

"No, I put masking tape on it."

"Well, Andy, let's take care of that patio."

Fifteen minutes later the job was done. Andy caught Cliff by the hand with a new familiarity and urged, "Come on, Mr. King. Let's play my new video game. Mom, you can come and watch us."

"I wouldn't miss that competition," she said indulgently, surprising Cliff for the second time. He'd expected her to make herself scarce this afternoon and was inordinately pleased that she was joining in.

"You get to play the winner," he told her.

Andy arranged three chairs in front of the small TV set in his room and took the middle chair, oblivious to the fact that his mother's presence gave him a decided advantage. He won the game by a good margin. Cliff had been too conscious of Jennifer to concentrate. He handed his control over to her. When she took it, her fingers touched his. He felt the contact all the way to his toes.

Andy easily defeated her and said, "You and Mom play each other, Mr. King. I have to go to the bathroom."

The chair between them vacated, Cliff suddenly found himself alone with Jennifer. She looked over at him. He gazed back at her, the urge to touch her a hunger inside him. Just the slightest encouragement and he would slide over and take Andy's seat, put his arms around her.

"Would you like something to drink?" she inquired hospitably.

No, what I'd like is to kiss you, hold you these few moments while Andy's gone. "Maybe later," he said.

"I have beer and soft drinks in the refrigerator. You can make yourself at home."

"Thanks. I will. Don't worry about me."

"Should we begin?"

"Might as well, I guess." Cliff could hear his own disheartened note. What had he expected? he asked himself. Had he been hoping for some scene out of a movie when he returned after a lonely, miserable week? For him and Jennifer to look at each other and suddenly have everything between them miraculously right? Yes, he guessed he had been hoping for that, and it hadn't happened.

Andy returned and slipped between them. After a few moments of watching the desultory competition, he started coaching both his mother and Cliff.

"Mr. King is being nice and trying to let me win," Jennifer accused.

"No, I'm not," Cliff denied, though it was true that his competitive desire was missing with her as his opponent.

Eventually, he did win, and he and Andy played another round before ending the session.

"Maybe Mr. King would like to unpack," Jennifer suggested, glancing at his open suitcase on Andy's bed.

"I'm used to living out of a suitcase," he replied, following her glance and noticing that the supply of underwear he'd packed was in plain sight.

"Andy emptied a drawer for you, and there's room in his closet for any hanging clothes." Her tone was gracious.

"This top drawer, Mr. King." Andy went over to pull out the drawer. "See? Mom put your clean clothes in here that she washed for you."

"I forgot all about those clothes," Cliff admitted. "Thank you, Jennifer, for washing them for me." He looked at her, remembering how he'd stripped off his sweaty clothes and showered with her after he'd mowed her lawn two Sundays ago.

She avoided his eyes, refusing to share the intimate memory with him. "You're quite welcome. I'll leave you two to settle in."

"Can I help you unpack, Mr. King?" Andy offered as his mother left the room.

"Sure, Andy."

It was a strain for Cliff to try to act his natural self. His frustration and dissatisfaction with the state of things between Jennifer and himself somehow made having his son call him Mr. King that much more intolerable. Making matters worse, the photograph of Frank Jennings sat on a shelf, having been moved from the table next to Andy's bed.

Who'd moved it? Jennifer? Andy? Cliff would like to have known, but he didn't trust himself to mention the photograph of the man he irrationally resented. It wasn't Jennings's fault that he'd been relegated to the role of impostor.

After they'd finished unpacking, Cliff and Andy went in search of Jennifer.

"She's probably taking a shower and changing her clothes," Andy conjectured, when they didn't find her in the living room or kitchen or laundry room.

Cliff had already come to that conclusion. As he settled down with Andy in front of the TV in the living room and sipped a cold beer, he wished he had the liberty to go seek Jennifer out in her bedroom or bathroom. But he didn't have that liberty and doubted it could be his unless they were husband and wife.

The picture was starting to be very clear to Cliff: Jennifer had been dead serious when she voiced her conviction, shortly after making love with him Sunday a week ago, that they couldn't be lovers. Looking back, he realized that she'd acted on that conviction, pushing him away to arm's length when Andy arrived home from his camping trip. Her cool goodbye when Cliff was leaving that night and her distant attitude all the past week were her way of drawing a boundary line.

He didn't think for a minute that she was employing the age-old female strategy of "holding out" on him to force his hand. She simply couldn't condone a casual relationship and evidently believed that was what Cliff wanted. But he didn't. What he felt for her wasn't casual. This wasn't just about sex. It was about caring, about...love.

The question was, did she return his feelings? If so, how could she erect these barriers and shut him out? His dejection weighed on him like a stone.

Jennifer appeared, looking dainty and fresh out of the shower. She was wearing a shorts outfit in place of the summery dress that she'd had on before. Cliff got a tantalizing whiff of soap and perfume as she curled up on the opposite end of the long sofa.

Andy was sprawled on the carpet, absorbed in the sport report on a local news broadcast. Shortly afterward the national news came on and he got to his feet, announcing that he was taking his shower now.

Cliff found himself alone with Jennifer. He shifted his body sideways toward her. Gathering his courage, he made a move to slide over closer.

"Cliff, *please*," she begged. "Don't make this any more difficult for me than it already is."

"Difficult for you? I hope you don't think this is an easy situation for me?" he demanded, his frustration welling up. "I feel like there's a plate-glass wall between us, and I have both hands tied behind my back."

"I understand," she said unhappily. "Can't we both just make an effort for Andy's sake? In time, it should get better."

"Look, I'll marry you." Cliff hadn't meant the words to come out so bluntly, like a concession. He tried to soften them. "If you're willing to gamble on me, that is. We both know I'm not the best husband material."

Jennifer shook her head. "I care too much about you to marry you, Cliff. You wouldn't be happy. And I wouldn't put any of us through a divorce."

With the gentlest language and in a tone of infinite regret, she was turning him down flat. Cliff turned his body forward again, too devastated to trust himself to speak.

At her end of the sofa, Jennifer gulped and fought back tears. Later tonight, when she was alone in her room, she would cry, but not now. In a few minutes, Andy would return. She couldn't afford to break down and give in to her emotions.

Refusing Cliff's halfhearted proposal—if it could be called a proposal at all—had surely been the wisest, the most unselfish and the most heartbreaking thing she'd ever done.

They both sat there, staring at the TV screen, until Andy rejoined them in time for the latest weather bulletin, which yielded no new information on Hurricane Freda.

"You win, Mom. Mr. King and I are both bankrupt."

"It's about time I came up the winner," Jennifer replied. She rose gracefully from the floor. "I'm going to say good-night."

"I'm ready to turn in, too," Cliff said, getting to his feet.

"Wait for me," Andy told them, hurriedly replacing the top on his board-game box and scrambling up. The three of them had been seated around the coffee table, playing the board game and eating pizza.

At the door to Andy's bedroom, Jennifer bent down and hugged him. "Sweet dreams. I love you."

He hugged her back. "I love you, Mom. Good night."

Cliff had been bringing up the rear. He stood back, observing them and feeling like an outsider.

Jennifer straightened and turned toward him. "Good night, Cliff." Before he could guess her intention, she moved close, rose on her tiptoes and kissed him on the cheek. His arms closed around her and he hugged her tight.

"Good night," he said huskily, releasing her. "Sleep well."

"You, too." She went on down the hall toward her bedroom.

Andy glanced after her and up into Cliff's face before he preceded Cliff inside his room. Taking his pajamas off a hook in his closet, he remarked, "Mom says that you and her knew each other in Florida."

"That's right. We did know each other."

Cliff stripped off his shirt, sensing that the subject wasn't closed.

"Did you know my dad, too?"

Cliff followed his son's gaze to the picture on the shelf. "I didn't know the man in that photograph."

Andy's brow creased thoughtfully, and he began donning his pajamas. "I don't think my mom was happy married to my dad. She told me she didn't know him all that well. What I wonder is why she married him instead of you, if she liked you better."

"Why do you think that?"

"Mom told me she liked you the best of all the men she'd ever known."

"She actually used those words, Andy?"

"Yes."

Cliff was down to his briefs. He pulled back the covers on Andy's bed and sat down on the edge. "Of all the women I've known, I like your mom the best," he confided. "In fact, *like* isn't quite a strong enough word. I love her." It felt good to make the admission aloud.

Andy came over and sat next to him. "Mom thinks you don't want to marry her. She says women know things like that."

"Well, she's wrong. I want to marry her and have the three of us be a family." Somehow, stating his desire to his son, committing himself, erased all of Cliff's tentativeness, all of his ambivalence.

"Boy, I'd like that. Did you tell Mom? Is that why she kissed you?"

"I did broach the idea tonight when you were out of the room. But it didn't come out quite the way I meant it. Her reaction wasn't very positive. She has serious doubts about me as a husband, for good reason. I think she probably kissed me out of sympathy."

"She said no?" Andy asked with dismay.

"Don't worry. With the two of us in favor of it, she's got to come around in time."

"She's *got* to."

Cliff looped an arm around his son's shoulders and hugged him. "Let's keep this between us for now."

"Okay." He sighed happily. "Where will you and me and Mom live? Will you move to Mandeville? Or will Mom and me move to Atlanta?"

"How would you feel about moving to Atlanta?"

"Kevin could come and visit me, couldn't he?"

"Sure, he could. And you could visit him. We could join a tennis club, although it isn't even necessary there. Atlanta has great public tennis facilities and lots of organized leagues and tournaments."

"What about *Windsong?*"

"We would move her to closer waters. Maybe Florida or the coast of Georgia. Possibly near Savannah, where my parents live. They would be your grandparents."

"And you would be my stepfather, huh?"

"I'd be your dad." Tomorrow, Cliff meant to get Jennifer aside and tell her that he couldn't go on playing the role of Mr. King. The bonds of father and son had already developed. It was time for Andy to know the truth.

"I sure hope Mom doesn't take too long to come around."

"Believe me, I'm going to work on her. I've been dragging my heels, which is part of the problem." He tightened his arm around Andy's shoulders, giving him another hug, and then patted him on the back. "Why don't you take first turn in the bathroom?"

Ten minutes later, they'd said their good-nights and had gotten into their beds, Cliff having doused the light. Andy spoke up in the darkness, his voice rather wistful.

"I guess when you and Mom get married, you'll sleep with her in her bedroom."

Cliff's answer was heartfelt. "Your mom and I will definitely share a bedroom. But you and I will still bunk together on some occasions. Camping trips or sailing trips, when she doesn't come along."

Andy's audible sigh was one of happiness. It was soon followed by a yawn, and shortly after that, he'd fallen asleep. Cliff could hear his regular breathing. The confidential session hadn't kept his son awake.

Cliff's wakefulness wasn't a tense, unhappy state. The news that Jennifer "liked" him better than any other man she'd ever known had done wonders for his low morale. *I care for you too much to marry you,* she'd said. Did "care" translate to "love"?

He was hopeful that it did.

For a man who made his living in sales, Cliff hadn't done a very good job of selling himself as a husband. Before now, he hadn't believed enough in his own qualifications.

Originally he'd doubted his ability to be a father, but as Andy had wormed his way into Cliff's heart, Cliff had found himself becoming Andy's dad. The responsibilities of parenthood were still daunting, but the joys were greater than he could have imagined.

The same was going to be true of being Jennifer's husband.

Taking on a family, Cliff now saw, wasn't tying himself down. It was embarking on a whole wonderful adventure.

Chapter Fourteen

The door to Andy's room was open. Jennifer hesitated outside it and glanced in. Andy's tousled blond head was burrowed in his pillow on the trundle bed.

The other bed was empty.

Where was Cliff? She gazed at the dent in the pillow that his head had made and noted the rumpled sheets, reassuring herself that he had slept in the bed. Or at least he'd lain in it. Had he been unable to sleep and gotten up and gone to a motel or to his boat?

Jennifer sighed, closing the door quietly, so as not to disturb Andy. Somehow, she could sense that Cliff wasn't in the house.

In the kitchen she turned on the coffeemaker, then went into the living room. After opening the blinds, she peered out through the slats. Her heart sank as she saw that Cliff's rental car was gone.

For all his good intentions, he couldn't spend a restful night in her house in this family subdivision.

Jennifer had to give him marks for effort. Last night she'd given him the option of going out to a pizza restaurant for supper, but he'd voted with Andy in favor of having a pizza delivered. They'd eaten in the living room, then played a game until bedtime. Had he sat there, trying to imagine himself spending many nights in the same way?

She plodded back to her bedroom, got dressed and returned to the kitchen. As she was pouring herself a mug of coffee, she heard the front door opening and closing. Wherever he'd gone, Cliff had come back.

"Good morning. I thought I smelled coffee." He spoke cheerfully from the open doorway.

"Good morning." She surveyed him, holding her mug. He wore jogging clothes that were damp with perspiration and held a newspaper under his arm. The blond stubble on his face only made him seem more vitally masculine.

"I drove to the lakefront and went for a run," he explained. "Have you caught the weather report this morning?"

"No, have you?" Jennifer had been too upset over his absence to give any thought to Hurricane Freda.

"Yes, on the car radio. During the night, Freda turned more westward and is now headed toward Vermilion Bay. Unless she changes course again, we should miss the brunt of the storm."

"That's wonderful news. For us," she added guiltily.

He handed her the newspaper. "I'm going to take a quick shower and then have a cup of that coffee with you. Be right back."

Jennifer carried the newspaper and her coffee mug over to the dining alcove and sat down. What accounted for his buoyant mood? Aside from relief about the weather, was he counting himself fortunate this morning, that she hadn't taken him up on his reluctant offer of marriage?

With a heavy-hearted sigh, she pulled out a section of the newspaper. By the time she'd turned the pages and scanned several articles, Cliff was back, not only showered but shaved.

"Can I pour you a refill?" he inquired.

"Please."

He brought his empty mug and the coffee carafe over to the table, poured coffee into both mugs and then replaced the carafe. Before he sat down, he bent and kissed Jennifer on the cheek.

"Did you sleep well?" he asked, sipping his coffee.

"I slept," she replied, the fresh, clean scent of him in her lungs. "What about you?"

"Once I got to sleep, I slept well." He was scanning the front-page headlines.

Jennifer pulled out another newspaper section. Before she'd finished looking through it, Andy entered, still wearing his pajamas, and went to the refrigerator to pour himself a glass of orange juice. Then, he joined them at the table. Cliff looked up from his newspaper to smile at him.

The scene was poignant for Jennifer in its very normalcy. A stranger looking into the kitchen and seeing them would make the mistake of thinking they were a family. But they wouldn't ever be a family.

"Did you want to go out for breakfast?" she asked Cliff a few minutes later, when the painful tightness in her throat had eased.

"Not unless you and Andy do."

A spattering of rain and a sudden gust of wind outside seemed to settle the issue. Andy got up and turned on the portable radio in the kitchen. They listened to the latest weather report while they ate cereal with fresh fruit.

A driving rain was falling within the hour, and the gusts of winds came with frequency, rattling the windowpanes. Tree branches falling on the roof made dull thuds. Jennifer got out her masking tape and they taped the glass patio doors.

At noon the electricity went off, eliminating video games and TV as entertainment. Andy and Cliff moved the coffee table in the living room closer to the windows, and in the gloomy light the three of them played cards and board games, the weather growing more violent outside. By midafternoon, it was too dark to see well and yet not dark enough for candles.

Jennifer had grown too nervous for playing games anyway. She sensed that Cliff was more nervous than he let on.

"I'm sure glad we're not getting the brunt of Freda," he remarked soberly, glancing out at the trees swaying and bending in the gale-force winds.

The weather commentary on the radio indicated that Freda had gone ashore at Vermilion Bay and was raging northward over land. They were experiencing the outer fury of her wide swath of destruction.

Jennifer curled up tensely at one end of the sofa. Andy came over and sat next to her. Cliff picked up the telephone to see if they still had phone service. "No dial tone," he reported and came over to sit close to Andy. He put his arm along the back of the sofa and squeezed Jennifer's shoulder reassuringly.

"Let's tell stories or something," Andy suggested.

"I'll go first," she said. "There once was a woman with a ten-year-old son, who foolishly insisted on staying home when a hurricane was coming. A concerned friend urged her to bring her son to a city in another state, but she refused. So he traveled to her state, putting himself in danger. In the middle of the storm she regretted being so stubborn."

"And he regretted not having come up with a better alternative plan," Cliff said, giving her shoulder another squeeze. Jennifer covered his hand with hers, and he grasped her fingers.

"You wanted us to come to Atlanta, Mr. King?"

"Very much. And not just because of the hurricane. I wanted you and your mom to visit me."

"Mom didn't even tell me."

"I have a story," Cliff said. "There once was a man who sailed in a race across a large lake to a small town. The next day he was jogging along the lake and happened to encounter a pretty brunette woman and her son."

"And her son's friend," Andy put in.

Jennifer met Cliff's questioning gaze. She knew what he was asking. Her mouth went dry. "Go on with your story."

He took a deep breath. "Well, the man thought the woman looked familiar. And it struck him that her son was very much like him in appearance. The man searched back in his memory and recalled that he'd dated a woman in Fort Lauderdale almost eleven years ago. The timing was perfect: the boy could possibly be the man's son.

"The man went up to talk to the woman, and she denied ever having known him. But he looked up her address and went to her house. She confirmed that he was the father of the boy."

"Mom?" Andy looked at her with solemn questioning.

Jennifer smiled nervously at him. "Please listen to the rest of the story, Andy. Can I take over here?" she asked Cliff.

"Please do." He was holding on tight to her fingers.

"The woman explained that she'd discovered she was going to be a mother after the man had left Fort Lauderdale. She hadn't known how to contact him. She'd moved to Louisiana and had lived happily with her son during the past ten years. During that time she'd made up a false story when her son questioned her about his father."

"Mr. King is..." Andy faltered, turning his head to look at Cliff.

"I'm your dad," Cliff confirmed huskily. He took up the explanation in parable form. "At first, the man didn't know how to deal with learning that he had a son. But he soon started feeling very proud and was glad that he'd been there on the lakefront that day. In time, not only did he come to love his son, but he fell in love with his son's mother. He wanted to marry her and have the three of them become a family."

"Oh, Cliff," Jennifer whispered, tears clogging her throat.

He went on gently, "The man did a botched-up job of proposing marriage to her, and she said no. But in the middle of a hurricane, he proposed to her again, saying,

'Would you marry me and make me the happiest man in the world?' ''

Jennifer took over. "And she said yes. Because she loved the boy's father with all her heart and soul."

Cliff lifted Andy onto his lap, and Jennifer scooted over close to him. He enveloped them both in a strong, encompassing embrace. "Want to finish the story, Andy?"

He grinned shyly at Cliff. "The man and the woman got married and moved their son to Atlanta, where his friend Kevin visited him."

"Last night Andy and I had a heart-to-heart discussion," Cliff explained to her. "He indicated that he would be willing to relocate to Atlanta."

"We'll move the sailboat," Andy said. "Maybe somewhere near Savannah, close to where..." His blue eyes widened.

"Close to where your grandparents live," his father finished his statement for him.

"I wish the phone was working," Andy commented, an undercurrent of excitement in his voice. "I'd like to call Kevin."

Jennifer and Cliff smiled at him and at each other. She was utterly content with their isolation, her world complete, and she sensed that Cliff was content, too.

"Do you mind relocating?" he asked. "If you do, I'll keep working as a sales rep until I can find a job in New Orleans."

"I don't mind relocating anywhere—as long as we'll be together."

"In that case, I'll take the regional sales manager position my company offered."

"Are you sure you want to give up the travel?"

He hugged her closer against his side and tightened his arm around Andy. "Very sure. Being on the road is no life for a family man."

"Andy?" Jennifer spoke her son's name lovingly to rouse him. After several huge yawns, he'd fallen fast asleep, lying on the carpet.

Hurricane Freda had spent her fury by seven o'clock. The three of them had eaten a supper of sandwiches by candlelight and then brought the portable radio back into the living room to listen to reports on the hurricane damage. Fortunately, the toll in lives seemed very small so far.

"Don't wake him up," Cliff said, getting up from the sofa where he and Jennifer had been sitting, holding hands. He knelt down by their son and picked him up gently in his arms.

Andy awoke, but he didn't assert his ten-year-old independence and insist that he didn't need to be carried to bed. Jennifer lighted the way to his bedroom with a candle and stood by while Cliff helped Andy undress.

"Good night, son," he said with a tender note in his deep voice that made happy tears well up in Jennifer's eyes.

"Good night...Dad," Andy answered. He hadn't addressed Cliff by name since the revelation that afternoon that Mr. King was his father.

Cliff hugged him tight, and Jennifer knew how precious the moment must be for him, hearing his son call him *Dad* for the first time. It was deeply special for her, too. A dream she'd never dared to dream had come true. The most she'd ever hoped was that Andy would have a stepfather who loved him like a son.

"I love you, sport," Cliff said huskily.

"I love you, Dad." The new-minted word came more easily this time.

As Cliff stepped back and reached for the candle Jennifer held, with his other hand he brushed a tear from his cheek. Her own cheeks wet with tears by now, Jennifer kissed Andy and told him good-night. Then she and Cliff left his room together.

In her bedroom, he set the candle on the dresser. Jennifer went into his arms. "I love you," she whispered in unison with him.

For several seconds they hugged each other tightly, weathering the emotional overload of almost too much joy and happiness. Then they spoke simultaneously again, "I missed you."

Jennifer raised her head as Cliff raised his. They gazed at each other and repeated the thrilling communication silently by candlelight. Then they kissed and repeated it again.

And again.

And again. It couldn't be repeated too often.

Eventually passionate dialogue was added. *I want you. I need you.*

They made love, taking precautions. Afterward, lying in his arms, happier than she'd ever believed possible, Jennifer sounded him out on whether he wished for her to start taking birth-control pills.

"For a while you could," Cliff said. "The three of us probably need an adjustment period as a family, before you and I give Andy a little sister."

Jennifer was surprised and thrilled. "Would you like to have a daughter?"

"I figure it's only fair for you to have a sidekick, too," he replied tenderly.

They kissed, carrying on the wonderful conversation of love.

* * * * *

Silhouette

SPECIAL EDITION™

COMING NEXT MONTH

#919 MAIL ORDER COWBOY—Patricia Coughlin

That Special Woman!

Allie Halston swore she'd conquer rigorous ranch life, even if it meant taking on all of Texas! Then she faced sexy Burn Monroe—who was more than just a cowboy with an attitude....

#920 B IS FOR BABY—Lisa Jackson

Love Letters

Beth Crandall's single passionate night with Jenner McKee had changed her life forever. Years later, an unexpected letter drew her back home, and to the man she'd never forgotten....

#921 THE GREATEST GIFT OF ALL—Penny Richards

Baron Montgomery knew determined Mallory Ryan would sacrifice anything for her young child. But when her boundless mother's love was tested, could Mallory accept his help and his promise of everlasting devotion?

#922 WHEN MORNING COMES—Christine Flynn

Driven and dedicated, Travis McCloud had sacrificed his marriage for career. Now a chance reunion with Brooke compelled him to open his heart...and to take a second chance at love.

#923 COWBOY'S KIN—Victoria Pade

A Ranching Family

Linc Heller's wild, hell-raising ways were legendary. Yet Kansas Daye wondered if becoming a father had tempered Linc—and if he was ready to step into her waiting arms.

#924 LET'S MAKE IT LEGAL—Trisha Alexander

John Appleton gave up the fast track to become Mr. Mom. Then high-powered lawyer Sydney Scott Wells stormed into his life, and John knew he'd show her the best of both worlds!

MILLION DOLLAR SWEEPSTAKES (III)

JINGLE BELLS, WEDDING BELLS:
Silhouette's Christmas Collection for 1994

Christmas Wish List

*To beat the crowds at the malls and get the perfect present for *everyone,* even that snoopy Mrs. Smith next door!

*To get through the holiday parties without running my panty hose.

*To bake cookies, decorate the house and serve the perfect Christmas dinner—just like the women in all those magazines.

*To sit down, curl up and read my Silhouette Christmas stories!

Join *New York Times* bestselling author Nora Roberts, along with popular writers Barbara Boswell, Myrna Temte and Elizabeth August, as we celebrate the joys of Christmas—and the magic of marriage—with

JINGLE BELLS, WEDDING BELLS

Silhouette's Christmas Collection for 1994.

The stars are out in October at Silhouette! Read captivating love stories by talented *new* authors— in their very first Silhouette appearance.

Sizzle with Susan Crosby's
THE MATING GAME—Desire #888
...when Iain Mackenzie and Kani Warner are forced to spend their days—and *nights*—together in *very* close tropical quarters!

Explore the passion in Sandra Moore's
HIGH COUNTRY COWBOY—Special Edition #918
...where Jake Valiteros tries to control the demons that haunt him—along with a stubborn woman as wild as the Wyoming wind.

Cherish the emotion in Kia Cochrane's
MARRIED BY A THREAD—Intimate Moments #600
...as Dusty McKay tries to recapture the love he once shared with his wife, Tori.

Exhilarate in the power of Christie Clark's
TWO HEARTS TOO LATE—Romance #1041
...as Kirby Anne Gordon and Carl Tannon fight for custody of a small child...and battle their growing attraction!

Shiver with Val Daniels'
BETWEEN DUSK AND DAWN—Shadows #42
...when a mysterious stranger claims to want to save Jonna Sanders from a serial killer.

Catch the classics of tomorrow—*premiering* today—
Only from

PREM94

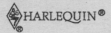 HARLEQUIN®   Silhouette®

The movie event of the season can be the reading event of the year!

Lights... The lights go on in October when CBS presents Harlequin/Silhouette Sunday Matinee Movies. These four movies are based on bestselling Harlequin and Silhouette novels.

Camera... As the cameras roll, be the first to read the original novels the movies are based on!

Action... Through this offer, you can have these books sent directly to you! Just fill in the order form below and you could be reading the books...before the movie!

48288-4	Treacherous Beauties by Cheryl Emerson	$3.99 U.S./$4.50 CAN.	☐
83305-9	Fantasy Man by Sharon Green	$3.99 U.S./$4.50 CAN.	☐
48289-2	A Change of Place by Tracy Sinclair	$3.99 U.S./$4.50CAN.	☐
83306-7	Another Woman by Margot Dalton	$3.99 U.S./$4.50 CAN.	☐

TOTAL AMOUNT	$
POSTAGE & HANDLING	$
($1.00 for one book, 50¢ for each additional)	
APPLICABLE TAXES*	$_____
TOTAL PAYABLE	$_____
(check or money order—please do not send cash)	

To order, complete this form and send it, along with a check or money order for the total above, payable to Harlequin Books, to: **In the U.S.:** 3010 Walden Avenue, P.O. Box 9047, Buffalo, NY 14269-9047; **In Canada:** P.O. Box 613, Fort Erie, Ontario, L2A 5X3.

Name: _____

Address: _____ City: _____

State/Prov.:_____ Zip/Postal Code: _____

*New York residents remit applicable sales taxes.
Canadian residents remit applicable GST and provincial taxes.

CBSPR

"HOORAY FOR HOLLYWOOD" SWEEPSTAKES

HERE'S HOW THE SWEEPSTAKES WORKS

OFFICIAL RULES — NO PURCHASE NECESSARY

To enter, complete an Official Entry Form or hand print on a 3" x 5" card the words "HOORAY FOR HOLLYWOOD", your name and address and mail your entry in the pre-addressed envelope (if provided) or to: "Hooray for Hollywood" Sweepstakes, P.O. Box 9076, Buffalo, NY 14269-9076 or "Hooray for Hollywood" Sweepstakes, P.O. Box 637, Fort Erie, Ontario L2A 5X3. Entries must be sent via First Class Mail and be received no later than 12/31/94. No liability is assumed for lost, late or misdirected mail.

Winners will be selected in random drawings to be conducted no later than January 31, 1995 from all eligible entries received.

Grand Prize: A 7-day/6-night trip for 2 to Los Angeles, CA including round trip air transportation from commercial airport nearest winner's residence, accommodations at the Regent Beverly Wilshire Hotel, free rental car, and $1,000 spending money. (Approximate prize value which will vary dependent upon winner's residence: $5,400.00 U.S.); 500 Second Prizes: A pair of "Hollywood Star" sunglasses (prize value: $9.95 U.S. each). Winner selection is under the supervision of D.L. Blair, Inc., an independent judging organization, whose decisions are final. Grand Prize travelers must sign and return a release of liability prior to traveling. Trip must be taken by 2/1/96 and is subject to airline schedules and accommodations availability.

Sweepstakes offer is open to residents of the U.S. (except Puerto Rico) and Canada who are 18 years of age or older, except employees and immediate family members of Harlequin Enterprises, Ltd., its affiliates, subsidiaries, and all agencies, entities or persons connected with the use, marketing or conduct of this sweepstakes. All federal, state, provincial, municipal and local laws apply. Offer void wherever prohibited by law. Taxes and/or duties are the sole responsibility of the winners. Any litigation within the province of Quebec respecting the conduct and awarding of prizes may be submitted to the Regie des loteries et courses du Quebec. All prizes will be awarded; winners will be notified by mail. No substitution of prizes are permitted. Odds of winning are dependent upon the number of eligible entries received.

Potential grand prize winner must sign and return an Affidavit of Eligibility within 30 days of notification. In the event of non-compliance within this time period, prize may be awarded to an alternate winner. Prize notification returned as undeliverable may result in the awarding of prize to an alternate winner. By acceptance of their prize, winners consent to use of their names, photographs, or likenesses for purpose of advertising, trade and promotion on behalf of Harlequin Enterprises, Ltd., without further compensation unless prohibited by law. A Canadian winner must correctly answer an arithmetical skill-testing question in order to be awarded the prize.

For a list of winners (available after 2/28/95), send a separate stamped, self-addressed envelope to: Hooray for Hollywood Sweepstakes 3252 Winners, P.O. Box 4200, Blair, NE 68009.

CBSRLS

OFFICIAL ENTRY COUPON

"Hooray for Hollywood"
SWEEPSTAKES!

Yes, I'd love to win the Grand Prize — a vacation in Hollywood —
or one of 500 pairs of "sunglasses of the stars"! Please enter me
in the sweepstakes!

This entry must be received by December 31, 1994.
Winners will be notified by January 31, 1995.

Name _____

Address _____ Apt. _____

City _____

State/Prov. _____ Zip/Postal Code _____

Daytime phone number _____
(area code)

Mail all entries to: Hooray for Hollywood Sweepstakes,
P.O. Box 9076, Buffalo, NY 14269-9076.
In Canada, mail to: Hooray for Hollywood Sweepstakes,
P.O. Box 637, Fort Erie, ON L2A 5X3.

KCH

OFFICIAL ENTRY COUPON

"Hooray for Hollywood"
SWEEPSTAKES!

Yes, I'd love to win the Grand Prize — a vacation in Hollywood —
or one of 500 pairs of "sunglasses of the stars"! Please enter me
in the sweepstakes!

This entry must be received by December 31, 1994.
Winners will be notified by January 31, 1995.

Name _____

Address _____ Apt. _____

City _____

State/Prov. _____ Zip/Postal Code _____

Daytime phone number _____
(area code)

Mail all entries to: Hooray for Hollywood Sweepstakes,
P.O. Box 9076, Buffalo, NY 14269-9076.
In Canada, mail to: Hooray for Hollywood Sweepstakes,
P.O. Box 637, Fort Erie, ON L2A 5X3.

KCH